D0365424

# kissing
# IN ITALIAN

also by lauren henderson

*Flirting in Italian*

• • • • • •

*Kiss Me Kill Me*

*Kisses and Lies*

*Kiss in the Dark*

*Kiss of Death*

# kissing
# IN ITALIAN

lauren henderson

DELACORTE PRESS

Visit us on the Web! randomhouse.com/teens

Educators and librarians, for a variety of teaching tools,
visit us at RHTeachersLibrarians.com

*Library of Congress Cataloging-in-Publication Data*
Henderson, Lauren.
Kissing in Italian / Lauren Henderson.
p. cm
Sequel to: Flirting in Italian.
Summary: Her relationship with Luca in jeopardy, English teen Violet plunges back into her quest to uncover her connection to an Italian family, but many surprises still await.
ISBN 978-0-385-74137-8 (hc) — ISBN 978-0-375-98453-2 (ebook)
[1. Identity—Fiction. 2. Dating (Social customs)—Fiction. 3. Tuscany (Italy)—Fiction. 4. Italy—Fiction.] I. Title.
PZ7.H3807Km 2014
[Fic]—dc23
2013009706

The text of this book is set in 12-point Goudy.
Book design by Kenny Holcomb

Printed in the United States of America

10 9 8 7 6 5 4 3 2 1

First Edition

*Non vi diró come finisce la storia*
*anche perchè non è finita mai*
*Se scorre un fiume dentro ad ogni cuore*
*arriveremo al mare prima o poi.*

*I won't tell you how the love story ends,*
*because it never will–*
*if a river runs inside every heart,*
*it will lead us to the sea at last.*
—Jovanotti

# kissing
# IN ITALIAN

# Plenty More Fish in the Sea

I'm looking at a portrait of a young woman, hung on the wall of an art gallery. And washing over me is the oddest kind of déjà vu, a dizziness that's making my head spin a little. I can see my own face reflected in the glass, overlaid on hers, and it's reminding me, suddenly, of the last time I saw myself inside an ornate gold portrait frame. Of how my summer Italian adventure started.

I'm in Italy, on a hot July afternoon, grateful for the thick stone walls of the Siena art museum, cooling the air. And the reason I'm in this country is that a few months ago, back home in London, in another museum, I saw another painting—of a girl who looked so like me that it made me feel something I had wondered about for most of my life might be true after all. That portrait sent me on a search to find out how I could possibly have had a twin in eighteenth-century Italy.

Thank goodness, this picture doesn't look anything like me. Quite the opposite, in fact. The girl, or young woman, is pale, with a long nose that seems to follow straight down from her high, extremely plucked, winged eyebrows. There's a flush in her cheeks, and her lips are dark pink, pressed firmly together, set with determination, the same determination that comes through clearly in the firm jut of her chin. And when you look down to the baby she's holding in her arms, you understand why she looks so resolved. Because that's not just any baby; it's Jesus.

"I like her," I say quietly to Kelly, who's standing next to me.

She nods, looking dazed. Kelly isn't used to going around proper museums. Unlike me, lucky enough to have been taken on trips and to lots of art galleries and sent to an expensive private school, Kelly isn't from a privileged background. These extraordinary paintings and sculptures we've seen in Siena today have hit her like a ton of bricks; she's staring in absolute awe at each one.

This Madonna and Child is definitely having a powerful effect on us. As I lean forward to look at the mother's expression, my face appears in the glass again, and I feel it's a reproach for having abandoned my quest. I came to Italy to find out why, when I don't look anything like my parents, I have a Tuscan double from the eighteenth century—only to find myself tangled in a web of family secrets that I had never anticipated. I thought I might have been adopted, or was maybe some weird kind of genetic throwback, and I was prepared for that. I love my mum and dad with all my heart, but I still needed to know why I look so very different from them.

What I hadn't expected—how could I have?—was to find myself falling for the son of the family that lives in the castle where the portrait was painted. And to have to face the fear that Luca, the boy I find so desperately attractive, might be—dare I even think it again—my half brother. That his playboy dad might be *my* biological dad too. I backed off my search when I realized that awful possibility.

But looking at the Madonna in front of me, at the strength of purpose I read in her face, I feel ashamed. I let myself be distracted from my quest by my feelings for a boy. I pushed the whole thing under the carpet, pretended it never happened, because I was scared to find out that Luca and I are blood relatives.

*Well, time to get back on track, Violet!* I tell myself decisively. *There are plenty more fish in the sea besides Luca di Vesperi! You have to woman up, as Paige would say. Finding out the truth about who you are is much more important than spending time with a boy you fancy. Boys come and go, but knowing who you are and where you come from is priceless.*

I feel myself setting my chin decisively. I have to write to my mum. I can't put it off anymore. I thought I could find out the truth without upsetting her; I was too scared to ask her before, since she's never said anything to me. We love each other so much that I've been afraid of doing anything that might make her sad. But I need to know the truth about myself. I can tell her some of the story—not that I came to

Tuscany on this mission, but that by coincidence, we visited the castello and I met the *principessa*—who blurted out that I looked just like the people in her husband's family. It's raised the question even more strongly of why I don't look anything like Mum or Dad, anything at all. . . .

I heave a deep sigh, fully understanding for the first time in my life the expression about a weight falling from your shoulders. The sense of relief is overwhelming. I feel as if I could float off the ground, like smoke rising gently into the air.

"I'm going to write to my mum and ask her to tell me everything," I say to Kelly, who knows the whole story and is quick enough to grasp immediately what I mean.

"I think that's a brilliant idea, Violet," she says seriously, and takes my hand. "You need to know. Do it as soon as we get back."

I nod, swallowing hard.

"Omigod, look at that *hair*!" Paige exclaims, coming up behind us. "It's like they had hot rollers in ancient times!"

She's not talking about the Madonna, whose hair is pulled back under a translucent white veil, but about the angel standing behind her. The angel's tresses are an impressive riot of golden curls. It's typical of Paige to focus on the most frivolous aspect of the painting.

"Painted by Francesco di Giorgio in 1471," Kelly says, reading from the plaque.

"They all look exactly the same," Paige continues, looming over us. "All these girls."

"It's what was fashionable then," Kelly explains. "Their

ideal of beauty. They only painted women who looked like you were supposed to look."

"That's *harsh*," Paige says, her wide mouth opening in surprise. "And *unfair*. Kendra?"

She turns, and with a wide swing of her arm, her bangles jingling, waves over the fourth member of our summer course, who strolls over to join us. Heads turn to look at Paige, mostly with disapproving expressions at the noise she's making, but Paige is oblivious. These two American girls are unself-conscious in public, with none of the self-effacing, be-quiet-and-don't-call-attention-to-yourself manners we British have.

"Hey, Kendra!" Paige continues. "Did you know that long ago you had to have a certain look for people to think you were beautiful?"

Kendra raises her eyebrows. "Times haven't changed that much," she says dryly. "I don't see many girls my color on the cover of fashion magazines."

Kendra is African American. I haven't thought about it before, but now that she makes the point, I see what she means.

"There are some girls like you on magazine covers," says tall, blond Paige. "Aren't there?"

Kendra says tersely, "Hardly."

Kelly, who's redheaded and definitely on the curvy side, says pointedly, "But all the girls in magazines are thin like you, Kendra."

A sharp clap interrupts my thoughts. We all turn as one, conditioned now by the sound that Catia Cerboni, our guide, uses to summon our attention. You don't mess with Catia, especially when it comes to the cultural side of things, the art visits and the language lessons that are the essential part of our summer courses. She takes those responsibilities seriously, though in other areas she's considerably more lax.

"Girls! We will move on now," she announces. Thin as a rake, her linen shift dress miraculously uncreased even on this hot and sweaty day, wafting Chanel Cristalle perfume, Catia is the epitome of Italian chic. Which, under the circumstances, is pretty ironic.

"We have seen the best of Sienese icon paintings, and now we go to the Duomo," Catia announces. "The cathedral. It is in the Italian Gothic style, one of the most perfect examples of medieval architecture."

Paige complains. "We're walking *so* much today! Is it far? Can we get a cab?"

"Honestly, Paige," Kendra says impatiently. "Everything here's really close. Siena is tiny."

"It's so hot . . . and my feet hurt . . . ," Paige whines, but she perks up as we leave the museum and emerge again into crowded and utterly fascinating Siena. It looks as if there hasn't been anything new built here since the Middle Ages. Its sun-warmed gray stone buildings are packed closely together, and because it's on a steep hill, the narrow streets are almost all sloped. No sidewalks, and when one of the orange city buses swings around a corner, perilously near, we all follow the lead of the locals and squish back against the wall of the closest shop. The bus turns within a foot of us, the driver calculating the angle perfectly.

We gasp at how close the bus comes. Our reaction would

be enough to identify us as tourists even disregarding the obvious physical evidence that we aren't Italian. Well, *I* look Italian: olive skin tone, dark curling hair and dark eyes. Because of this, no boys give me a passing glance; their attention is for the exotic threesome I'm with.

*I wonder if I fell for Luca because he was the only boy who noticed me. That's all, no other reason. I wish I could believe that.*

"Shoes!" Paige is sighing, her face lit up with the same kind of ecstasy Kelly showed when she was looking at the Madonna and Child. "*Look* at those stunners in that shop! Can we—"

"*After* the Duomo, *perhaps* we visit some shops," Catia says, whisking us up the street, past so many enticing places to spend more money: leather goods, stationery boutiques, lace makers.

We find ourselves in a little piazza with a church looming in front of us, and on the left, a steep flight of marble stairs leading high up the hill. Catia climbs briskly, calling, with the voice of a woman who has led many groups of excited teenage girls up these very dramatic steps, that we can take photos later. And at the top of the stairs, we go through a high arch and reach our destination, right at the top of Siena: the Duomo.

It does take your breath away.

"It's like a wedding cake!" Paige breathes, and actually, I know what she means. It's the layers. The cathedral, looming above us, is built of white and greenish-black marble, layered in stripes, and as we reach its façade, our heads tilt back almost as far as they can go to take in the icing on the cake, ornate carvings and sculptures and gargoyles, red marble added into the mix. Catia's voice flows over us with an impressive array of information she's clearly trotted out many times before. It's impossible to separate her descriptions of which bits are Gothic, which classical, and which are Tuscan Romanesque, and I doubt any of us are even trying.

As we walk inside, we gasp in unison at the sheer scale of the cathedral. The breathtakingly tall marble pillars, striped in black and white—Siena's civic colors, Catia is telling us—the dome above, the ceiling painted in rich blue with golden stars. In the center of the opulently gilded and carved dome, a golden lantern lets in the bright light, like the sun itself. Jewel colors dazzle as the sun pours through the round stained-glass windows. I swivel around, feasting my eyes, as silent as the rest.

We wander down the nave, into the chapel, into the library, following the sound of Catia's voice. Our heads go back to look at exquisitely painted ceilings, tilt down again to stare at elaborately inlaid marble floors. Oxblood-red, sapphire, emerald, and white marble glow like mother-of-pearl in the mosaic work, which Catia informs us is called intarsia. Finally, we take in the bright frescos wrapping around the walls. We are completely quiet, overwhelmed by this much lavishness, by the incredible amount of work that has gone into creating this place of worship.

Catia is so pleased by our subdued demeanor that she lets us stop for photos on the marble steps, plus visit the shoe shop Paige spotted on the way up here. Paige is actually the only one who goes, and she can't focus enough to buy anything. In the gelato shop next door, we don't agonize loudly over our choices, either: we're quiet, still under the spell of the Duomo. We look down at the amazing shell-shaped Piazza del Campo as we pass, walking back up the Banchi di Sopra, our heads full of beauty, quite ready to drive home.

But then, crossing Piazza Matteotti, the day takes a totally unexpected turn. There's a staircase on the far left with an iron balustrade, leading up to a church. It's Kelly who spots them, nudging me excitedly, as the boys vault over the railing, whooping, and land lightly on the warm stone of the piazza. Two lean, handsome Italian boys, slim in their pale shirts and tight jeans, their hair falling forward over their foreheads, and just behind them, an American, much more casual in a T-shirt and loose jeans, his hair cropped close to his head, his blue eyes bright in his deeply tanned skin.

"Andrea!" Kelly exclaims. If we didn't know already that she has a huge crush on him, she'd have completely given herself away with the squeal of excitement with which she calls his name. "Leonardo," she adds swiftly, "and Evan! What're you doing here?"

Leonardo is Catia's son, and Andrea is his best friend; they're party boys, out for a good time, nothing more, in my opinion. They're fun but shallow. I'm always a little wary of boys who know exactly how good-looking they are. Evan, one of Paige's many brothers, just arrived two days ago. He's been backpacking around Europe with friends on his summer holidays, and came to crash at the villa while the friends go to a folk-music festival in Umbria that he didn't fancy.

There's an Italian word I've learned, *"solare."* It means "sunny" and it's used to describe people. That's Evan. He's sunny. He has a lovely big smile that crinkles his eyes and lights up his whole blunt-featured face; like his sister, he reminds me of a golden Labrador: friendly, good-natured, easygoing. But he's also clearly more mature than Paige, and not just because he's three years older. Paige is wild, uninhibited, gets drunk and falls over; I can't imagine Evan behaving like that. He seems sensible, sober, reliable. I haven't had much chance to get to know him, but already I like him a lot.

"*Ragazze!*" Leo calls. He's always the leader. And he's relishing the envious stares from the other boys in Piazza Matteotti as he lopes toward our group, takes our hands, kisses us on each cheek, throws his arm around Paige's shoulder, and announces:

"We have come to kidnap you! We take you away to have pizza and go dancing all night!"

Moments ago we were hot, wilted, limp, like string beans left too long before picking. But these words have a miraculous ability to refresh us. We perk up as one, turning to Catia, our expressions pleading.

"*Mamma, possono venire?*" Leonardo asks, tilting his head to one side, flashing his most practiced, charming smile. "*Dai, perchè no?*"

Catia looks tired too, her eyes sunken into hollows rimmed by dark liner, her red lipstick dried into faint lines around her mouth. Catia is a mystery to me. She comes across as totally Italian, and yet her daughter, Elisa, told me that Catia's actually American, pretending to be Italian, married to an Italian man, never breathing a word about her real nationality. It's totally weird.

"*Perchè no?*" she echoes. "Why not?" She's probably happy

to be rid of us, to be able to drive home in peace and quiet and put her feet up instead of having to supervise dinner, ready to pounce on every error we make in table manners. *"Non fare troppo tardi,"* she adds. "Don't be too late."

We all break into smiles; we know these are just words. Catia may be in loco parentis to us, but she's a pretty slack chaperone. We had to lug Paige home a fortnight ago, drunk as a skunk, and Catia barely batted an eyelid. All she did was trot out a speech about learning to hold your drink, and then she let us go out with the boys again practically the next evening.

*"Fantastico!"* Leo claps his hands. *"Andiamo tutti!"*

He kisses his mother enthusiastically, turns, and dashes off toward the *fortezza,* gesturing that we should all follow him. I hesitate, wondering if we should follow his lead and kiss Catia goodbye, but she's already heading toward La Lizza, where she parked the jeep, one ringed hand held up in farewell to us.

No adults! We're on our own, out for the evening, ready to party. And now that Evan's here, we won't have a repeat of Paige drinking too much. Nothing like a looming big brother to keep his wild younger sister in line.

I've been feeling so confused, so messed up recently. Now that there's the prospect of some release for my stress, I'm so happy I could scream. I dash along the pavement and trip on a cobblestone in my haste. Evan grabs my elbow, catching me. It feels as if he could lift me off the ground as easily as if I were a little girl. I look up and smile at him in thanks.

"You're in a hurry!" he says, and I laugh and agree.

"I really love to dance," I say, beaming at him. "I can't wait."

"I really love pizza!" he says, letting me go. "*I* can't wait!"

We're on a total high, all seven of us, as we pile into two cars and sweep out of Siena in convoy, driving around the walls of the old fortress and onto a narrow highway that Leo says is the road to the sea. The evening sun is a golden haze, and since we're heading west, it's blazing into our eyes, wrapping us in warmth, as if we're driving into the heart of a fire. We have all the windows down, the wind whipping our hair.

"It's like being in a film," Kelly sighs to me, her hazel eyes glowing.

"It *is*," I agree. *But what kind?* I find myself wondering. *A romantic comedy or a gritty family drama?*

The car crosses a little bridge and then starts to slow down, and Kelly oohs at the sight of our destination, a sound I echo. It's a big sprawling stone building set back from the road, behind a large gravel parking lot bordered by trees strung with brightly colored paper lanterns. As we pull in, I see that the bridge we just crossed spans a little river, which flows by the side of the dining area, below a wall lined with long terra-cotta planters of flame-red and fuchsia geraniums.

My heart lifts. I jump out as soon as the car comes to a halt, taking in the sight. The air is rich with the perfume of wisteria and jasmine, which are trained over a big trellis behind the patio. Now that the noise of the car engine has died away, I can hear the running water of the river, and music drifting out from the restaurant.

Everyone piles out, the other girls exclaiming in delight as we walk across the gravel to the entrance. We go through a high wooden arch wreathed in more wisteria, and after we're led to a table and given menus we exclaim all over again at the sheer number of pizzas they have—fifty choices. We order, and moments later the pizzas arrive. They're huge, the size of cartwheels, but so thin and light they're not too filling, easy to eat, and we finish every last scrap, even Kendra, who's always watching her weight. They're the best thing I've ever eaten. Evan, halfway through his, calls the waitress over and orders another one; we all roar with laughter, but he's quite unembarrassed, saying he has a big appetite, and the waitress, flirtatiously, agrees with him, squeezing his broad shoulders, commenting on his size, offering to bring him a third if he wants.

Paige squeals with amusement. And when Evan's pizza comes, the waitress leaning over him sexily as she takes his old plate and slides the new one in front of him, he turns to wink at me, saying:

"Hey, I told you I really loved pizza! I wasn't kidding!"

After the pizzas, we have sorbet, served in the shells of the fruit: lemon and orange, tangy and sharp, and coconut, smooth and creamy. Then coffee, then little chilled glasses of limoncello and arancello, lemon and orange liqueurs, the glasses frosted from the freezer, the liqueur sweet and heady and sugary. The American girls still can't believe that no one asks for proof of drinking age.

Night has fallen. The candles are all lit and flickering above our heads, their wax melting gently into the iron setting. The lanterns are illuminated and glow red and yellow and green and blue. The music's grown louder, no longer soft jazz; now it's booming pop, the bass cranked up, echoing gently off the paving stones, summoning us inside to dance.

And we do. We dance our feet off. We shed all embarrassment about the tackiness of the music. It's all Top 40 and, yes, the *Grease* medley that drove me off the dance floor in Florence a few weeks ago. But now I have a group to be silly with, and we sing all the words, or, to be honest, howl them, our heads back, our mouths wide open, sharing the pure, silly, dizzy fun, making the Italian boys sing "Ooh ooh ooh, honey!" after every "You're the one that I want."

Suddenly, it's midnight. When Leo drags us off the dance floor, all of us sweaty and shiny, and announces what time it is, Paige actually wails like a banshee in disappointment, thinking that he's announcing a curfew, that we're Cinderellas who have to leave the ball.

"No!" Leo gestures out of the open doorway at the side of the dance floor, which leads outside; we've been nipping out there to cool down. "Now we go swim! In the river!"

"Everyone go!" Andrea chimes in eagerly. "Everyone swim after dance here."

This, in our overheated state, seems like the most brilliant idea in the world. I glance out the door, and now that I'm looking, I see a few dark shapes bobbing in the water. Someone dives in with a splash I can see but barely hear over the music, and people squeeze past us, making for the door. I see a girl start to pull off her dress; underneath it is a brightly striped bikini. They've all come prepared.

Kendra gets it in a flash.

"We don't have bathing suits!" she points out.

"Oh, no problem!" Leo responds, a gleam in his eyes. "We swim in our *intimi*—our underclothes."

"Underwear!" Paige yells, swatting him. "*Underclothes?* That's hilarious!"

But I turn to look at Kelly and see the same panic in her eyes I'm feeling myself.

*No way am I going outside to swim in my underwear in front of a bunch of boys!*

# Things I Can Never Have

Mad, screaming giggles and squeals come from Paige and Kendra as their elbows fly, clothes falling on the floor of the little bathroom as they squish up to the mirror to look at themselves in their underwear. Behind them are Kelly and me, our faces pink, caught between panic and excitement: our eyes shining, our lips parted. We're freaking out, swaying, almost dancing on the spot, the music pouring through the thin wall that separates the loos from the rest of the club, the bass line pounding as insistently as our own heartbeats.

"Paige, you cow!" I sigh in jealousy, looking at her matching underwear. Pink bra and knickers (of course, Paige *lives* for pink), dotted with white and trimmed with white lace.

And best of all, better even than matching, it's not see-through at all but made of opaque cotton, the bra structured and lightly padded to contain Paige's abundant upper half.

I look down at my strapless lace bra and grimace so hard that my mouth practically stretches to my ears. No way can I go swimming in this. My pants are all right—not very pretty, just plain black, but they do cover my bum. Still, what am I supposed to do? Run outside with my hands over my boobs, jump in the river and spend the whole time underwater with just my head showing?

I think longingly of my swimsuits back at the villa. I'm not usually comfortable wearing a bikini around boys, but even that would be infinitely preferable to my underwear. I glance at Kelly, wedged next to me, who's pulling exactly the same face; she's been caught out too, and even worse than me—she's in thong underwear that shows pretty much her entire bum cheeks. No way can she be seen by boys looking like this.

"What am I going to *do*?" she wails hopelessly.

"Go in your dress?" Paige suggests, trying to be helpful. But when she glances down to the dress puddled at Kelly's feet, she can't help wincing; Kelly's in a maxi, with a smocked bodice. Way too much fabric to have billowing around you swimming in a river.

"Tie it around your . . . ," Kendra starts, but trails off when she realizes that Kelly can't knot the dress up around her waist—it's her bum that's the problem.

"Oh, *why* didn't they let us know we were doing this! We could have tried to buy bathing suits in Siena!" Kelly's on the verge of tears, the pink of excitement deepening perilously into a hot red of embarrassment and disappointment that clashes badly with her ginger hair. Her voice wavers, becoming a wail. "If I don't go in, Andr"—she's about to say Andrea, we all know. But she bites off his name, corrects it to—"*they'll* think I'm a spoilsport."

Paige, Kendra, and I exchange glances in the mirror, biting our lips, unable to think of any reassurance to give. There's no point lying: Kelly's right, as she pretty much always is. Everyone else will be in the river, and if Kelly sits on the side, she'll be a wallflower.

I feel I should tell her that I'll sit with her, keep her company, make sure she isn't alone. But I'm ashamed to admit that I'm not nice enough for that. My blood's racing around my veins, so hot it feels as if I'm boiling up. I'm desperate to get back out into the club, to dash through it and outside into the warm night air, to jump into the river, splashing and laughing, to burn off the energy that's still rushing through me even after having danced like a maniac for a couple of hours. Kelly's my ally here, my best friend in Italy, and I'm still not prepared to give up my midnight plunge for her.

I suck, as Paige would say.

Kelly's eyes are welling up. She's madly keen on Andrea, and Kendra, at my request, has released him into the wild, snubbed him hard enough that he's got the message and stopped chasing her. But that still leaves a big gulf between Andrea's cheerful, friendly attitude to Kelly, and the doglike worship he used to pay to Kendra.

I don't know if Kelly can bridge that gulf in the weeks we have left in Italy. But she's quite right; she won't get any further by sitting glumly on the riverbank while we all dive in and get wet.

"Hey!" Someone's banging on the door of the ladies' loos: we all jump. Kelly blinks, and one big tear is released. It starts to trickle down her red cheek.

"Hey!" the voice calls again. It's a guy, and not an Italian; they don't yell "Hey!" here, but "*Oh!*" instead, which is weird until you get used to it. I'm closest to the door. I grab my dress, hold it over me with one hand, and ease the door open a crack with the other.

Behind me, the girls, overexcited, scream at a pitch that would deafen bats. We're all ridiculously worked up at the thought of a man seeing us in our underwear, even though we're planning to go into the river in exactly that.

In front of me is a wide male chest. I look up, over the swell of the pectorals, the broad tanned neck, the square jaw, to the cheerful blue eyes and cropped blond hair of Evan, Paige's brother. Like Paige, he's built on a massive scale, especially by comparison with the slender, slim-hipped Italians. He completely blocks any view of the club behind him.

"Violet!" he says. His eyes widen as he takes in my state of undress, but he's manfully resisting looking anywhere but my face, which I thoroughly appreciate. "Look, I made the other guys give me their shirts, okay? I thought you'd need all of them."

He's holding a bunched-up ball of fabric in one big fist, which he pushes toward me; it leaves me in a quandary, as I don't have my hands free. I wedge the door with my shoulder, which means I can still hold my dress over me and take the shirts with the other.

"Thanks!" I exclaim gratefully, realizing that this means Kelly can come swimming with the rest of us, that I can cover my bra up.

But Evan isn't done. He reaches down, takes the hem of his own T-shirt, and pulls it up in one swift movement, dragging it over his head, baring his tanned chest. I can't help staring. Evan is at college on a football scholarship, apparently, and from his muscle definition, I can't imagine he gets any time to study. He looks as if he spends every waking minute in the gym.

And he's really close to me. I feel a blush rising to my cheeks, and I try to step back a little, confused by my feelings about this sudden striptease, his physical proximity. His hand reaches out to me again, giving me the T-shirt still warm from his body, still smelling of him. I take it, realizing that my mouth has fallen open at the sight of him. I clamp my lips together as he says, grinning, his white American teeth perfect:

"Give this to Paige, okay? Those skinny little Italian guys' shirts won't fit around her, and I don't want my little sister showing her junk all over town."

"*Hey!*" Paige shouts back crossly. "I do *not* show my junk all over town! You better not go around telling people that!"

Evan's grin deepens as he looks down at me; he winks.

"It's just too easy to get her going," he says to me confidentially, seeing my eyebrows raised: I've rarely heard Paige this wound up. Evan certainly knows how to press her buttons.

I back inside the bathroom again and close the door. Kelly rips a shirt from my hands and drags it on, buttoning it as best she can, as Andrea is very slim and Kelly's definitely curvy. Of course, it's Andrea's shirt she's picked. She's beaming now, tears forgotten. I hand Paige Evan's T-shirt and then look hesitantly at Kendra. We're one short.

"You take it," she says nonchalantly, slender as a wand in the white underwear that contrasts beautifully with her dark skin. "I'll be okay without a cover-up."

*Of course she will,* I think, glancing at Kelly. Kendra is an athlete, with a perfect body; I'd be more than happy to show it off too.

"Evan's such an idiot," Paige says, still cross, pulling on his T-shirt.

"Oh, ignore him," Kelly says quickly. "I never listen to a word my stupid brother says. Come on, I'm dying to go for a swim!"

She's pulled her dress on over the shirt—she's very self-conscious about her legs—then winds her arm through Paige's and pulls her toward the door. Paige follows obediently, and as soon as they emerge, I hear wolf whistles from boys waiting outside. They're for Paige, of course, just as the sighs that issue as Kendra and I come out are for her, not me. Kendra has slipped her dress on again, but she doesn't need to be half naked to drive Italian boys crazy; they adore blondes as well as black girls, loving the difference from the local brunettes, I assume. And Kendra has a grace and elegance to her carriage, a goddesslike way of walking with her head up and her shoulders back, that particularly draws the eye.

Evan, Andrea, and Leonardo form a phalanx around us and whisk us along the side of the room, skirting the dance floor with its mirror balls twirling and sending cascades of silver sequins over everyone's bodies. Thank goodness for Evan. I've pulled Leo's shirt on, and when we get to the river I'll tie its tails below my boobs, covering my lacy bra. For now, they're hanging down to my upper thighs, perfectly decent enough to walk through a club where some of the Italian girls are wearing miniskirts barely longer than their tiny bums.

We emerge into the warm night air and I smell the honeyed wisteria, hear an owl hooting across the fields on the far side of the river. I'm eager to dive in; I love to swim. I'm picking my way down the little slope when, behind me, I hear a commotion and look back to see Paige braced between Evan and Leo; she's tripped on her wedge heels and is cackling like a banshee.

Kendra looks at me and rolls her eyes.

"Hopefully the cold water'll sober her up a bit," she says resignedly.

I don't answer, even though I completely agree. Because, leaning against the wall of the club on our left, long legs crossed at the ankles, shoulders propped square to the stone, black hair falling over his face, is a silhouette that looks eerily familiar, like a ghost that haunts my dreams. There's a book called *The Beautiful and Damned,* by F. Scott Fitzgerald, that I found in the villa's library, and I've been reading it. I don't quite understand it all; to be honest, I pulled it off the shelf because the title spoke to me, made me think of him. Luca. Definitely beautiful, and the damned part fits too, because he's so dark, so brooding, so sad; it feels sometimes as if he doesn't want to reach for happiness, as if he actually pushes it away—

*But he saved me when I was in danger,* I remind myself. *He saved my life. And then he told me he thought I might be his half sister. Which meant we couldn't see each other anymore, in case that was true . . .*

A red dot flashes in the blue-black night as the figure raises a cigarette to his lips.

*It can't be Luca,* I tell myself. *We're beyond Siena, miles and miles from Chianti, where he lives. It can't be him.*

Everyone's already passed me, brushing by as I stopped to stare at the lean boy draped against the roadhouse wall.

"Violet!" Kelly calls, her voice high and thrilled. "Come *on*! Wait till you see this!"

I turn back toward the river and plunge down the little path as if I were being chased by the hounds of hell. Away from a silhouette that's making me think of things—*want* things—that I can never have.

## *"Ciao, Violetta"*

"Look, Violet!" Kelly's positively shrieking with excitement. "*Look* at this!"

I tumble down the last few rough steps—really, they're just slabs of stone wedged into the steep riverbank. I would have caught myself in time, but Evan holds out a hand in case I need to brace against him. He does it nicely, not in a patronizing, look-at-you-silly-girl-falling-over-again way; he just puts his palm out at chest height, leaving the choice to me whether I take it or not.

Because he's being so nice, I touch his hand briefly for balance, so he doesn't look silly with it out like that, as if he's carrying an invisible tray. And then I gasp as I take in what Kelly—and the other girls—are so worked up about.

"They're hot springs!" Kelly exclaims. "Now, this is mental!"

"*Thermal* springs," Kendra corrects her snottily.

Kelly and Kendra are both brainy, and they know it. Unfortunately, that isn't enough for either of them, as on this summer course they've been engaging in a competition to see who's cleverer. It's beginning to break into open warfare, and certainly Kendra's tone is sharp enough to make Evan turn to look at her, obviously taken aback.

But I'm staring at the thermal springs. I've never seen anything like this before. Along this bank of the river, several have bubbled up through the stone and formed pools, irregular ovals, beside the main river. They're like hot tubs made by nature, and the steam rising off them is visible, pale swirls like vapor coming off a witch's cauldron. No wonder the locals knew to wear swimsuits.

Maybe the most amazing thing is that the water itself is white. Milky, cloudy white. The people sitting in the closest pool are completely invisible below the waist. I bend down and run my fingers through the water, but it's clear on my fingers; it's not the water itself that's white.

"It is the *calcare* that makes it white," Leo says, seeing my disbelief. "Under, the stone under the water."

"Chalk!" Kelly says swiftly, scoring a point back at Kendra. "It's chalky—that's why it looks like that. '*Calcare*' means 'chalk.' "

Dark freshwater flowing beside us, white steamy hot tubs dotted along the riverside, stars overhead, and a glowing white moon hanging low in the sky over the patio, beyond the lanterns; it's magical, otherworldly. I stare at the steam rising from the white pool, hypnotized, and only snap out of it when Kendra's dress comes flying past me and drops onto the grass bank. I know that, cross at Kelly's one-upping her by knowing the word for "chalk" in Italian, Kendra has retaliated with her best weapon: her fantastic figure. It's cheating, really, as the battle is about who knows more, who has the best brain, not who's the slimmest; but as Leo and Andrea both rush to hand Kendra into the hot pool, and as a boy in there already openly sighs "*Bellissima!*" and kisses his fingers to her, it does feel as if Kendra's won.

Which is depressing.

I pat Kelly's arm in silent sympathy, but she's not letting Kendra get to her. Pulling off her dress, she's stepping into the pool as well, following Andrea. It's packed in there, and they're all squeezing up, laughing and squashing and obviously tremendously enjoying pressing in like sardines.

But that's the last thing I feel like. By the sounds they're making, everyone in that thermal pool is attracted to someone else; it's as if I'm the only one who doesn't want to jump in and hope that the boy I like will throw an arm around me and pull me close. In a split second, I turn on my heel, kick off my own sandals, and slip away into the dark. A couple of steps take me to the edge of the river. Remembering that I've seen people diving in, which means the water must be reasonably deep, I take a deep breath and launch myself into a shallow dive, cleaving the surface, bracing myself against the shock of anticipated cold.

But it isn't cold. It's lukewarm. Even though the water is flowing, not sitting in a swimming pool, it's still been heated by the July sunshine, and it's like swimming in a mild bath.

Clear water, lapping all around me. I take a few strokes underwater, pulling hard with my arms, letting go of as much tension as I can, of the shock of seeing someone I mistook for Luca. The water holds me up; I stop swimming and float to the surface, letting the flowing river carry me along. I only need to make small movements with my arms and legs to stay buoyant. My hair is submerged, waving around me like river weeds; my face is upturned to the night sky. I watch the stars twinkle, and make out Orion's Belt, the bright glow of Venus, the Big Dipper.

The stars cut out as I'm carried slowly under the bridge, which seems to be a cutoff point for the party people flooding down from the dance floor. There's no one around. I'm emptying my brain, feeling as if I'm in a flotation tank. My hair is heavy and damp around my face, and I move my head slowly back and forth, enjoying the sensation of the wet locks on my cheeks, like a cool compress on my skull, as I emerge on the other side of the bridge. . . .

"*Ciao, Violetta.*"

The sound of his voice, low and almost caressing, is such a shock that for a moment I think I've hallucinated hearing it. But as I jerk my head back, I see his shoes, his jeans, and swiftly I swing my legs under me, scrabbling for a foothold in the squishy mud of the riverbank, digging in my toes, and stand up waist-high in the water. Luca has bent his long legs now, and is sitting down in front of me, halfway down the bank on a stone outcropping, so we're almost level. I stare at him, still disbelieving.

"It *was* you!" I blurt out, and then feel stupid.

"*Cosa?*"

He lifts his dark brows. I can see his face clearly in the moonlight, the pale skin, the perfect bone structure, the black lock of hair that falls over his forehead, inky-dark.

"Before," I say. "Up by the club. You were smoking."

He nods. "Which you think is a disgusting habit," he observes, amusement in his voice.

"Yes, I do," I say firmly, glad of the way the conversation is going; ticking him off is much easier than . . . anything else. "It's revolting. *Schifoso,*" I add, having learned the word in Italian.

*"Bene."* He pulls the packet from his jeans pocket, raises it to show me, and then, quite unexpectedly, releases it, his long fingers empty, the packet falling into the river beside me. "No more cigarettes," he says. "Since you say they are *schifoso.*"

"You're stopping? Just like that?" I fish out the packet before it becomes so waterlogged it sinks, and put it on the grass.

He shrugs. "*Perchè no?*"

I swallow. "You shouldn't just throw things in the water like that. It's bad for the environment," I say, sticking with the severe, ticked-off voice, as it makes me feel safe. If I lose this voice with him, I'm in much deeper, more dangerous waters than this pretty little river.

*"Mi scusi,"* he says lightly, an apology with not a flicker of contrition in his voice. "You are good for me, Violetta. The only one who tells me when I do wrong."

When he calls me by the Italian version of my name, I can't help it: I feel like I'm melting. Dissolving, help-less, gone. I dig my toes deep into the yielding, sucking mud, clear my throat, and attempt to say his name firmly. But to my dismay, it comes out really feebly. A plea, not a reprimand.

"Luca," I say, and he leans toward me.

*"Sì, Violetta?"*

"Luca, we said we weren't going to be alone together."

I'm almost whispering now. The water lapping around me, flowing past me, is a soft, gentle, seductive background noise. I'm aware, all at once, that I'm wet from head to toe, that the borrowed shirt is clinging to me, my bra probably showing through, and I don't dare to look down to see if it is.

"I know," he says quietly and sadly. "I see you go down to the *pozze termali* with all your friends, and I watch you, to see if you're happy, if you laugh and jump in with them. If you are happy, I leave. But you don't laugh with them. You dive into the river and you swim away, and I think you are all by yourself, and maybe not very safe, so I walk along the . . . *riva* . . ."

"The bank," I prompt as he trails off, unable to find the word in English.

"Sì. I walk along, and then I see you floating like a mermaid, and I want to say something to you."

He shrugs again, but it's very different from the last one; that was casual, dismissive. This is . . . wistful. And, to my horror, I hear myself confessing:

"It's nice to see you."

Stupid, silly, banal little words. Luca smiles, his dark blue eyes sparking.

"Nice?" he says, and he starts to take off his shoes. "This is a very strong word in English, *non è vero?*"

"No," I say quickly. "It's not a strong word at all."

"Oh, *peccato,*" he says cheerfully, which means "what a shame."

He's pulling off his socks.

"What are you doing?" I ask, which is stupid too, as it's obvious; he's standing up now, his hands at his waistband, unbuckling his belt. The sight is incredibly disconcerting. I back away, into deeper water, on the tips of my toes now. "Luca—"

"I am hot," he says. "That's correct, isn't it? Not 'I have hot.'"

I know what he means: in Italian, you say you "have" hot or cold, not that you "are." It takes a bit of getting used to. Especially with the double meaning, which I'm certainly not going to explain to him now.

"Yes," I say even more feebly as Luca's jeans drop to the ground and he steps out of them. Thank goodness he's wearing boxers! His legs are long and almost too thin, a bit storklike. I'm ridiculously glad to have found a defect in him. As he starts to unbutton his shirt, I take another step back and find myself treading water frantically, out of my depth now. I can't look at his mostly bare body: I turn away, feeling a blush suffusing my cheeks. So I hear, rather than see, him dive into the river.

He surfaces next to me, shaking his wet hair back from his face. It plasters down to his skull, and that makes his bone structure much more pronounced, his cheekbones sharp as knives. I stare at him, tongue-tied, as he treads water easily next to me.

"Now you must be cross with me," he says, a thread of

laughter in his voice. "You must tell me that I'm wrong, that we must not be alone together."

"We mustn't," I say, suddenly angry. "You know we mustn't." I can't keep treading water; my legs feel too wobbly. I put my head down and swim away from him, a couple of strokes to the far bank, where I can stand.

He follows me; he swims right to me, and when he comes up, he's so close, so tall, that he blocks out the moon. His bare chest is dappled with drops of water clinging to his skin. I can't look anymore, so I raise my eyes, and then I'm looking into his, and oh no, that's a really terrible idea, that's the worst idea in the world. . . .

*"Se scorre un fiume dentro ad ogni cuore, arriveremo al mare prima o poi,"* he says, looking down at me. "More Jovanotti," he adds, smiling, as he sees me staring at him in confusion.

Jovanotti is Luca's favorite singer; he's quoted songs of his before to me. But I don't know this one.

"'If a river runs inside every heart, we will arrive at the sea,'" he translates. "I think of this because we are in a river."

"It's very pretty," I mumble.

"The rest of the song is maybe not so pretty," he says. "It is a love song, but Jovanotti tells the truth about love. That it is sometimes not pretty at all."

I nod, even though hearing the word "love" spoken by Luca is enough to make me feel as if I'm blushing all over.

He reaches out to stroke my wet hair, smoothing it back from my face. "Just once," he says softly. "Just now, just for a few moments . . ."

We lean into each other at the same time, wet skin pressed against wet skin, cold water over cold skin, warming each other, heating up so fast it feels as if the river droplets are burning off us already as our lips meet. I've never kissed anyone in the water before, never been so—comparatively—naked as I press against someone, and it's dizzying. My hands slip over his shoulders, run over his back, feel the lean muscles there, the strength as his arms tighten around my waist, pulling me up toward him, onto the tips of my toes again. He's kissing me hard, his tongue cool in my mouth, and I can't help kissing him back just as hard.

His hands slide under the loose shirt I'm wearing, up my bare back, and I moan against his lips; I press against him and feel his nipples, hard little points, through the cotton fabric of the shirt, the lace of my bra. It's an odd, entrancing sensation, and it makes me want to rub against him even more. I'm clinging to him, my hands rising up to stroke his scalp, burrow into his wet hair, and he almost purrs against my mouth with pleasure, a sound that starts deep in his chest. I feel the vibration. It makes me think of a cat, a big, predatory cat, and I shiver from head to toe and pull my mouth from his and bury my face in the bony hollow of his shoulder, against his bare skin, and just hold on to him.

I'm shaking. It's too much, it's not enough. Luca's hand closes over the back of my head and smoothes my hair down, his other hand still firm around my waist, holding me to him. I feel his lips press to my scalp, kissing it.

"*Violetta,*" he says, with utter desolation in his voice. "*Violetta, cosa mi fai?*"

"What are you doing to me?" he's saying. And I want to repeat his words back to him, but I know he doesn't expect an answer.

I keep my face pressed into his shoulder, because it will be the last time. I try to smell his skin, but the fresh flowing water carries scents away, and when I eventually pull back, there's an extra little rush of heartbreak because I know it means that I will never have Luca's scent in my nostrils again, will never again be close enough to him to have that luxury.

There's nothing to say. His hands fall from me and he steps back, enough to let me slip past him, turning my face away, because I'm shallow, and the sight of him with his hair slicked back and his mouth red from kissing will make me do what I know I can't: throw myself at him all over again.

I dive down and swim as many strokes as I can underwater. Coming up briefly for air, I dive straight down again, swimming against the current, pulling hard with strong strokes of my arms, beneath the bridge, out the other side, emerging breathless to find Kelly, Paige, and Kendra in the river, splashing one another with squeals and shrieks. The boys, of course, are joining in eagerly, a commotion that completely camouflages my reappearance. Kelly glances at me and says:

"Oh! There you are!" and then some boy cannonballs in, drenching us all, and she screams happily along with the rest of them, and I make my way to the bank and slide into the now-empty thermal pool, soaking in the milky-white, sulfur-smelling hot water, watching them all cavort blissfully and saying to myself, over and over again:

*He can't be my brother. He can't be my brother—half brother! He can't be! How could I possibly feel like this about him if he were my brother?*

I keep my eyes away from the right bank of the river, the side with the roadhouse restaurant. In fact, I turn my back to it. That's simple enough. I don't want to see Luca, and somehow I know that he won't stay in the river; he won't want to come and join our merry group now. There's no danger of that, of having to smile and pretend that everything's okay while being horribly, intensely aware of Luca's presence; or worse, having to watch him talk and laugh with other girls. The thought of that makes me shiver in repulsion. I remember how jealous I've been of Elisa, Leonardo's sister, who's made a huge play for Luca. Even though I know that I'm the one Luca wants, what difference does that really make when Luca and I can't be together?

Bodies crash back into the thermal pool, slippery as they slide past me, chilly from the cooler river water, wet hair slapping against backs, breath being caught; Kelly, plopping in next to me, wraps an arm around my shoulders, drops her head against my arm, and says blissfully:

"This is the best night *ever*!"

Andrea and Leo, squashing up opposite us, have their hair plastered over their faces, their eyes shining with the success of their evening plans. I look at them and see that Leo's arm is around Paige, who's half on his lap. Andrea is staring at Kendra, who's ignoring him, chatting with Evan; I give her points, because even with the rivalry she has with Kelly, she's not using the fact that Andrea prefers her to wind Kelly up.

"Andrea—" Kelly says, and I watch him turn to look at her, his eyes passing over me, not in an unfriendly way, but simply as if I'm not here. To Andrea and Leo, I'm part of the furniture, just another girl who looks like so many other Italian girls: not different, not special in any way, not a strapping blonde or a black goddess or a redheaded, charmingly freckled Irish girl.

As Andrea decides to push himself off his side of the thermal hot tub and over to Kelly, I reflect that maybe that's why I'm so obsessed with Luca. He's the only boy I've ever known who looks at me as if I'm the only girl in the world, as if, when he's with me, he doesn't even notice anyone else. As if he and I are in a bubble, suspended out of time.

Andrea is hugging Kelly now, whispering in her ear, snuggling up next to her, setting his shoulders against the stone surround of the pool, pulling her familiarly back against him. I know how happy this will make her, that the boy she's so keen on, has been crushing on since she first saw him, is finally singling her out, showing her attention. I cross my fingers, hoping that it isn't just to make Kendra jealous, that Andrea has realized now he has no chance with Kendra and is turning his focus to someone who actually likes him back.

But as I glance sideways, I see that Andrea, though stroking Kelly's arms, is not looking down at her head, nestled below him. His chin is up, his gaze directed to the other side of the pool, where Kendra is chatting with Evan about some people they both know in the States, her skin glowing dark and luminous against the milky water and the white of her bra. Her hair is pulled back into a short ponytail, showing off her strong jaw and full mouth.

*Oh dear*, I think feebly.

And just then, Evan, probably sensing that I'm looking his way, turns and grins at me.

"Having a good time, Violet?" he calls.

I nod, and find myself thinking:

*Why does it feel so special when someone uses your name? Didn't some ancient society have a custom that you had a secret name that only the people you really trusted knew, because using it gave people power over you?*

*If that's true, and not just something I read in a novel, I really understand it now. There's something so nice about a boy saying your name. As if he likes you for yourself, what's inside as well as outside. Not just your boobs and face, but your brain, too.*

Deliberately, I make myself smile back at him.

*I'm getting over Luca*, I tell myself. *I have to start somewhere.*

# A Girl on a Mission

"Oh, my *head*!" Paige moans, but none of us cares. Not even the littlest bit.

We're all still waking up slowly, acclimating to the bright daytime after our late night—we didn't get back from the hot springs till two in the morning—and we all feel a little bit delicate, as if we're missing a protective layer of skin. Paige always wants the most attention, gets ratty if she isn't the loudest in the group. *Which is annoying right now,* I think crossly, *as she's the tallest and the blondest–can't that be enough for her?*

Clearly not.

"Oww!" she tries again, but the three of us keep ignoring her.

Thank goodness we don't have lessons this morning; it's Saturday, which means market day in the village, Greve in Chianti. Market day is a huge deal. Greve has a pretty triangular piazza filled with shops, but the prices are way beyond our budgets; plus, they mostly sell stuff girls don't want to buy. The stores are geared toward older, richer tourists—ceramics, olive-wood bowls and chopping boards, household items.

But the market on Saturday is another thing. It could have been designed especially for teenage girls. Elisa goes down to the village in the Range Rover every Saturday at ten, and we can join if we want, but we got up too late today and had to tumble down the rough path that leads down the hill. It's like a goat track, narrow and rocky, and it won't be much fun going back up, but we were still determined not to miss out. Lorries are pulled up around the three sides of the piazza, the stalls folding out from them, metal frames hung to the rafters with cheap, enticing clothes on hangers, and tables covered with secondhand lucky dips or shoes lined up on their boxes. Every week we lose ourselves in the market for a couple of hours, trying things on, working out what we can afford, doing deals like "if we split this, I'll wear it this week and you can next week."

Paige shoots toward the hat stall. As always, the only people browsing there are foreigners, Japanese and English; the Americans usually wear baseball caps, and the Italians wouldn't be caught dead in hats for some reason. Paige is picking up a soft, broad-brimmed straw hat in stripes of white and blue, its crown trimmed in a wide dark-blue satin ribbon; when she plops it over her blond curls, she looks like

Brigitte Bardot in an old film. Even squinting at her through our sunglasses, we have to admit she looks great.

"She's so lucky, being tall like that," Kelly says wistfully. "She can carry anything off."

Pirouetting in the hat, Paige is getting what she wants from the crowd, what we're too knackered to give her: she's the focus of all eyes.

*"Che bonona,"* says one guy devoutly, which we've learned is a compliment paid to girls who aren't skinny-thin: it means "curvy and beautiful."

I'm not in the mood for Paige's antics today. And I've stopped spending money on clothes at the market; I've discovered something I like much better. I gesture to Kelly to let her know where I'll be, and weave my way a few stalls down, to a *banchino* where a lady sells art supplies. Sketchpads, pastels and crayons, brushes, tubes of watercolor and oil paint, all kinds of paper . . . it's a treasure trove for me. Learning to draw and paint has been a huge revelation since I came to Italy. I thought I wanted to study art history, but more and more, with the art lessons we're having here, I think I want to do art itself instead. And from the encouragement I've been getting from our teacher, Luigi, I honestly think I might have some talent.

The problem, though, is that I'm on one track already; the exams I've done, the path I've chosen, all lead to a different destination. I can't believe, talking to Paige and Kendra, how much better the system is in the US. There, you study all sorts of subjects till you're eighteen, and even when you go to college, you don't have to choose what you're going to focus on for at least a year or two. It sounds brilliant. Kelly and I have grown up in a very different setting, where, at sixteen, you pick three or four subjects to concentrate on, and by eighteen you've decided exactly what you want to study at college.

I had no idea there was so much more freedom in the US for what you could study. Every time I think about it, I'm riven with jealousy. It's so unfair. The choices I made at sixteen have trapped me in a way I never anticipated, and so has the choice my mum made when she sent me to a trendy London private school that didn't teach anything as unfashionable as formal art lessons. It never occurred to me that I might actually be able to draw, to paint; the girls who studied art at St. Tabby's were all doing installations, conceptual pieces where they took photographs of one another and scratched them up, performance work where they wandered around the school in tight-fitting bodysuits, striking poses and being really significant. They were all very thin and pretty—to be honest, I think the photos and bodysuits were mostly about showing off how thin they were. We might have visited proper museums, but St. Tabby's was obsessed with being modern, cutting-edge; it wouldn't have occurred to the art teacher to give lessons in something as conventional as drawing properly.

Which is what I long to be able to do. I'm determined to ask my mum for art lessons as soon as I get back to London, continuing what I'm learning here with Luigi. But I'm worried that a few months of art lessons won't be remotely enough to put together a portfolio that will get me into art school. . . .

"*Ciao!*" says the woman behind the stall, smiling at me. "*Bentornata!*"

That means "welcome back." I smile, saying "*Ciao,*" and she continues:

"*Posso aiutarti?*"

"*Sì,*" I answer. She's asking if she can help me. I point to the pastels. "*Questi–e carta?*"

I'm asking, I hope, what paper goes with the pastels. She pulls out a sheaf, and starts to lay them out in front of me in a fan. Her eyes flicker sideways, and her smile deepens as she exclaims:

"*Oh! Luigi!*"

She bustles around the side of the stall to greet the man beside me, Luigi, our art teacher, kissing him on both cheeks, the way they do in Italy. Luigi calls a "*ciao*" to me in greeting, and the two of them rattle away to each other, much too fast for me to understand. I start pulling out pieces of paper, concentrating on the things I want to try to sketch, plus the budget I've allowed myself for today, and I get quite distracted.

By the time I've assembled my selection, Kendra is next to me, managing to patter away pretty well in Italian. She's propped her bum against the table, blocking the view of the stall so the person talking to her can't be distracted by its contents and has to look straight at her. She's tilted her head to one side and is playing with a lock of hair, her lips parted as she stares at the man she's focused on with her huge, dark, slightly slanting eyes.

I wince in a mixture of shock and revulsion. Because it's

definitely a man, not a boy. The person at whom Kendra is directing the full force of her considerable flirtatious wiles is Luigi.

It makes me incredibly uncomfortable to watch. I realize that, for the first time ever, flirting so openly, Kendra looks needy. Vulnerable.

Luigi is in profile to me. I notice his wide neck, his stocky body, the shirtsleeves rolled up above his elbows, displaying his muscly—and hairy—forearms. Hair sprouts from the open neck of his shirt, between the glinting links of his gold necklace, tight dark curls like the short ringlets that cover his skull closely, and I can even see hair at his neck . . . eww. Everything about Luigi is adult. Not like the boys we hang out with, boys our own age. Evan's muscly, but there's a solidity about Luigi, a confidence that comes with time. He must be well over thirty—double our age.

They're oblivious to me, and that makes me even more uncomfortable, as I'm so close that I could reach out and touch them both. They're pretty much the same height—Kendra's tall, easily as tall as many men here in Italy—which means that as they lean closer to each other, their faces are on the same level. Luigi's voice is a deep rumble, Kendra's soft, a tone I haven't heard from her before. It's as if she's speaking quietly to draw him in. And if that's her goal, it's working. He shifts, takes a step nearer to her, and as I watch him reach his hand toward her, clearly about to touch her arm, I can't stand it anymore.

"Kendra!" I say loudly, and I barge sideways, interrupting Luigi's gesture, catching it on my shoulder and ignoring it completely. "Look what I'm getting!"

She looks dazed. Her eyes are wide and shiny. It takes her a moment to turn her head toward me, and even then there's another long moment before she blurts out:

"Oh! Hi, Violet! I didn't see you there."

*Oh, please,* I think, and even in my thoughts my tone is withering. *You knew perfectly well I was here. You mean you forgot all about me because you were so busy making googly eyes at Luigi. And he was so busy perving after you.*

"Are you getting anything?" I ask, still loudly. "I'm going to pay for my stuff, and then we should find Kelly and Paige. So are you getting anything?"

I sound like I'm on an endless loop. But I can't think of anything else to say; the sight of Luigi about to stroke Kendra's arm has turned my stomach. I'm babbling from embarrassment.

"*Brava, Violetta!*" Luigi says to me, wrenching his gaze away from Kendra with what looks like a major effort, and glancing down at the pile of paper, pastels, and crayons I've assembled. "*Ti dai proprio da fare, eh?*"

I work through the Italian carefully, translate it as "you're working hard," and say "*Sì*," handing the pile to the stall owner. The trouble is that Luigi is a great teacher, enthusiastic and strict in good balance, and I'm the only student of his who's really keen. Paige and Kelly dropped out of art classes almost immediately, and, to be honest, I've wondered before why Kendra didn't too; she doesn't have much talent or much interest. Now it's hit me like a ton of bricks why she keeps coming to class.

I pay for the art supplies and take the bag, my brain racing. Luigi and Kendra are still standing there looking at each other. I take a deep breath, link my arm through Kendra's, and physically pull her into the fray again, joining the stream of people who are flowing down the wide aisle between stalls.

"I hope Paige got that hat!" I observe, loudly again. I'm stuck on one volume setting and can't get it down. "'Cause then it'll be really easy to spot her!"

I sound like an idiot, but I feel so awkward, icky, confused, that it's hard to get words out at all: I don't know how to process what I just saw. It's with huge relief that I do spot the blue and white brim of Paige's hat bobbing above the crowd; my arm still twined through Kendra's, I navigate us toward it. I feel that if I let go of her she'll slip right back to Luigi.

"Hey!" I say brightly as we reach Paige and Kelly, who are looking at shoes; this stall is too expensive for us, but the stock is amazing. Stacked leather wedges trimmed with suede flowers, fastened with narrow silver and gold straps that wrap around and around the ankle; crazy stiletto heels that would be mad to wear here on the cobblestones but are just ridiculously beautiful.

"I keep hoping she'll lower the price," Paige says, "because they're all here week after week, but it's still forty-nine euros. . . ."

"*Way* too much," Kelly says, turning away with a sigh.

"I need to talk to you," I hiss at her. "Let's hit the library now."

"Are we going to the rotisserie chicken stall?" Paige asks. "I'm getting hungry."

"Why don't you and Kendra go and get lunch," Kelly says, coming over all organized, "and then join us in the park with the benches in half an hour? Opposite the cinema? Violet and I want to go to the library."

"Okay!" Paige says happily. I fumble for some euros to give her, but she waves me away. "I got this," she says cheerfully. "You can treat next week."

"Get lots of the fried veggies," I say. "I love those."

"And the polenta," Kelly says eagerly.

I hesitate for a moment, wondering if I should tell Paige to keep Kendra away from the art stall and Luigi, but then I realize that's impossible and silly. It would be for nothing, anyway; we'll see Luigi this afternoon, for our art lesson. My plastic bag of art supplies swinging from my wrist, I follow Kelly through the crowds.

We turn under the stone colonnades that run around the sides of the piazza. In front of the bars are casual wrought-iron tables and benches, and chic dark-brown woven chairs and tables covered in cream cloths outside Nerbone, the smart restaurant. I always look with envy at the people lunching or dining in Nerbone; the food smells delicious, the tinkle of glasses and cutlery is enticing, the clientele is so smart.

And then I see Luca and Elisa, Catia's daughter, our implacable enemy, having lunch at a table beside the hedge that wraps around Nerbone's dining area. They look—perfect. Elisa is, as always, chic, wearing a slightly transparent shirt over a miniskirt that shows off her long, thin, tanned legs. Luca is in a white linen shirt and jeans. They're each holding a glass of straw-colored white wine, talking and laughing without a care in the world. It's as if he and I hadn't had that dark, deep, passionate moment in the river yesterday, as if he could dismiss me, completely, from his mind. . . .

Kelly hasn't seen them, I think. I turn my head so he won't catch my stare; I believe we have a bond, which means he'll sense I'm looking at him. And I couldn't bear to see Luca raise his glass at me mockingly, saying with a glint in his dark-blue eyes, *You ran away from me last night, so why shouldn't I go out with Elisa? I'm free to see whoever I like, aren't I?*

He *is* free. Of course he is. I scurry away as fast as if the cobblestones were burning my feet, around the corner of the piazza, past the big stall that sells plants and herbs and flowers set out in pots and vases all over the pavement. We shoot across the traffic lights, crossing the little bridge over the Greve River, quacking ducks below calling to one another as they float on the shallow water. We pass the huge iron sculpture of a black rooster, the symbol of Chianti and its wines, turn left before the cinema, and walk down the path to the village library. Kelly discovered it first—in part, I think, as somewhere to hang out when the rest of us were wandering around the shops or sitting in the piazza having coffees and debating purchases. She has very little cash, and saying she wanted to go to the library was a clever way to avoid spending money while simultaneously looking good.

That's Kelly in a nutshell. She thinks things over, works out solutions, plots and plans, uses her considerable brainpower to her best advantage. Of course, I would have bought her coffees, as many as she wanted, but she's too proud for that. She'd see it as charity. And I admire her for her pride too, this clever new friend I've made in Italy.

"Did you see Luca?" she asks as we trot down the path.

"Yes," I say shortly, flinching at the pain that every mention of Luca's name gives me. "And I saw Elisa, too."

Luca's father is a *principe,* which means "prince"; Luca will inherit the title, and the castle, so Elisa is utterly focused on snagging him. Ditto Catia, who's very ambitious for her daughter. We've all seen Catia working her friendship with Luca's mother, the principessa, to maneuver their children together; we're all regularly snubbed by Elisa, who called us pigs the first time she saw us; and we all, in consequence, hate her guts.

Kelly comments obliquely:

"That's why we need to find out about you."

I nod. The chink in Elisa's armor is the attention that Luca pays me, the genuine feelings he has for me. It annoys her tremendously, and though of course that's not the reason I'm so keen on Luca, I can't help admitting that it's an extra bonus, the icing on the cake. If somehow we can prove that he and I aren't closely related, if we can be free to see each other, apart from making me ecstatic, it will drive Elisa crazy.

"I'm emailing my mum as soon as we get back to the villa," I say. "I've already got it mostly written in my head."

"Good," Kelly says, turning to give me a very direct gaze, her hazel eyes clear. "And now we'll start on the research side of things."

She reaches out and squeezes my hand. We walk together the last part of the way still holding hands, something I'd never do in England, where it's for little girls only; but in Italy, people are much more openly affectionate. They kiss each other's cheeks on greeting; they embrace when they feel affectionate; grown men walk down the street with their arms around each other.

"*Ciao, Kellee,*" says the librarian, smiling at us as we come in. "*Buon giorno.*"

"*Buon giorno, Sandra,*" Kelly says. "*Questa è mia amica Violetta. Abbiamo bisogno di aiuto.*"

"We need help," she's saying. I nod and smile. I hatched this idea yesterday, on the drive home from Siena, but since Kelly's Italian is better than mine, she launches into the words that explain what we're after: I make out the words "Castello di Vesperi," Luca's home. The librarian's nodding, standing up, leading us over to a section of books against the far wall, and I follow Kelly as we sit down where she indicates. We look at each other excitedly as the librarian pulls a large coffee-table book from the shelves, opens it, and places it triumphantly in front of us.

It's called *Castelli di Chianti,* Chianti Castles. We're looking at a beautiful, glossy photograph of the Castello di Vesperi high on a hill, with its vineyards and olive groves below, and the cypress-lined drive curving up to it.

"*Grazie,*" I say to Sandra, beaming as we turn the pages and realize that there's tons of history about the castello here. Exactly what I'm after.

And then I gasp, and nudge Kelly so hard she tips on her plastic chair.

"*Look!*" I hiss.

In a black-and-white thumbnail photograph, in a cluster of other reproduced family portraits, is a head-and-shoulders picture of the girl I saw in the painting in London. She's very like the other members of the di Vesperi family: as the principessa said when she saw me, the family features are distinctive.

I know it's the same girl. I pull out my phone, call up the photo I took in London of the portrait, and hold it against the picture in the book. The hair is subtly different, and so is the neckline of her dress; it's not the same portrait. But it's definitely the same person.

Kelly points wordlessly to the footnotes at the bottom of the page, which give details of all the pictures. *Fiammetta di Vesperi,* we read. *Nata 1732, mortà 1754, della febbre tifoide.*

"The typhoid fever," I say sadly, puzzling out the words. "She was so young!"

I can't even imagine having only a few more years to live. It feels like my life has barely begun; I've got so much I want to do, so many places I want to go. To have that all closed down so fast, to feel an end coming so soon, is unimaginable.

Did Fiammetta have any idea of her impending death when this portrait was painted? I stare down at the picture of Fiammetta di Vesperi, who was, more than likely, a distant ancestor of mine. Her dark eyes look back at me, their gaze steady and determined; her forehead is smooth, unworried, and her lips are set together firmly.

I take courage from that look of hers. She's a girl on a mission, like me. I sense that even in her short life, she knew what she wanted and pushed to get it, made every moment count.

I resolve to do the same.

# It's Definitely a Boy

Darling Mum,
There's something I have to ask you, and I really, really need you to get back to me right away. Please believe that I wouldn't be bringing this up if it weren't incredibly important to me. You're the best mum in the world, okay? And you always will be. I know how much you and Dad love me—up to the sky and back again, remember saying that when I was little?
But something really odd happened here a few days ago, and I can't stop thinking about it. . . .

I sketch in a summary of the events at the Castello di Vesperi. I don't just describe the principessa being struck by the resemblance between me and her husband's family, but also my likeness to so many portraits in the gallery, how many times my face appeared there, in different historical periods, different dresses, different hair arrangements—yet still my face. The di Vesperi female face.

I say that I've always known I didn't look like my tall, skinny Scottish father and Scandinavian mother, with their long freckled pale limbs and their blond (Mum) or sandy (Dad) hair, their pale blue eyes; that it never bothered me (which is a lie), but that I suddenly started thinking about it after the visit to the castello (another lie). That I love her, will always love her just the same whatever she tells me (the truth, the absolute truth), but that I want to know if there's any remote reason she could possibly think of to explain this weird resemblance. . . .

I wish she weren't alone. My parents divorced years ago, and my dad lives in Hong Kong now with the horrible girlfriend he left my mum for, a Danish woman called Sif who hates me, resents how much Dad loves me, and tries out of jealousy to pretend I don't exist. (I console myself with the reflection that her name sounds almost exactly like a brand of loo cleaner.) But although he doesn't notice awful Sif doing her best to snub me when I visit them, he's still, thank goodness, an amazing dad.

He isn't with Mum anymore, and I've accepted that. Mum isn't seeing anyone, though. She's on her own. I brighten up, remembering that her sister, my aunt Lissie, was going to come to London and visit her while I was away; Aunt Lissie used to model too, like my mum, and she's a stylist now, traveling all over the world for magazines. Hopefully Aunt Lissie's there now, when this email arrives.

Mum usually talks everything over with me. This, I realize, will be the first time she can't.

I knew that Mum and I were maybe a bit too close. That coming away to Italy might not be the worst thing for either of us. But this is truly bringing it home to me.

I swallow as I read through the email again.

I love you so much, and I always will. Whatever you might have to tell me could never change that, I promise. I know how much you and Dad love me! But please, if there is anything to tell, please do it now! You could email or ring me, whatever you want. But please, please, Mum, let me know.
All my love,
Violet x x x x x

Before I can think it over, I hit Send. It's gone. I watch the blue line at the bottom of the screen grow, stretching from left to right as the message is in transit, a heartbeat in which, conceivably, I could—shut the laptop? Jam my finger on the off button? Throw it against the wall?

I don't know if any of that would work: whether, as soon as you send an email, it shoots up into the cloud like a puff of air. And anyway, it happens so fast; it's gone in a split second. Before I could even try to stop it, the possibility has vanished.

*This had to happen,* I tell myself. *You didn't have a choice. You had to ask her. And it was better to email her, to give her time to think this over and decide how to handle it, not to put her on the spot in person by ringing her, or waiting till you see her again.*

I could never have been brave enough to ask her to her face if I was adopted—or if Dad wasn't my real father. . . .

I jump up, slam the laptop shut, and dash out of the bedroom I share with Kelly as if I were being chased by a pack of wild dogs. I can't think about this any longer. I tear down the stairs, my bare feet slapping on the stone, through the hallway, out the front door, and around the house to the swimming pool. Pulling off my cover-up, chucking it on the stone flags, I dive in, the shock of the cool water on my overheated skin exactly what I need to stop me thinking. I do a length underwater as fast as I can, and when I come up, gasping and shaking my head, I realize that everyone's staring at me.

"Wow," Evan says, looking over his guitar, which is propped on his lap as he sits cross-legged on a towel. "You in a race with the Invisible Man?"

I giggle at this image.

"*Violet,*" he sings, strumming a chord. "*Running a race with a serious face–so did you win? Or was it him? Don't forget, Vio*-let–*Dive in!*"

He ends on a high falsetto note, grinning at me.

"That doesn't make much sense," he adds. "But hey, at least I rhymed your name."

"Violet's pretty easy," I say, propping my arms on the edge of the pool and smiling back at him. "Regret, forget, net, jet, yet, set, bet—"

"Try Evan," he suggests. "Apart from numbers and heaven, which gets old *very* quickly, there's practically nothing."

"Numbers? Oh! Eleven . . . seven . . ." I furrow my brow.

"Devon," Kelly calls over. "That's a county in England."

"Leaven," I add. "You do it to bread."

Evan's expression is comical, his blue eyes stretched as wide as they'll go as he plucks a string and, in a singsong nursery-rhyme voice, intones:

*"From the age of seven to eleven*

*Before he tragically went to heaven*

*Evan leavened bread in Devon."*

He throws his hands wide. "See? Not much to work with."

"At least you don't have rude stuff that rhymes with you," Kelly says gloomily. "They called me Smelly Jelly Belly at school for years."

"And Kendra isn't that great either. It sort of sounds like bend-ya," Kendra adds.

I can't help smiling that Kendra and Kelly are competitive in everything, even down to whose name rhymes with worse stuff.

*"Kendra,"* Evan sings, playing a chord, *"I would never bend ya,*

*or lend ya*

*or send ya . . .*

*Oh, the words I can engender*

*thinking about Kendra . . ."*

" 'Engender'!" Kelly exclaims. "That's really good!"

I pull myself out of the pool and walk over to a lounger, picking up a towel and wrapping it around myself; I sit on one side of Evan, Kelly on the other. Even cool-as-a-cucumber Kendra has sat up to watch Evan playing his guitar.

"What about Paige?" I ask, looking over at his sister, the only one uninterested in her brother's talent. She's got a moisturizing pack on her hair—her head is wrapped in the special leopard-skin towel she uses when she's doing a hair treatment—pink headphones on her ears, and a magazine in her hands as she reclines on her lounger.

"*Paige goes into a rage when you tell her she's not yet legal drinking age–*" Evan sings immediately, and Paige, who must have been listening after all, promptly throws her magazine at his head. He ducks easily, and it flies past and lands on the tiles.

"You haven't done me yet!" Kelly says wistfully, twisting her hair over one shoulder, playing with the ends. She's got some sun since she's been here, taking it slowly and carefully after a couple of days where she went bright pink; now her fair skin looks sun-kissed, her freckles standing out prettily across her nose, and she's been squeezing lemon juice over her red hair to lighten it, which has worked a little. She looks very pretty staring at Evan imploringly. He grins, strums a series of soft chords, and starts to croon:

"*Oh, Kelly,*
*you make my legs weak like jelly.*
*Oh, Kelly . . .*
*I get butterflies in my belly.*
*Oh, Kelly,*
uh, *your perfume is so sweet and smelly, Kelly . . .*"

She's giggling now.

"Sorry," Evan says, plucking a final chord. "Turns out even I can't make smelly into a compliment."

"Two out of three isn't bad," I point out, very impressed with Evan's skills. He can sketch out a tune really fast, and switch between styles; one moment he's doing a blues song, then pop, and the one he made up for me was like something from a musical.

As if he's reading my mind, he echoes, turning to look at me, drawing out the syllables:

*"Don't forget, Vio-*let*–Dive in!"*

This time he ends the line low and gentle, and it isn't a musical number anymore. It's almost a love song.

"You mind if I work on that?" he asks, leaning on the guitar, looking at me. "That's kinda nice. I could do something with that."

"Oh!" I don't quite know what to say. "Sure," I add.

"Ooh! Evan's writing Violet a love song!" Paige whoops, coming over and retrieving her magazine. "Evan and Violet sitting in a tree, K-I-S-S-I-N-G!"

I expect Evan to look embarrassed, or to tell Paige to shut up, but he just grins again, bending over his guitar, starting to strum it again, quite unaffected by his sister.

"*Paige,*" he sings to me,

"*needs to act her age. . . .*

*Such a shame*

*She's such a pain*

*It's a* terrible *strain. . . .*"

I laugh and settle back on the lounger, watching him play, his hands moving with surprising lightness and dexterity on the strings. Kelly is watching him too, and so's Kendra, who has slipped into the pool and is propped up on the side, her dark limbs gleaming with the water, sunglasses on her nose; we're circled around him, enchanted by someone who can make music this easily.

*Well,* I admit, *a* boy *who can make music this easily.* Let's be honest, if it were one of us, we wouldn't all be gathering around like worshippers at a shrine. And if it were a girl playing, would a bunch of boys be sitting around her? Or would they be trying to grab the guitar from her so they could show off themselves?

That's not fair, though. Evan isn't showing off; he's genuinely enjoying himself. His head ducked over the guitar, his lips moving as he tries out lyrics under his breath, he's completely unaffected, I can tell; like his sister, he's very open and outgoing, but unlike Paige, he doesn't crave attention.

*He's so nice,* I think. *Why can't I like Evan? Why can't I feel as excited when I see Evan as I do when I see Luca? It would make my life so much easier!*

As if sensing my thoughts, Evan raises his head and looks directly at me, his blue eyes clear and candid. The blond eyelashes glint in the sunshine, tiny gold threads, and his tanned skin creases into fans of equally tiny white lines as he smiles at me.

I like Evan a lot, I realize. And as he bends his head once more, his thick fair hair close to his scalp, I wonder what it would feel like to run my hand over it, whether it would be bristly under my palm, or unexpectedly soft and silky. . . .

I feel a shiver running down my back, as if someone trickled a few slow, icy drops of water down the beads of my spine, running between my shoulder blades. I wriggle a little; the sensation's unexpectedly pleasant. I'm still staring at Evan's bent head, and suddenly I connect the two things.

*Oh. Maybe I could like Evan that way after all.*

I'm so absorbed in my thoughts that I haven't seen the flash of sunlight on metal that means a car is coming up the winding drive, working its way around the switchback bends. I don't notice the other girls stir, sit up, because a car approaching at this time of day is very likely to contain precious cargo: i.e., at least one boy.

Up this steep hill, without our own transport, and a long, sweaty walk to the village, we've quickly got attuned to the rhythms of Villa Barbiano, the times that people come and go. The post lady drops off the mail between twelve and one—we've learned not to get excited at the sight of her white Panda chugging up the hill. Catia goes down to the village early, to do the marketing, but after that her jeep stays in its ivy-covered shelter and doesn't go out unless she's taking us on an excursion or, occasionally, leaving us in the evening for dinner with a friend. So, in the afternoon, a car might be Elisa, Catia's unpleasant, skinny daughter, which would be a definite negative.

Or it might be Leonardo. And Leonardo almost always means Andrea, too; they're like a two-for-one offer.

I only hear the car when the wheels spin loudly, whisking up the gravel of the parking area, set on a terrace below the pool. That means it's definitely a boy: only boys drive like that, announcing their arrival with a whirl of loose stone on rubber. And the swift, imperative series of honks that follow confirm it. Catia would be furious if Elisa disturbed the afternoon peace by pounding the car horn like that, but her son gets away with much more. Catia may be American, but she's fully adapted to the Italian way of parenting, where boys seem to be pampered to an almost limitless extent.

*Like Luca with his mother, the principessa,* I reflect. *She fawns on him as if he were already the prince he'll be when he inherits from his father.*

Then, because I'm not thinking about Luca, I determinedly push that idea away and look up to the terrace of the villa, where a distraction is being offered in the shape of Elisa. She's leaning over the stone balcony like a modern Juliet, all streaked hair and dangling gold earrings, a huge pair of sunglasses obscuring most of the upper part of her face, her lips pouting as she blows a theatrical kiss to the parking lot, then raises one thin arm to wave, gold bracelets clinking so loudly we can hear them over the soft strumming of Evan's guitar and the chattering of the crickets.

*So it's not Leonardo or Andrea,* I realize. *Elisa wouldn't bother to put on a full charm offensive for her brother or his friend.* I turn to glance down at the parking lot just as Elisa yodels:

"*O! Ciao, bello! Arrivo!*"

"I'm coming," she's saying. I realize who she's calling to just a flash of a second too late; I've already turned my head, am gazing at the car that's pulled up at an angle across the center of the lot, not parked, but waiting to pick up a passenger. The driver's door is open, and Luca's leaning on it, elbows propped on the top, in a white linen shirt, his black hair raked back from his brow, sunglasses dangling from his long fingers.

As soon as I catch sight of him, he lifts his head, as if he's sensing me. Our eyes meet.

*Oh no. I can't do this.*

I get a flash of sapphire, and it's awful, it's too intense. How can just a momentary glance do this to me? It's ridiculous, beyond stupid, and when Luca promptly lifts his sunglasses, slides them onto his nose, and raises his head further, chin tilted up, clearly avoiding my gaze, I'm grateful. I really am. I tell myself so, very firmly.

But then I see him looking at Elisa, raising his hand to wave back to her as she positively dashes along the terrace on her high stacked heels, pale layers of chiffon wafting around her top half, her lower half almost completely visible in her taupe cuffed shorts. She has really good legs, and she knows it: long, slim, bronzed, enviable. Elisa flits across my eyeline and then, mercifully, disappears as she heads down the steps at the end of the terrace. Going to meet Luca.

The other girls are all glancing at me to see how I'm dealing with this. I reach up to my hair, lifting it, squeezing water out of it down my back, and I know that the movement summons Luca's attention back to me. I can feel his eyes on me now as I move closer to Evan on the lounger, looking at his hands moving on the strings, the typical girl admiring a boy playing a guitar. Evan flashes me a smile and keeps strumming away, quite unaware of the little drama being enacted around him.

"*Don't forget, Vio*-let," he croons softly. And though I can't really sing, not properly, I know the tune now, and my head leans in toward his as I join in on the last two words:

"*Dive in!*"

He finishes on a last, rising chord and lifts his head, our faces close now. The sunshine beats down on us; the blue water of the swimming pool glints brightly in the heat, the breeze raising tiny ripples on the surface. Evan's eyes are as clear and blue as the water, with no hidden currents, no unexpected, dangerous undertow. The rosemary and lavender bushes planted around the verge are wafting a lovely, sun-warmed scent, bees buzzing in the lavender. It's paradise. It *should* be paradise.

In the parking lot below, tires screech. We all jump. Luca must be executing the tightest, sharpest three-point turn in history: the car scrapes, churns, tears up the gravel, and shoots out of the lot and down the drive so fast we wince. It snaps back and forth like Road Runner as he speeds downhill. Only a very good driver could make those switchback turns so fast without crashing—and he's very lucky he didn't meet anyone coming up.

"Wow! I guess they have somewhere they really need to be," Paige observes.

"More like someone to get away from," Kelly says dryly under her breath, so only I can hear her.

"Whatever," Kendra says, standing up. "We've got art class coming up, Violet."

"Really?"

I glance up at the sun, still high in the sky; art class doesn't start till five-thirty, and it can't even be near five yet.

"I'm going in to change," Kendra says, pulling her sarong around her, tying it at her slender waist. Slipping her feet into her flip-flops, she pads back to the house, watched by the three of us girls; none of us say a word until she's well out of earshot.

Then Paige turns back to me and Kelly and says:

"*Riiiiight.* Because it takes nearly an *hour* to get ready for art class."

"It does if you have a crush the size of Big Ben on the art teacher," Kelly zings back.

"She isn't even any good at art!" Paige giggles. "I mean, not like Violet!"

"Violet's *brilliant,*" Kelly says, very pleased to have found an opportunity to both praise me, her friend and ally, and get in a dig at Kendra, her rival for Brainiest Girl in Villa Barbiano. "Her paintings are *gorgeous.*"

"Oh yeah?" Evan says to me. He's very good at tuning out girl talk and focusing only on the important information—a skill doubtless acquired from a lifetime of living with Paige. "What do you paint?"

"Still lifes, at the moment," I say, feeling self-conscious. "But I'd really like to do portraits. We need a life model, though, and Kelly won't do it and Paige can't stay still for long enough."

"I fidget," Paige says cheerfully.

Kelly ducks her head and doesn't say anything; she's too self-conscious about her looks to want them immortalized. Though she's finding out that curvy girls, in Italy, are considered attractive, she's still not as slim as she'd like; she's definitely cutting down on pasta and bread.

"I'll do it," Evan offers. "If you want."

"Oh! Would you?" I say eagerly. "That would be *great.* Luigi said if one of the girls would do it, he'd teach me figure drawing—you could come along to class this afternoon and see if he'll be okay with starting now."

"Ha! Evan's going to take his clothes off, Evan's going to

take his clothes off!" Paige yodels. "Violet and Kendra are going to draw Evan's pee-pee!"

Evan goes bright red.

"Um—I really don't think I'll be okay with—" he starts to blurt out.

"No!" I say just as quickly. "I'm sure you don't need to!"

"That would be like, from zero to a hundred," Kelly observes, grinning now. "One day you're drawing flowers, the next day a big naked American!"

"I'm *sure* you could just take your shirt off," I say firmly to a still-red Evan. "That's more than enough to be getting on with."

*Definitely,* I reflect, remembering Evan's naked torso in the club, his big, defined muscles. *More than enough.*

And I stand up quickly, mumbling something about going to have a shower, because I have the suspicion that I'm going red too.

# Spill the Beans!

I still haven't heard from Mum. It's been a whole six hours since I sent the email. She could be out for the day, I suppose, seeing a film, going to a museum. Maybe Aunt Lissie's visiting and they're out to dinner. Or maybe she simply hasn't checked her email. Mum isn't remotely technological and barely goes online. She doesn't even like booking airline tickets on the computer—she's always moaning about the olden, pre-Internet days, when travel agencies did all that kind of thing for you. I can't even imagine how slow that would have been.

So it's totally, a hundred percent normal that Mum hasn't got back to me yet. She'll have her phone with her, on silent if necessary but never turned off, in case I need to get in touch with her urgently; she'll check it constantly for messages or missed calls, but it wouldn't occur to her to keep checking her email.

She probably hasn't even read it yet. It's just not possible that she's sobbing on her bed, curled up in a ball, reduced to an absolute tearstained mess because I wrote to her asking if there's something about my birth that she and Dad haven't told me. . . .

And yet, I can't relax. I can't sit still.

Unfortunately for my restless mood, it's a quiet night in with no outside distractions. We've had dinner, at which Leonardo and Andrea didn't make an appearance. So no offers from them to take us to the village for coffee and gelato, which we often do now. In Italy all the teenagers eat at home and go out afterward—in the summer, anyway—strolling down to a bar to sit outside, play table tennis or table football, say hi to all their friends, like a never-ending party that rolls over from one night to the next.

But tonight we're party poopers, curled up in the small living room, what Paige and Kendra call the den, watching a film. It's one of those American rom-coms with a lot of rude jokes and a hero who isn't half as attractive as the heroine: he's a bit doughy and plump, and loads older than she is, which seems unfair, as she's in a bikini half the time and absolutely gorgeous. Everyone else is howling with laughter as the hero and his best friend accidentally crash their car into a septic tank and get drenched in poo, but though I'd normally be laughing along too, I can't get into it.

My thoughts are completely elsewhere. It's as if there's a glass wall between me and the rest of them. I'm sitting on the end of one of the big sofas, next to the open french doors, and when I get up and slip out onto the terrace I don't think anyone even notices.

It's a warm, velvety night. I'm wearing a T-shirt and light pajama bottoms, and the soft evening breeze is lovely on my bare arms as I pad around the side of the villa, cross the front lawn, and go down the short flight of steps into the ornamental garden, heading for the art studio on the far side. The moon is big and bright, almost full, and the outside lights are on to illuminate the parking lot for Elisa and Leonardo, neither of whom are home yet. I close my mind firmly to the implications of Elisa's absence as I lift the big wooden bar that latches the studio door, swing it down, and pull the door open.

Flicking the bank of switches on the wall floods the studio with clear white light. I blink, my eyes accustoming themselves gradually to the sudden brightness; then I shut the door behind me and walk over to my easel, where my last sketch from this afternoon's class is propped. Evan's face, rendered in charcoal, looks back at me.

Well, sort of. I don't think that if you showed it to someone who knew him, they'd recognize him. I do need to learn the basics. I found it hard to sketch Evan in black-and-white, maybe because his coloring is so strong: without his blond hair, his tanned skin, his blue eyes, it was hard to get a likeness. His features are neutral and even: regular, Luigi called them. To get the resemblance, I needed to focus on the eyes.

And I didn't do a brilliant job. His squinch up more at the corners, and they have more of those fine white laugh lines in his tan.

I rub gently with my thumb around the contour of Evan's eyes, erasing the outer corners. Then I pick up a stick of charcoal, think for a moment, and start to try to get the shape right.

I've discovered over the past few weeks that drawing or painting is the only thing in the world that can completely absorb me. It distracts me from any outside worries. When the art studio door closes, when I'm inside with paint or pastels or charcoal and a subject to focus on, I'm vacuum-sealed. The world beyond disappears.

I feel beyond lucky to have discovered this. Kendra has it with her physical exercise and sports, I think; Paige doesn't need it, she never seems to have a care in the world. And Kelly? I don't know if she's found hers yet.

*I should ask her,* I think vaguely as my hand carries on without me, erasing, redrawing, until I've gone over the outline so many times the paper's getting dirty and I need to start again with a fresh piece, sketching Evan's face partly from memory now, using the old one, propped up, as a rough guide to what worked and what didn't. I have all the time in the world. Catia doesn't keep a curfew on us; if they're all going to bed, someone will work out where I am from the studio lights and come and get me, but I have hours yet.

I lose myself in what I'm doing, stepping back to look at what I've just done, stepping in to make corrections, the only sounds my slippered feet on the stone floor shuffling back and forth, and a quiet hum coming from between my slightly parted lips, a habit I've fallen into when I'm working. It isn't a conscious decision when, eventually, I stop; my body seems to decide it for me. I know that I'm done when

I yawn, put down the charcoal, start rolling my head in a circle, and then shrugging my shoulders, easing out the stiffness that's come from—I look at the clock—over two hours, working solidly.

I feel amazing, though exhausted from concentrating. I realize I'm grinning from ear to ear. I look at what I've done, drawing in a deep breath, letting it out with a whoosh. The portrait isn't perfect, not by any means. But it's definitely improved. Evan's eyes look more the way they did when he smiled at me by the pool, crinkled at the outer corners; it was really hard to get those crinkles done without making them look like crow's-feet, turning him into an old man, and I haven't quite managed it.

*Luigi's coming the day after tomorrow for another art class,* I think as I yawn again, switch off the studio lights, and step outside into the dark. *I can show him this. I bet he'll be impressed I've been working on my own.*

It's past eleven. Lights are still on in the house, streaming out from the french doors of the den, and I hear the TV still going. The film must have finished; they'll be on to something else by now. I walk slowly through the garden, coming down from the high of a successful sketching session, past the rose beds, and up the little flight of stone steps.

It's so lovely and peaceful out here. I sit down on the top step, enjoying the calm and the varied sounds of the Tuscan night. An owl, hooting as it dives for its prey, its wings beating softly, and the squeaks of a mouse as the owl's talons close around it. Bats, rustling in the cypress trees where they nest. A dog, barking far across the valley, probably at the wild boar that come out at night to forage for berries and hazelnuts and walnuts. I've never seen a live one, but there's a stuffed boar in the village outside the butcher's, and it's so formidable that I'm quite happy to have skipped that experience so far.

Then I hear a heavy rustling sound in the neatly clipped bay hedge that borders the lawn, and I stiffen, listening intently. It stops, and I relax, thinking it must have been the wind: but then it starts again, and I know it definitely isn't the wind. It's like an animal trying to push its way through, or rooting at the base of the hedge for food.

*Oh no, not a boar! Not this close to the house, surely!* I stare nervously at the hedge. It's dark, but I can see the leaves moving in a clump. There's definitely something in there. I would think it was a dog, but there are none at the villa, and though we see the occasional half-feral cat, no cat's big enough to make that much noise. . . .

This is crazy.

My brain's spinning, working out what I'll do if a wild boar comes through the hedge. I picture the spot where the sounds are coming from and visualize what's below it, another short flight of stone steps that leads to a smaller lawn below. I can't get to the house: the boar will emerge onto the lawn, blocking my access. I could try to nip back to the studio, but then how would I know when it was okay to come out? I could be in there all night!

*You idiot,* I tell myself furiously. *Why did you have to start thinking about boar? It's like you made one appear by thinking about it!*

I'm biting my lip, trying to keep really still, as the bushes rustle more and more. I'm tucked in, my back against the stone pillar at the top of the steps, and there are no lights anywhere near me. I'm completely in the dark; if I don't move, the boar might not spot me. And if it does, I can dash down the steps and make for the studio.

Dry leaves crackle against each other as a dark shape emerges from a gap in the hedge. I stifle a gasp, biting on my lip harder.

I can't believe I'm thinking this, but I wish it had been a boar.

Because what I'm seeing, unmistakably, is Luigi and Kendra, tightly linked together, their arms around each other's waists. That's what caused all the rustling: the gap in the hedge is big enough for one person, but not two, unless they're wrapped around each other so closely their shape is like a two-headed beast. As they emerge from the hedge, they stop and turn to each other, Kendra's arms winding around Luigi's neck as they kiss passionately.

I don't move. Not a muscle. If it were a boar prowling the lawn for stray bits of food, I couldn't stay any more still.

Kendra is wearing a pale dress and Luigi a white shirt and jeans; the light-colored clothing shows up against the hedge, a black background in the shadowy night. I see her hands running up and down his back, her face pressed against his. I wonder if Luca and I, kissing in the river, looked like this, wrapped up so tightly in each other's arms that we were utterly oblivious to anything else around us. The memories of that night flood back so vividly that my eyes close as I remember the feel of his bare chest pressed against me, his bare arms around my waist, his wet skin so close, his skin slippery with river water. . . .

My eyes snap open. I mustn't do this. I can feel my body melting just at the thought of Luca, and it's much more dangerous to give in to these feelings in the warm, dark, romantic Italian night. I do understand Kendra and Luigi sneaking around, having a secret rendezvous by moonlight; what's more, I have to admit I'm jealous, because I would love to do that myself. I know where they've been—set into the retaining wall of the lawn below is a curving alcove with a marble seat inside it, a perfect place for a couple to sit together and make out, with a spectacular view of the valley below by day and the stars in the sky at night. If Luca had asked me to sneak out and meet him there . . . if we were free to be together . . . I'd do it in a heartbeat.

Kendra and Luigi are still kissing passionately, so absorbed with each other that they haven't even taken a moment to look to see if there's anyone around. They've stopped just by the hedge, where they're sheltered from the main terrace, but there are windows along the side of the villa, and gardens surround them, stepped on levels up and down the hillside. They could be spotted from so many different angles that the recklessness of what they're doing makes me terrified for them.

The gravel border of the lawn is barely a foot away from me. I sneak my hand out, pick up a handful, and scatter it lightly as I slip down a couple of steps so that only my head emerges at the level of the lawn. They won't be able to see me; I just hope the gravel noise did the trick, reminded them that they're not alone out here in the moonlight. And that if they're caught by Catia, or Elisa, they'll both surely be in major trouble.

It works. From my low vantage point, I see them start and pull apart. Their whispers are soft; I can't make out any words, but they must be asking themselves what that sound was, if anyone saw them. Luigi ducks back into the shadowy gap in the hedge. Kendra disappears briefly too, presumably for a last kiss goodnight, before emerging once more onto the lawn, smoothing down her skirt, strolling around the house with the aplomb of someone who has just been out for an evening walk alone, with absolutely no intention of meeting an art teacher who must be more than fifteen years older than her.

Only the occasional quick turns of her head give her away. She's trying to see if there's anyone else out here too, who might have spotted her and Luigi. But she's looking much too high to see me kneeling on the fourth step down, and in a minute she's looped around the side of the villa, presumably to go in by the kitchen door and sneak up to her room, so that no one will know she's been out tonight at all.

No one but me. I stand up slowly, and then cross the lawn at a normal pace, just as I would if I were coming back directly from the studio after a sketching session. I feel like my head's about to burst with what I've just seen, all the implications. When I reappear in the den, Paige, Evan, and Kelly are just finishing an old episode of *Friends* and are turning off the TV and DVD, heading for bed: my timing's perfect. I mumble about being in the art studio, and no one even cares; they're all sleepy and wound down. We stumble up to bed, saying goodnight to Evan, who's crashing in the den while he's here. Despite my pretense of sharing their sleepiness, my brain's racing as fast as Luca shooting down the hill earlier today. I don't know what I should do now, whether I should tell anyone or pretend that, as far as I'm concerned, Kendra and Luigi's secret meeting in the garden never happened. . . .

But the decision's made for me. As soon as we get into the bedroom we share, Kelly shuts the door, sits down on her bed, and says to me:

"What's going on?"

I stare at her, amazed.

"Violet!" she snaps, still keeping her voice down. "I know you. You look like you just saw a ghost! Something's definitely up. Come on! Spill the beans!"

To be honest, it's a huge relief. I didn't know if I should tell or not, but I didn't want the weight of carrying this secret all on my own. I flop down onto my own bed, take a deep breath, and tell a stupefied Kelly exactly what I just saw out in the villa grounds tonight.

# The Principessa-in-Waiting

"We need to get into the castello," Kelly says to me firmly the next day.

My head jerks up and I stare at her. Then I raise my hand and wipe a drop of sweat off my forehead. We're in the dining room, one of the coolest places in the house in the baking-hot hours after lunch; the thick stone walls keep out some of the heat, and we have the french windows open and the door propped to let the air circulate as much as possible. The trouble is, the air is so heavy and still that there's no breeze at all. The thermometer has hit forty degrees—or, as Paige and Kendra would say, over a hundred Fahrenheit, which I actually prefer to Celsius: "over a hundred" definitely conveys that it's boiling hot. Not a leaf or blade of grass is moving; they're drying out in the heat, turning brown and crispy. Even the water of the pool is still and gradually reaching bathtub temperature.

Our room under the eaves is like a sauna. We're staying well away from it till night falls and it cools down even a little bit. Like most places we've been in Tuscany, there's no air-conditioning in the villa. Catia sneered at Paige and Kendra when they asked if she could turn it on. Paige took umbrage, and I can't say I blame her. Catia looked right down her nose at Paige, which, considering Paige is much taller than her, was pretty impressive.

The American girls are lying in the shade, fanning themselves, waiting for the blazing sun to start to sink in the sky and loosen its iron grip on the countryside. Kelly and I thought we could convene in the dining room to look at the info on the di Vesperi family we photocopied from the book in the library, but it only works if we stay really, really still. Any movement makes us sweat, and my forearms, propped on the polished table, leave long damp marks on it when I peel them off.

"I can't go to the castello," I say firmly. "Not after . . . I can't."

Kelly's not aware of all the details of my terrifying encounter at the castello a fortnight ago: I promised Luca I wouldn't tell a soul, and I've kept my promise, which hasn't been remotely difficult. All I want to do is forget it, and I know he feels exactly the same.

The trouble is that the horrible scene we went through together was a confirmation of our worst fear—that we might be related. Luca's mother, the principessa, barely clapped eyes on me on our first visit to the castello before she was commenting that I was the spitting image of her husband's family in general, and his sister Monica in particular. And after my second visit—well, it's out of the question that I ever go back.

*Luca and I really are doomed.*

"O-kay, *you* can't," Kelly says, her hazel eyes assessing me, clever enough to know that she mustn't push me on this, mustn't ask any questions. "But *I* can."

My eyebrows shoot up. Even that small gesture brings out a bead of sweat.

"That's true," I agree. "What would you—"

"The portrait gallery, for starters," she says immediately; she's clearly been thinking this out. "I thought I'd like to see if there are any other pictures around the same period as Fiammetta di Vesperi." She goes pink. "I know that isn't anything to do with you, Violet—I mean, about you specifically—but I'm really curious now to know how that picture of her left the family castle, when the walls are, like, *lined* with family portraits! I thought it would make a really interesting project. I need a scholarship, you know that. Maybe it would help with my uni application if I researched something like this on my summer course."

"Definitely," I say, realizing once again, as if I needed any extra proof, how smart Kelly is. It's something I know instinctively, with my expensive private education, that university boards love something that makes you stand out, shows that you went the extra mile: a project like that would be really effective in her interview.

"*And*," she continues, "once I'm there, hopefully I can poke around and see what I can find out about you!"

I have a blinding flash of inspiration.

"Look at family photos," I say slowly. "They have those everywhere at the castello—framed ones all over the place. If there's any chance of working out"—I calculate quickly in my head—"where the principe was at the start of 1995 . . ."

"The start of 1995?" Kelly looks puzzled.

I swallow, and explain, looking down at the photocopies instead of at her:

"I was born in October 1995. So, um, nine months before then would be the start of 1995. . . ."

I feel as if my entire body is burning with prickly heat at the embarrassment of this conversation.

"I'm sorry," she says quickly, reading the expression on my face. "I should have got that."

"It's okay," I mumble. "I mean, we're *thinking* it, we should be able to talk about it."

Kelly averts her eyes.

"I'll talk to Catia about my project," she says. "She loves any excuse to contact the principessa or go over to the castello—she'll be fine about it."

I pull a face.

"She loves any excuse to shove Elisa and Luca together even more than they are already," I mutter. "She's just dying to see Elisa become the principessa-in-waiting."

That's so true that Kelly, sensibly, doesn't say anything to contradict me. Instead she looks at the clock on the wall above my head and comments:

"It's nearly three—I might have a shower to cool down and then come back to make project notes to show Catia or the principessa in case they ask to see 'em."

"Okay," I say. "I'll have a shower after you. I'm *so* sweaty."

She nods as she leaves the room. I stare down at the photocopied images of the Castello di Vesperi, but I don't really see them. Three in the afternoon: that means it's been over twenty-four hours now, and Mum hasn't answered my email. I'm longing to ring her but sense I should wait till she's ready to get in touch. Still, it's so hard not knowing what she's thinking or feeling.

And here I am, actually discussing with Kelly the month I was conceived! No one wants to think about their parents having sex, let alone their parents having sex with someone else. If I could stop this right now, never think about it again, I would: but how can I? I have to know! I have to know, not just for Luca, but for myself, and the fact that my mum hasn't got back to me is the clearest of indications that I'm not making a mountain out of a molehill. There truly *is* something about my birth that I need to find out.

In the hallway, the house phone's ringing. I listen to it absentmindedly, grateful for a sound that's cutting through the downward spiral of my thoughts. Catia's heels come ticking down the hallway, and I hear a rapid stream of Italian as she talks to her caller; she sounds lively, excited, punctuating her conversation with a lot of theatrical gasps and cries of "*Ma davvero,*" which means "No! Really?"

However, it hasn't taken us long to learn that Italians almost always sound lively and excited. Benedetta, the cook, and Catia once had what all of us thought was a huge fight over something really important, with lots of screeching and throwing hands around, and it turned out to be about whether you melt an anchovy into the sauce for the pasta and chickpeas that Benedetta was cooking for dinner. So I don't pay any attention until Catia comes clickety-clacking into the dining room, her eyes bright with anticipation, and says:

"Violet! Where are the other girls?"

I start to tell her, but she's too hyped up to listen: she rides right over me, continuing:

"You must tell them to get themselves ready for this evening!" she announces imperiously. "We have all been invited to a party at the Castello di Vesperi!"

My eyes bulge; I can feel the skin around them stretching. I must look like one of those frogs on the nature channel whose eyeballs pop out on stalks.

"The—the," I stammer. "Are you *sure*?"

Two weeks ago, after the-thing-Luca-and-I-don't-ever-mention, the principessa took to her bed in a nervous collapse following the departure of her faithful maid, Maria, who had looked after her for her whole life. The castello was, to put it bluntly, really dusty and cobwebby and not very well cared for, as Maria, who had run it for years without much help, hadn't been able to keep it remotely clean, and a lot of it looked like something out of a Dickens novel. The principe, Luca's father, left to live in Florence with—according to Luca—a string of young model girlfriends when Luca was very young, and ever since then the principessa had been letting the castle go to rack and ruin.

The idea that suddenly, in just a fortnight, the principessa has recovered from her nervous collapse and decided to throw a big party—and to invite *me* as part of the Villa Barbiano group, when my resemblance to her husband's family is what started the whole mess in the first place!—makes so little sense that I'm sure Catia's somehow got everything wrong.

"*Sì!*" Catia says, her eyes sparkling. "Luca's father, the principe, has returned from Florence, and he is throwing the party to celebrate!"

"It's so . . . *sudden*" is all I can manage to say.

Catia gives me a narrow look.

"The principe has always done exactly as he pleases. When you have money," she says cynically, "you can make anything happen. We will have a light dinner at seven and leave the house at eight. Everyone must be ready and dressed in their best clothes."

Her mouth twists in a knowing smile.

"You should probably tell the other girls immediately," she adds. "They will want at least three hours to get ready."

*Ooh, snarky!* But to be fair, Catia has a point. I get up obediently, my brain racing. And behind me I hear Catia snapping open her phone, tapping the touch screen, and after a pause, saying excitedly:

*"Elisa! Carissima! Indovina cos'è successo! Ho appena ricevuta una chiamata dalla Donatella–"*

She's calling Elisa to let her know the exciting news. The party. The return of the prince.

*But with the amount of time that Elisa's been spending with Luca,* I think sadly, *surely she already knows everything that's happening with the di Vesperis. . . .*

# None of This Is My Fault

To my great surprise, Paige and Kendra are shockingly unenthusiastic about the news. I thought they'd be over the moon: they love parties, they love dressing up for parties, and they particularly love the attention they get at Italian events, where their unusual looks draw huge numbers of males flocking around them. But although they've turned themselves out with their usual gorgeously groomed attention to detail, they've been lackluster about the evening's activities, and positively sulky during the early dinner Catia gave us, presumably to make sure our stomachs were lined before the wine started flowing at the castello.

"What's up with you two?" I hiss to Kendra as we get into the jeep. "You're acting like you don't want to come!"

"I *don't*," she whispers crossly. "Paige and I were going to go out after dinner with a couple of the boys who've been texting us. Ones from the village."

"I bet it'll be all oldies at the party," Paige adds. "Friends of Luca's mom and dad." She pulls a huge, theatrical grimace. "Bor-*ing*. We were going to go hang at the Casa del Popolo and maybe go dancing after."

"Thanks for asking us along," Kelly says teasingly, twisting around from the front seat. She looks amazing: Paige has spent time this afternoon doing her hair and makeup in exchange for Kelly's helping her with her Italian homework assignment. Hot rollers have given Kelly's fine red hair body and bounce, like something from a shampoo ad, and she's made up with more makeup on than usual but actually looks as if she's got less on because Paige has spent so much time applying it subtly.

It's obvious that Kelly's joking: her tone is light, and there's no reason Paige and Kendra should have to take us with them. We're not all joined at the hip. So I'm briefly surprised when Paige shuffles nervously in her seat next to me, tilts her head to look at Kendra, and emits a high-pitched giggle. Something's up with them. Kelly looks at me and raises her eyebrows, but I'm too nervous about what's awaiting me at our destination to wonder what Paige and Kendra aren't telling us.

The prince, back from Florence, throwing a party to celebrate. The playboy father whose behavior his son, Luca, resents so violently that he doesn't have a good word to say about him. The playboy who might, just maybe, have met my mother at the start of 1995.

*Does the principe know anything about me?* I'm asking myself. *Does he know why Maria left the castello, why the principessa's so upset? Did she or Luca tell him what really went on?*

*Or will the sight of me be a total surprise to him?*

For a minute or so, I did consider pulling a sickie. Insisting at the last moment, that a headache or period pain had just hit me, rendering me unable to go to the party. I knew Catia wouldn't fuss too much about it; you can't physically drag a whiny girl complaining of cramps out of the house. I'm scared of going back to the castello, of meeting Luca's father. Of seeing Luca, the principessa—of everything there.

But clearly my curiosity is stronger than my fear. Because here I am, in my best dress, a silk jersey my mum picked out for any smart parties I might be invited to in Italy: black, boatneck, with a swirling print of red roses and green leaves. My makeup is as carefully done as I can manage, and I'm wearing high-heeled red sandals bought from the market that are probably going to leave me blistered but that give me a few precious extra inches of height and make my legs look nice.

I swallow hard. My palms are already sweaty. I'm trying to make my mind as calm as possible, to keep my breathing even. By the time the jeep bumps up the hill to the castello, however, I can't even swallow anymore; my throat has locked up. There's a huge lump at the back of it. I can't speak: my mouth is completely dry. As I climb down from the Range Rover, my legs are actually wobbling. Kelly notices and quickly winds her arm through mine. It looks as if she's just being girly and friendly; actually, she's helping me stand up, helping me walk across the gravel parking area, past the other cars that signal that plenty of guests have arrived already, through the high arched gateway, and up the sloping path to the huge wooden carved double doors.

Immediately, I see the difference from my last visits. Before, we gained access through a smaller door set into the left-hand one, creaking like something out of a haunted house when it eventually swung open. Now, both doors are open wide, propped back with a matching pair of huge wrought-iron lions, and light spills from the entrance, as warm and inviting as it was bleak and forbidding before. Candles burn in sconces set along the hallway, their light flickering prettily, and a smiling waiter stands just outside the front door, carrying a silver tray laden with Prosecco.

We all gasp. From a haunted house, the castello has turned into a setting for a fairy tale. Even Paige and Kendra, who've been sulky at having their plans for the evening curtailed, perk up, stepping to take a glass each from the waiter; he's slim and elegant, his dark hair slicked back, and Paige looks him up and down with barely concealed appreciation.

"I don't know which she's leering at more—the Prosecco or the waiter," Kelly comments to me. Paige, overhearing this, flashes a smile at us, tossing her blond curls in a way that makes the waiter swivel to watch her sashay into the castello.

"Both!" she says over her shoulder, winking at him and us. Clearly, she's got over her sulks about the last-minute change to her evening plans.

"That girl could win an international flirting competition," Kendra says dryly.

"International? She'd win a *galactic* flirting competition!"

Kelly adds, one-upping Kendra, and even Catia allows herself a quick snicker of amusement as we follow Paige's swaying hips into the great hall of the castello.

Another waiter is stationed at the foot of the carved staircase, with a tray of canapés in one hand and linen napkins in the other. He directs us into the Gold Salon, where we had drinks before with the principessa. It's a beautiful sitting room with gold brocade walls and pale-yellow-silk-upholstered furniture, everything trimmed with reams of gold braid and dangling tassels. There's a harpsichord made of inlaid wood against the wall, and a lady is playing tasteful, soft music, the ivory keys tinkling gently, the kind of background music that's perfect for a grown-up drinks party, filling in any conversational gaps.

The room is impressive in itself, but at one glance I know the guests are real Italian high society. The women are in tailored linen dresses and Hermès silk scarves, their jewelry glistening, their tans even. The men are in light summer suits, their leather shoes as gleaming as their hair. They're mostly older, Catia and the principessa's age, and the sheen of wealth and status gives them the confidence that money really can buy.

Beside me, Kelly comes to a dead halt. I know this is incredibly intimidating for her, and the need to reassure her helps me. Now it's me who tightens my arm through hers, me who gives her the courage to start walking again, to cross the room behind Catia and be officially introduced to our host.

It helps too that everyone's looking at Paige and Kendra. As always in Italy, they're the ones who draw attention, and we can follow comparatively unnoticed in their wake. Knowing that my resemblance to the di Vesperi family might be commented on, I did the best I could to change my usual style; I straightened my curly hair, which is exactly the same as the hair of all the women in the family portraits, parted it in the middle, and pulled it back into a smooth ponytail. I don't think it's a very flattering look for me, but it's definitely different. I look more fashionable, older, but mainly conventional. Less likely to call attention to myself.

"*Che bella nera,*" I hear someone comment, which means "what a beautiful black girl"; it sounds distinctly odd, but we've learned here that it isn't meant badly, just a statement of fact in this country. Kendra doesn't bristle as she hears it.

We come to a halt by the fireplace. Catia is embracing the principessa, lightly holding her upper arms while air-kissing each of her cheeks. And the principe, seeing us file up and stop in front of him, removes his arm from where it was nonchalantly resting along the wide marble mantelpiece and holds out both hands to greet us all.

"*Ma che bellezze!*" he exclaims, smiling widely. "What beauties!" he's saying, and he has such an air about him that even Paige and Kendra, who are by now utterly accustomed to hearing lavish compliments in Italian, preen and giggle as he places his hands on their shoulders and kisses their cheeks. And then they fall back, and I have my first proper look at the principe.

I saw photographs of Luca's father on my first visit here. He barely looks any older, even though those were taken years and years ago; his frame hasn't bulked out at all, his navy silk suit fitting him sleekly. His tight dark curly hair has silver laced through it, but it looks distinguished, and his brown eyes are bright and sparkling with life. His tan is deep mahogany, his teeth white as an American's, and charm rolls off him in waves.

*What a contrast to Luca,* I find myself thinking as the principe's warm hands close briefly on my shoulders and his lips touch my cheeks. He smells of tobacco and very expensive aftershave. *It's as if Luca doesn't want to be anything like his father—easy, charming, friendly. As if he's deliberately chosen to be difficult, grumpy, offish so that no one can possibly say he's like his dad.*

To my enormous relief, the Principe di Vesperi doesn't pay me any more attention than he does to the other girls; we all get a quick up-and-down flick of his bright eyes, a frank assessment of our looks, before we politely greet the principessa. You have to kiss everyone twice every time you meet them; I suppose I'll eventually get used to it, but it still feels strange.

"The young people are on the terrace," the principe says to us. "You will want to join them, not stay here with the boring old ones, eh?"

I glance at the principessa, whose face is a polite mask. I can't read how she feels about me returning to her home, about her husband greeting me, kissing me on both cheeks. She's far too well bred to show emotion. She seems very pale, but she's always pale. Luca gets his looks from her, his white skin, his slanting blue eyes, his high cheekbones. But her skin feels paper-thin as I brush it with my lips, fragile as tissue.

I back away as swiftly as I can. I don't want to stay with

them, but I don't want to go outside either and see Luca: I feel like I'm caught between a rock and a hard place. The other girls swirl around me, sweeping me along with them, moving outside. Paige exclaims happily as she sees Leonardo and Andrea, who are both dressed in suits and ties and look, I have to say, absolutely gorgeous.

"Suits make boys look so grown up," I observe to Kelly, trying to sound nonchalant, as if I'm completely okay with the introduction to the prince; I'm impressed that my voice comes out relatively normal, though I have to clear my throat first.

The group of young people outside is just as smart and shiny and scary as the adults in the Gold Salon. Thank goodness Kelly and I have each other. We stand a little back as Paige plows happily toward the boys she knows; I glance at Kelly and see that she's staring longingly at Andrea.

"Did you ever text back Giacomo?" I ask her, trying to jolt her thoughts to a boy who's shown interest in her, away from one who hasn't.

"Who?" She hasn't taken her eyes off Andrea, who's fiddling with his silk tie, fashionably loose around his tanned throat, as he fixes his gaze on Kendra.

"The guy at the party who took you outside to see the stars!" I remind her, a bit crossly, because I do think she's being silly, crushing on Andrea like this when there are plenty more fish in the sea. Nothing like pointing out mistakes someone else is making to help you ignore your own.

"He was cute," I continue. "He had very curly hair—*you* know! He definitely texted you the day after. Did you ever get back to him?"

She shakes her head.

"You should," I say firmly. "He seemed really nice. You know, sometimes it can really help to go out with one boy if you, um, aren't getting anywhere with another."

I've never been this blunt with her: somehow, it's a lot easier in the twilight, when we're standing next to each other, not face to face, to blurt out the truth. And I genuinely want to make sure she has the best time possible in Italy, not waste it mooning over a boy who only has eyes for Kendra. Kelly's still looking at Andrea, who's running his fingers through his hair as he looks longingly at Kendra. True to her promise to me to back off Andrea, Kendra is paying him no attention, but in the end, that's only made him even keener.

"It doesn't even matter that she's sneaking out to see Luigi," Kelly observes quietly. "She doesn't pay any attention to Andrea at all. Just her being there is enough for him. If she weren't here . . . that's the only thing that would possibly make him notice me. If she just—weren't here."

*"Kelly,"* I start to say, but just then there's a flurry of movement in the group, and Evan's blond head appears. He's dressed up as best he can, in a shirt and chinos; backpacking around, he didn't have anything smart, and Leonardo found the idea that he should lend Evan something to wear hilarious, as Evan's built so much more broadly than he is.

Still, the Italian girls don't seem to mind that Evan's not up to their sartorial standards; in a flash, they're fluttering around him like pretty butterflies. I don't see Elisa, and for a moment my heart lifts: but then, as the crowd moves and re-forms, I spot her a few steps down, the thinnest, most tanned, most made up, chic-est girl in the whole group. The silk layers of her minidress simply emphasize how thin her arms are, brown sticks laden with bangles. And I notice her arms particularly, because they're gesticulating, waving in the air, using the movement to isolate the person she's talking to from the rest of the group.

*Of course. It's Luca.*

I take some comfort in the fact that, though Elisa has singled him out like a skinny, starving lioness cornering her prey, he looks bored and irritated. His mouth is set in a straight line: his shoulders, propped against the side of the stone staircase, are like a clothes hanger from which the rest of his body is drooping limply, as if the only reason he isn't crumbling to the ground is that his bones are stacked one on top of the other. His black hair tumbles thickly forward. I can't see his eyes at all. The glowing red tip of Elisa's cigarette traces circles in the air, a force field she's building to ward off anyone getting close to Luca.

*But Luca isn't smoking himself,* I think suddenly, my heart racing. *He'd always have been smoking before in this kind of situation—*

"Hey, Violet!"

I jump, jolted out of my thoughts, to see Evan standing in front of me, holding out his hand.

"Wanna dance?" he's saying.

I stare at him blankly. Then, around the side of his big frame, I see Kendra being waltzed around the terrace by some boy I don't know.

"*Ev!*" Paige reprimands her brother, giggling. "You say, 'May I have the pleasure of this waltz?' "

Evan goes one better: he bends over in an awkward bow as he repeats the words. I don't feel remotely like dancing, but how can I possibly say no? So I take his hand and make a sound like "Oof!" as he pulls me toward him. I put my other hand up on his high wide shoulder and do my best to follow him as we trip and stumble at first, trying to get the one-two-three rhythm of the waltz. I'm mainly worried that he'll tread on my feet, but he doesn't, by some miracle, and gradually we sort of get it; I look up at him and he's grinning down at me.

"Paige dared me to ask someone to waltz," he says confidingly, "and I picked you 'cause you're such a good dancer."

"Thank you!" I say, flattered.

"No, thank *you*," he says, swinging us in a semicircle to make a turn and avoid crashing into the wall of the castello. "You're actually kinda making me look like I know what I'm doing."

So all of a sudden, I'm waltzing on the terrace of a castle. Disney Cinderella in her pale-blue dress, dancing with her prince, her skirt belling out. In my ideal picture, it would be Luca I'd be waltzing with, his lean, slim body in my arms, not Evan's wider frame, his big solid shoulder under my hand.

*But Luca didn't ask you,* I tell myself firmly. *He can't ask you. He's probably too bloody cool to dance in public anyway. Remember what you just told Kelly? It doesn't help to moon after a boy you can't have when another boy likes you and isn't afraid to show it.*

Because I'm definitely beginning to get the sense that Evan likes me. And if Luca's hanging out with Elisa, coming to pick her up from the villa to make the point to me that she has a date with him, why shouldn't I dance with Evan, smile up at him, have a good time instead of moping around?

My body lightens, my steps move faster. Evan's whirling me around enthusiastically, his confidence growing. Out of the corner of my eye I see other couples dancing; who knows how the waltzing started, but now it's snowballed, reached critical mass, and lots of other twinned shapes spin by us. They're just shapes because Evan's bulk blots out almost everything else: I focus on his wide, tanned neck, remembering that in ballet class years ago, the teacher said to look at a fixed point when you do pirouettes to stop yourself from getting too dizzy.

The adults in the Gold Salon notice the dancing outside and cluster at the windows to watch. I'm clinging to Evan for dear life now, a fistful of his shirt in one hand, his big fingers wrapping around the other, and I'm laughing with sheer pleasure and exhilaration at the speed, at the fact that Evan is now physically lifting me off my feet and whirling me every time we do a turn, his arm around my waist picking me up as easily as if it were a lever. When we finally stop, I'm still clinging to him, laughing and laughing, and Evan's laughing too.

I tilt my head back, gasping for breath, and past Evan's shoulder, I see the principe and the principessa standing at one of the windows. The principe is clapping enthusiastically, eyes and teeth sparkling, applauding our efforts, looking from side to side at his guests, exhorting them to clap too; the ones who aren't are raising their Prosecco flutes to us like salutes. Golden light floods out from the salon, the spectators lit up as if they're onstage, not us. The principe looks like the conductor of an orchestra, gesturing at us all, and the principessa—

Oh. She's the only one who's doing nothing. Not clapping, not raising her glass. Her hands are empty, and she's looking straight at me, her face dead white, framed by hair that's dyed too black, making her look like a ghost. I flinch as I meet her eyes.

*I'm not dancing with your son!* I think frantically. *I've stayed away from him. And I was invited here by your husband! None of this is my fault. . . .*

Then I realize that the prince is looking directly at me too. Husband and wife stare at me, panting, still twined in Evan's arms. I feel horribly self-conscious: I know I'm sweaty, but hopefully I'm not too shiny, as the evening breeze is cooling me down. The principe, having whipped up his guests to applaud, is taking this opportunity, while they're all distracted by the spectacle, to observe me, his gaze sharp and focused, and I understand with a shock that his seemingly nonchalant greeting earlier was all an act, a cover-up for the chance to scrutinize me when he could do so without anyone else realizing.

Anyone, that is, but his wife. Because now the pressure of her stare eases as she glances at him instead. Her husband, looking at a girl who might be his daughter. I can't imagine what it feels like for her.

And another thought hits me now like a physical blow as I look at the man who could be my father. *Was this all planned? Did he come back from Florence because he heard of my existence? Did he make his wife throw a party so he could get a look at me in the most completely unsuspicious, neutral way possible?*

I tear my head away swiftly, burying it in Evan's shoulder.

"Hey!" he says above me, sounding understandably surprised. "You okay? What's up?"

"Everyone's looking—I feel shy," I manage to say.

It's not completely a lie. He turns me with him, his arm still around my waist, walking away from the lit windows and into the comparative shadow at the back of the terrace.

"*Complimenti!*" a high voice trills, and I look sideways as we pass to see Elisa smiling at us, extremely complacent to see me in another boy's arms.

And beyond her, Luca, not smiling: positively glowering. I can see his eyes now, and they're burning as blue as if there were a miniature gas flame in each one. I feel scorched by the anger in his stare.

How dare he be angry with me! At this moment, I swear, I'm done. If I could run away right now and never come back, I would. Because I never want to see any of the di Vesperis again. I cling to Evan as if he were a life raft in choppy seas.

"Violet!" Kelly hisses next to me. She's a little out of breath, which surprises me, as I don't think she was dancing. She pushes her hair back with both hands as she says quickly:

"Come with me! There's something I really need to show you!"

# Cougar Bait

I feel awful, because Evan's been so nice; asking me to dance, which is always lovely—no one likes to feel like a wallflower. And he was kind enough to whisk me off the center of the terrace when I was overwhelmed by the di Vesperi family drama. But if Kelly's found something out, there's no question that I have to go with her.

"I'm just nipping to the loo," I say to him, and as I slip away with Kelly, a woman with hair dyed blond, her makeup plastered on, sashays across the terrace toward Evan. She's wearing a purple knit dress that clings to every single curve of her tall body and she's smiling at Evan like Shere Khan in *The Jungle Book* when he's contemplating eating Mowgli.

"'Ello!" she says to him flirtatiously. "You dance *very* well. My name is Sunny, what's yours?"

"Wow, cougar alert!" I mutter to Kelly, who looks back and giggles.

"Hey!" Paige says as we pass, clutching Leonardo's arm with one hand and pointing at Evan with the other. "Did you see? Evan's got a new dancing partner!"

It's another waltz: Sunny's drawing Evan onto what's become the dance floor, sliding one hand around his neck to pull him close.

"She's, like, *ancient*!" Paige howls happily. "Where's my phone? I've got to take photos!"

Kelly pulls my arm to guide me along the terrace, leading me into a room with paneled walls that smell deliciously of wood polish. I imagine an army of cleaners tearing through the castello over the last week now that the principe is back with his money to take care of things. It reminds me of the animals and birds in Disney films that whisk away any dirt in the blink of an eye. Hard not to keep thinking of fairy tales when you're at a party in a castle.

"Here!" Kelly says eagerly, almost running over to the far side of the room, dodging past a grand piano with a silver candelabra on top and a mahogany stand carrying a huge, elaborately decorated Chinese vase that must be three feet tall. "I found some photo albums, and you're not going to *believe* what's in them. . . ."

She reaches a long table against the far wall, laden with leather-bound albums embossed in gold. I open one at random. Each page of photos has its own translucent protective covering sheet, and I raise the one on top to see neatly pasted black-and-white photos with those old-fashioned white scalloped edges. The middle one is a trio of girls, their arms around one another's waists, dressed up in forties-style wide skirts and small fitted jackets, smiling at the camera. Their hair is curled, their faces are bare of makeup apart from lipstick and powder, and the one on the right is the spitting image of me. I slam the album shut with a crash.

Dust puffs out.

"I don't want to see any photos that look like me," I say in a small stifled voice. "It's making me feel weird."

"No, that's not what I was going to show you," she reassures me. "But—"

Her hand slides across the page of the album that she's just opened, covering the picture.

"It's not going to make you feel amazing, though," she continues nervously.

"Let me see," I say curtly, before I can change my mind.

She moves her hand away from the page that she was concealing, and I lean over to look. It's a color photo of the principe. Younger, with no gray in his hair, and fewer lines around his eyes. But really, apart from those small differences, he hardly seems to have changed.

"He looks almost the same, doesn't he?" Kelly comments, as if reading my thoughts. "That's what happens when you have tons of money." She grimaces. "You should see *my* dad in a photo from nearly twenty years ago. You wouldn't even recognize him."

The principe is smiling broadly at the camera. He has one arm around a beautiful girl who's towering above him in her high heels. They're clearly at some sort of fashion show. She's in a tiny, acid-bright lace dress, her legs seeming endless, her shoes a tangle of little straps reaching up to mid-calf. Behind them is a catwalk; I can make out the rows of delicate gold chairs behind it. It looks as if the fashion show has finished; there are groups of people milling around, chatting.

And on the far right—Kelly's pointing her out, but I've found her already, I know now why she's showing me the photo—on the far right is my mum. Wearing another tight little lace minidress, her long slim body making it look elegant rather than vulgar. Her blond hair is teased up into a crazily high arrangement like the one on the model the principe is embracing. Mum's talking to another woman, a scary-thin blonde with poker-straight hair in tight leather trousers and so much black liner around her eyes that she looks like a full-on Goth.

"That's Donatella Versace," Kelly says in awe. "Your mum was really a proper model, being in a Versace show."

I nod absently, unable to take my eyes off my mum. She looks so beautiful, the makeup and the hair turning her into a goddess. She never wears much makeup nowadays; she says she had enough in her modeling days to last her the rest of her life. Her cheekbones are so high with the contoured blusher that her face looks almost alien.

"So you know what this means," Kelly's saying, and I realize that I've been focusing hard on my mum's gorgeous face to avoid coming to the real conclusion. Reluctantly, I nod again.

"This is September 1994," she says, "in Milan. I mean, it doesn't prove anything at all. But it shows that they were together, they could have met. Before you were— *Anyway*, they could have met."

She's right: it doesn't prove anything. But it's another nail in the coffin of my hopes that Luca and I aren't related. And for a moment, horribly, I resent Kelly with such intensity that my fists clench, my nails digging into my palms. She's too good at researching, too clever. She's only seen a couple of photos of my mum on my phone, and she still managed to locate these albums, work through the ones with the correct time period, and spot Mum in the background of a photograph that didn't even feature her.

I should thank her. But instead, I want to kill her.

"Violet?" she starts, and I swallow hard, because my anger has suddenly transformed itself into a desperate wish to burst out crying. And I absolutely can't burst into tears, not here, not at this party. . . .

Then we hear footsteps outside, on the terrace, a swift pattering of heels on stone, coming closer. We stare at each other in panic. Under the circumstances, the last thing I want is to be caught here, looking at family photograph albums. Kelly moves like lightning. She shuts the album, grabs my arm, and pulls me to a small sofa, ducking down to hide behind it. One of my sandals twists under me and I wince, but I can't move to adjust it now, not a muscle, because the footsteps are clattering onto the parquet floor, and Paige is saying breathlessly:

"Are you really upset about tonight?"

"Yes!" Kendra sighs in a rush. "Oh God, I feel like I'm going mad!"

"Is he—"

"Yes! He's waiting, to see if I can sneak off, but he can't hold on for much longer—he's got to go and help out a friend later with something—"

"Oh *no*!" Paige gushes.

"I feel like I'll *die* if I have to wait till tomorrow to see him!" Kendra bursts out passionately. "And it was going to be so lovely tonight—he was going to take me out to dinner somewhere far away, where no one would recognize either of us, a little restaurant in a sort of secret garden—it was going to be so romantic. He's *so* disappointed! He's been texting and texting me—"

"*Oh!*" Paige is clearly completely caught up in the romance of all this sneaking around. "But hey, we can do it anytime, though—we'll just say we're doing the double-date thing again. I can always find someone to go out with, and then you can take off with Luigi—"

"Shh!" Kendra hisses. "Don't *ever* say his name!"

"Sorry!" Paige is contrite.

"He says Catia would go *mad* if she knew," Kendra whispers.

Squashed beside me, I feel Kelly's head nodding in vigorous agreement at this.

"Oh, she *totally* would," Paige agrees. "And we have to be really careful around Evan, too. He'd go crazy."

"It's so *unfair*!" Kendra laments. "Just because he's a bit older! Why can't people *understand*? I don't *want* to date boys my own age!"

"I'll *totally* help," Paige assures her enthusiastically.

"Hey!" cuts in a deeper voice, and I can hear the two

girls start, their feet shuffling, their dresses rustling, at the interruption.

"Ev!" Paige says quickly. "What's up?"

"I'm hiding out," her brother says. "There's this, um—*lady,* who—"

"Omigod, I *know*!" Paige says in a happy rush. She's having a fantastic evening; so much drama she doesn't have time to keep up with it all. "She was, like, all over you!"

"She said she feels much more at home with all us young people," Evan recounts, sounding very uncomfortable. "She said her husband was really boring and everyone inside was really old—"

"*She's* really old!" Paige exclaims.

"It was pretty embarrassing," he says. "I mean, she made me waltz with her and she was kind of rubbing my arm and talking about my muscles."

"Cougar bait!" Paige trills. She giggles. "I bet you'd rather've been dancing with Violet, right? Did you head in this direction 'cause Violet came this way?"

Evan mumbles something unintelligible.

"You're mean to tease him like that," Kendra says after a few moments; I presume Evan's left.

"What? He likes Violet!" Paige says. "And she's not after Luca anymore—or she messed up with him, 'cause he's with Elisa now. I'm almost positive. I thought he was into Violet, but something went wrong there."

"She played that badly," Kendra agreed.

Eavesdroppers hear no good of themselves. I jerk furiously, fighting the impulse to stand up and yell at them that they don't know what they're talking about: that Luca still really likes me, that Elisa's only second-best to him, that he looked beyond jealous just now when I was dancing with Evan. . . .

"We should get back," Paige is saying.

"I don't want to." Kendra sighs miserably.

"You'll see Lu—er, *him* tomorrow!" Paige says. "You can sneak out into the garden again! Just wait till ten, like last night. I'll get us all watching a movie like the last time—no one had any idea you weren't reading in bed. Come on, we should get back."

"I wish I could be like you," Kendra says as they go out onto the terrace. "You just don't *feel* things like I do."

"That's me. Easy, breezy, beautiful CoverGirl. Deep as a puddle of water," Paige says lightly as their voices fade away.

" 'You don't feel things like I do'?" Kelly hisses, hauling herself to her feet. "That Kendra's beyond arrogant. Ow, I've got a cramp in my foot. . . ."

"She's lucky it's practically impossible to offend Paige," I say ironically. "Paige was kind of messing with her there."

I stand up, wincing, swiveling the ankle that was caught underneath me and now has the worst pins and needles. We both limp across the room, shaking out our feet, and head back down the long terrace. The harpsichord music has been replaced by jazz, and Sunny has got hold of poor Evan again, backing him against the balustrade and swaying in front of him. "I used to be an air hostess," she's saying. "Only in first class, though. They put the prettiest girls in first class, did you know that?"

Elisa, meanwhile, has maneuvered Luca onto the dance floor. She has her arms around his neck and is wriggling her narrow hips in time with the music, doing the dancing for both of them.

I take a deep breath, march over to Evan, and say over Sunny's shoulder: "Hey, I thought we were going to dance again."

"Oh yeah!" he says with flattering enthusiasm. "Excuse me, ma'am," he mumbles to Sunny, sliding past her and out toward me. I grin at him as he mouths "Thank you!" and we take each other's hands, starting to move to the music.

I have no idea how to dance to jazz, and clearly neither does Evan; but what we have in common is that we want to have fun. I honestly don't know whether the impulse to save Evan is stronger than my jealousy of Luca and Elisa, but right now it doesn't even matter. I can't have Luca, that's clear enough. So I need to move on.

I'm not one of those girls who rush from one boy to another, scared of being alone. I'm not going to suddenly throw myself at Evan, snog him one night and declare that he's my boyfriend the next day, as I've seen girls do. But dancing has always been one of the main ways I've distracted myself, and this kind of dancing needs a partner, and Evan needed rescuing, and I can't chatter away to Kelly while watching Luca and Elisa out of the corner of my eye. . . .

My head is spinning. Really, all I can think of is the photo that proves Mum and the principe could have met before I was born. It's almost as if that image is projected on Evan's wide chest, as if on the pale-blue fabric I can see the principe, smiling with his arm around that model, Mum in the background. I put a smile on my face and I keep it plastered there as we dance around the terrace. And I'm doing fine, I really am.

Until I get back to Villa Barbiano that evening and find the text from Mum waiting for me.

# You Did the Right Thing

**Darling, I got your email. Hold on. Hold on. I love you so much. Please just wait to hear from me. Please!!! I love you!**

I must have read Mum's text a hundred times. I have no idea what it means. But I know what it doesn't say: *Of course Dad and I are your parents! Why on earth would you think anything different? I'm on the first plane over to give you a big hug and tell you I love you!*

I've actually gone weirdly calm, as if my brain's suffused with a drug that's flowing gently through me. I woke up feeling outside of myself: I'm floating above my body, looking down at the Violet who's going about her day, observing her with detachment as she eats breakfast, goes to her Italian lesson, eats lunch, goes to the pool. Fights the desire to ring her mother and beg her to explain what's going on.

Luigi comes in to teach an art class; that doesn't faze this strangely detached Violet. She sits there and sketches Evan and doesn't even blush when Luigi convinces him to take his shirt off. She concentrates on trying to render, as accurately as possible, the cap of muscle on Evan's shoulder, the one that's turned toward her. Luigi is making her draw Evan in three-quarter profile, and it's surprisingly hard to get the proportions right.

Violet has the feeling that if she let herself tune in to the vibrations between Kendra and Luigi, she'd pick up all sorts of things. Nothing even that overt. The briefest of touches, maybe, as Luigi leans over Kendra to make an alteration on her drawing, or as Kendra turns to him to ask him a question. It's more the way they communicate, the haze in the air around them, a sense that they're scarcely aware, when they look at each other, that anyone else even exists.

But this Violet, to be honest, couldn't care less anymore about what's going on with Luigi and Kendra. It's not her business if Kendra's being a stupid idiot, or Luigi an old creep. Violet has more than enough of her own to cope with. Violet feels as if she's carrying a brimful vase of water, and she has to move very carefully to keep it level. Because if that vase tilts even a little bit, and even a drop spills on her, she'll start crying and she'll never stop.

Evan can tell something's up with Violet, but he's too nice and tactful to push at her. He asked her this morning if she was okay, and she said yes, but she knows she sounded so aloof and disconnected that it was a total snub. And after that, he's been polite but respectful, keeping his distance.

Which would make it strange, seeing him with his shirt off, if Violet were really in her body. Since she isn't, however, she can just take him for granted as the life-drawing model, whose squarish features are particularly hard to draw in three-quarter profile, and focus entirely on the work of conveying what she sees in front of her to the sketchpad. She is constantly aware of the phone in her skirt pocket, resting on her thigh, starting if she hears even the slightest sound that might be an incoming call, feels something that might be the vibrating buzz of a message. And a text does come in, but it's from Milly back in London, and Violet doesn't answer it because she feels so disconnected from almost her entire life that she wouldn't know what to say.

After art class, Violet showers and then goes to dinner: spaghetti with mild green peppers called *frigitelli,* sautéed in olive oil, and then cold sliced veal dressed with tuna mayonnaise and capers, which sounds bizarre but is actually tasty. She has a glass of red wine with the food, and coffee afterward. And then Paige suggests that they all watch a movie or two in the rec room, and Violet says that she'll probably go back to the art studio and keep working on her sketches, and Paige exchanges a glance with Kendra that clearly tells Kendra to keep an eye out for Violet in the studio when she sneaks out to see Luigi, and Violet really wants to say that as far as she's concerned, Kendra and Luigi could be lying on the main lawn snogging each other's faces off and she, Violet, would just step over them and keep going, because she couldn't care less about the mess that anyone else is making of their lives right now.

As the rest of them debate what film they want to watch, Violet goes back to the studio, which is the only place where she's sure of keeping the vase of water steady and balanced. She looks at her sketches of Evan and decides that she can't cope with the demands of another human being. So she puts them aside and starts instead to draw a still life of a jar of brushes and some tubes of paint. She's so absorbed in that task that she almost completely forgets about anything else until, a couple of hours later, outside the studio, she hears someone screeching their head off, and she drops the pastel she's using and sprints for the door, because frankly, it sounds as if someone's being murdered—

And what she sees outside jerks her back into her body instantly. Me. Jerks *me* instantly back into my body with a fizzing electric shock.

All the outside lamps are on. The front of the villa is lit up as brightly as a stage, the green of the lawn shining iridescently in the artificial light. From the lower level of the formal garden I might be a spectator looking up at a stage on which a melodrama's raging away. Catia, standing in the middle of the lawn and screaming in a mix of English and Italian, is definitely the leading actress; she's dominating the scene. She's yelling at Kendra, who's emerging from the gap in the hedge. Kendra has changed from the simple dress she wore at dinner and is in a sexy slip that might actually be a nightie, which is pretty gross, considering the circumstances.

"*E tu! E tu, Luigi! Fatto vedere! Tanto so che ci sei!*" Catia is yelling. She's telling Luigi to come out and show himself.

*If they were meeting in that stone alcove again,* I think, *there really isn't any way out from there apart from the steps to the lawn. Could he jump down? Is it too far?* I picture the area, and think there's quite a big drop—but Luigi looks strong, he might be able to climb down the wall, or jump for it. . . .

He hasn't. He's here. Coming out behind Kendra. I can't read his expression, but his body language looks distinctly hangdog. *Busted,* as Paige would say.

On the terrace above, Paige, Leonardo, Evan, and Kelly are spilling out from the rec room, looking down at the scene below. Paige squeals as Catia strides across to Luigi and slaps him so hard across the face that we all wince at the sound.

"*Ma sei scemo!*" she yells. "*Cretino, idiota, scemo! Cosa cazzo avevi in mente?*"

Swinging around, she confronts Kendra.

"And you!" she shrieks. "Stupid little girl! What the hell were you thinking, sneaking out at night to see a married man?"

I gasp. So does almost everyone else: I hear Paige squeal again in surprise. I nip up the steps and onto the terrace to join the rest of the group; you want company in these moments, someone to turn to when you need to share the shock.

"*Married!*" Kendra exclaims, such misery and disappointment in her voice that we all wince again in sadness for her.

Luigi cringes as she turns to him.

"Tell me it's not true!" she says, and I can hear tears in her voice.

"Not just married—he has a little daughter and another baby on the way!" Catia announces.

"*È vero,*" Leonardo says to us. "It's true," he translates. "His wife is—uh, *in dolce attesa,*" he adds, clearly not knowing how to say "pregnant" in English.

Kelly's ears prick up at learning something new.

"'In sweet waiting'?" she asks, translating it literally. "That's actually a nice way to say pregnant—"

"It's not true!" Kendra screams, not having heard Leonardo's confirmation. She throws herself at Luigi, grabbing hold of the collar of his shirt with both hands, trying to shake him, but Luigi is stocky and muscular, and he doesn't move under her assault. This failure makes Kendra collapse onto his chest, still holding his shirt.

"Tell me she's lying," she wails against his neck.

"You seemed like the clever girl!" Catia says furiously to her. "The one who wouldn't be stupid enough to be caught out by some man!"

"Uh, *thanks,*" Kelly mutters. Paige snorts.

"And *you,* Luigi!" Catia continues, even more viciously. "You swore up and down to me two years ago that you'd learned your lesson! I was an idiot to give you a second chance! I should never have allowed you to come back to teach in my summer school! I should have been on the lookout as soon as I heard that Annalisa was pregnant again!"

"Oh my *God,*" Paige says as the full horror of the situation sinks in.

We exchange stares of pity for poor Kendra. It's not only that Luigi's done this before, that she isn't unique in having a fling, or whatever she's doing, with him: this isn't some big love affair, some grand passion. Kendra was just a distraction for him while his wife was pregnant. As, presumably, the first girl was too.

"*È vero*," Luigi says to Kendra, so quietly that we can hardly hear him. "*È tutto vero. Mi dispiace, Kendra.*"

It's true. It's all true. I'm sorry, Kendra.

Kendra bursts into heartrending sobs. And Paige shows her true worth. She bounds down the steps to the lawn, tumbles across it, and grabs hold of Kendra, pulling her away from Luigi with one arm; with the other, she hauls off at him. *She* doesn't slap Luigi, though. For the rest of my life I'll remember the sight of Paige landing a punch square on Luigi's jaw. I honestly don't think any man could have done a better job. Kendra's shaking couldn't budge Luigi, but Paige's roundhouse punch sends him reeling back, grabbing his jaw as if she just broke it.

"You stay away from her from now on, you hear?" Paige yells. "If I see you anywhere near her, if you try to call her, I'll track you down like a dog and beat the hell out of you in front of your wife!"

Wrapping both arms around Kendra, she helps her friend stumble across the lawn and back up the steps. Kelly runs down and together, one on either side of Kendra, they guide her up and into the house. I follow them upstairs to Paige and Kendra's bedroom. Poor Kendra's making awful, stifled, whimpering sounds, like a puppy that's been kicked.

There's nothing we can say, nothing at all that will make this situation better, or give her any consolation. Heartbreak's bad enough, but these circumstances are so terrible that we can't even meet one another's eyes. That scene was so embarrassing I want to pretend it never happened, and I sense that Paige and Kelly feel the same.

They sit Kendra down on her bed, and she promptly collapses like a floppy toy, unable to even sit up. I make myself useful by unbuckling the ankle straps of her pretty sandals and taking them off. There's an unspoken consensus that we can't undress her, and she clearly isn't going to do it herself. We're all just sleeping with a sheet to cover us, the nights are so warm, and as Paige and Kelly smooth down her silky slip-dress, I pull up the sheet and fold it at Kendra's armpits. She's lying completely still, those awful little moans still coming from her lips, and Paige sits down on the bed next to her and takes her hand, stroking it.

*He's a lying horrible cheat,* we could say. *Plenty more fish in the sea. No boy's worth getting this upset.* But we've all heard those same phrases in attempts to console us over some boy who's messed us around, and we all know that they don't help. They can make it worse, actually: they can make you sob more, insist that he's the only one you'll ever love, the only one you'll ever want, that he *is* worth it. And the more you struggle against the truth, the worse you feel. The more stupid you feel.

So what Kendra's doing—lying there, letting it sink in, the full knowledge of how badly Luigi's behaved—is the right thing to do. And I think what we're doing—being quiet, not trying hopelessly to make things better—is right too.

Paige gives us a small jerk of her head toward the door, telling us we can go. It's as if we're at a funeral: no one wants to say anything, not even in a hushed voice. We stand up and walk out of the room, trying to make as little noise as possible. Out of respect for Kendra's suffering, I suppose. It's for us, not for her—I don't imagine she gives a toss how loud our feet sound on the stone floor. I put my hand on the light switch and meet Paige's eyes: she nods, and I turn it off, leaving them in darkness. The only sound is Kendra's poignant sobs of misery as I close the door.

Kelly and I turn to go to our bedroom and promptly jump, squeaking together in shock like frightened mice, because Catia is standing right there. She's directly under the overhead light, and it sends weird shadows over her face, hollowing out her eye sockets, making her look like a corpse. When she speaks, her voice is dry and grating, adding to the corpselike effect.

"Kendra's gone to bed?" she asks us, and we nod, tongue-tied.

"Good," she says. And then she looks at Kelly. "You did the right thing telling me," she adds. "At least I stopped it before it went any further."

I freeze.

"Go to bed now," Catia says wearily. "We all need some sleep. Tomorrow I will make some serious decisions."

We watch her go down the stairs, her shoulders sagging under her linen sweater; Catia's posture has always been perfect till now. I don't move until we've heard her go into her suite on the floor below, the door closing behind her. Then I swivel my head to look at Kelly, hardly able to believe what I just heard. And simultaneously, the door of Paige and

Kendra's bedroom swings open and Paige appears, pale with fury under her tan, as tall and blond and beautiful as one of the avenging angels in a fresco from Siena Cathedral.

"You *bitch*!" she hisses at Kelly.

And I don't say a word in Kelly's defense.

## We Can Never Trust Her Again

**Coming over very soon, darling. Please hang on. Will be there very soon. I love you up to the sky and back again! Please just hold on and wait for me. Love you.**

Mum's coming to Italy. She texted first thing this morning. A huge relief has settled over me at the knowledge that I'll see her. Excited as I was to get away, to explore the world without her, Mum has always been my rock, my anchor. Although I know that the fact she's coming means she has something to tell me that I won't want to hear, it also means she'll *be* here, physically. I can't wait, I just can't. I'm desperate to hug Mum, to cry on her shoulder, to hear what she has to tell me and pour out everything that's been happening.

Well, almost everything. Obviously, I can't ever tell her about Luca.

*But why can't she come straight away? She could have got on a plane this morning and been here by lunchtime.*

*Something's holding her up—something that must be very important. But if I speculate about it, my brain will start to whir faster and faster until it explodes, so my job until she comes is to try not to think about it at all. . . .*

On the positive side, the Luigi/Kendra drama has certainly provided quite a distraction from the routine at Villa Barbiano. It isn't exactly a normal morning on which to wake up, shower, and go down to breakfast.

On the negative side, however, the atmosphere is almost unbearably tense and poisonous. I've barely exchanged a word with Kelly so far, apart from a mumble about who's going to use the bathroom first. I've never seen a girl look so miserable; she hasn't met my eyes yet. As we emerge from our room, Paige and Kendra come out from theirs. I don't know if the timing's deliberate, but it's like something out of a play, a highly charged moment where all the characters come onstage at the same time and the audience holds its breath, anticipating a fight.

No—on second thought, it's more like something from a soap opera. Paige has clearly got up early to do herself and Kendra up to the nines. Her equivalent of going into battle is dressing up and working on her hair and makeup till her entire appearance is like a suit of polished armor. Her hair cascades in waves, her makeup is impeccable, her tight white T-shirt fits her like a glove, her blush-colored linen mini is equally smart. She's even wearing wedge heels instead of her usual daytime flip-flops.

Behind her, Kendra is ashy pale under her naturally warm-toned skin. But she's holding her head high, and either she or Paige has curled her ponytail into a big fat ringlet that bounces bravely at the back of her neck. She's in a short-sleeved button-up dress, and she too is carefully made up, with lavender eye shadow to contrast her dark-brown eyes and eyelashes that look as if she's taken a curler to them.

"Hi, Violet," Paige says.

"Hi, Violet," Kendra echoes.

"Hi," I mutter, thinking: *Oh no. Really? Please let this not be what I think it is—*

"Come on, Kendra," Paige says, raising her chin in a clear snub to Kelly and walking downstairs as elegantly as a Vegas showgirl with a huge headdress of feathers. Kendra follows, and I don't dare look at Kelly. I have a nasty sense of what tactic they've decided upon, and over breakfast, it becomes abundantly clear. They're sending Kelly to Coventry, which is British for what the Americans call a freeze-out.

Catia, presiding as usual at the head of the table, barely says anything after a token "*Buon giorno,*" and we follow her lead; we're not keen to chatter away after the events of last night. But somehow, the fact that Paige and Kendra aren't addressing a word to Kelly makes it more obvious, rather than less, when hardly anything is being said. Clearly, Paige has cast herself as the friend who's going to avenge Kelly's betrayal of Kendra's secret. She makes a point of asking me politely a couple of times to pass the *macedonia*, the big glass bowl of fruit salad, and offers me more orange juice or Danishes while ignoring Kelly completely. In short, she behaves in exactly the ladylike way Catia has been trying to ding into her for the last few weeks, and it's so disconcerting and awkward that I barely manage to respond to her.

Because I'm very much on the fence myself. Yes, it's uncomfortable to be singled out by Paige for this kind of overgracious treatment, but at the same time, I can't blame Paige, not at all, for having her friend's back. Kelly's actions broke the most important rule of the girl code: not to tell tales on her friends to parents or teachers. She exposed Kendra to a scene so humiliating, so public, that I shiver at the mere memory; it makes me want to scratch my face up with my nails just to get the image out of my head. I give Kendra huge points for managing to get up and come downstairs this morning. I honestly don't think I could have done it. My guess is that Paige gave her the courage to do it by promising her they'd make Kelly's stay here a living hell from now on. And honestly, if that's what Paige did, it wouldn't be a bad strategy at all.

I can't defend Kelly. Frankly, she deserves what she's getting. But it's very hard to watch.

Breakfast can't last more than twenty minutes, but it feels like at least a couple of hours before Catia rises, puts her hands on the table, and says:

"We will not have lessons this morning. Kendra, I will see you now in my study. The rest of you may work on your

Italian grammar with particular attention to the past historic tense."

We stare up at her, all mute now. I think we were hoping that everything would go back to a sort of normal, as it did after Paige came home tipsy: that Luigi would never be seen again, and that Catia would pretend nothing had happened.

*Oops. Well, scratch that faint hope.*

There's a pause, and then Kendra pushes back her chair and stands up too. Paige reaches out to squeeze her hand in support for a moment before Kendra follows Catia from the room. It makes me think of scenes from films where people are going off to their executions.

We wait until the door at the far end of the corridor has closed behind them. I start to say something, but Paige is clearly dying to start laying into Kelly, and she gets in the first word:

"Violet, you can tell your friend that as far as we're concerned, from now on she doesn't *exist* for us, okay? We're not going to talk to her, help her out, be in the same room with her—after what she did, she doesn't deserve *anything*. To think I helped her with her hair and makeup for the party! She's a nasty little ungrateful *snitch*!"

I bite my lip. Kelly's started to cry; she grabs her napkin and holds it to her eyes to cover her face under Paige's onslaught.

"She should be ashamed of herself!" Paige continues passionately.

"I'm so, so sorry," Kelly whimpers from behind the napkin. "I never meant—I didn't think—"

Paige rounds on her furiously, her chair squeaking on the floor as she turns to confront her; then she realizes that she isn't talking to Kelly, which makes things a bit difficult to yell at her directly.

"I just thought Catia would warn off Luigi," Kelly sobs. "I never *imagined* that she'd go down and drag them up and make a huge scene in front of everyone! And I never thought that Luigi was *married*! How could I have known? Or about his wife being—" She gulps. "And it *is* a good thing we found out about that sooner rather than later. Can you imagine if things had gone any further—I mean, I don't know how far things had gone—but can you *imagine . . . ?*"

I realize I'm nodding in reluctant agreement.

"She *snitched*," Paige says with absolute loathing in her voice. "That means we can never trust her again. I'd be really careful, Violet. I wouldn't tell her *anything*."

I take a deep breath.

"Kelly," I say as calmly as I can, "why did you do it? If you were worried about Kendra, you should've come to me and Paige and we could have talked about it and tried to think of something to do."

"I know it was totally wrong, but I was jealous," Kelly sobs. "We were at the party and Andrea wouldn't even look at me, he wouldn't even say a word to me when I tried to talk to him. He wasn't rude—it was *worse*. It was like I didn't even *exist*! All he could do was gawk at her like she was the most beautiful thing in the world—and she doesn't even *want* him! I know I shouldn't have done it, I *know. . . .*"

"Well, that's, like, totally *pathetic*," Paige says contemptuously. "So you just wanted to pull her down 'cause Andrea's into her? That's not her fault!"

"She knows that, Paige," I cut in swiftly. "She *knows* that. She was an idiot and she's really sorry. And look, Paige, you must have had a sense of what was going on. You two went out together, you must have known Kendra was sneaking off with Luigi. . . . Don't you feel a bit bad about that, now we know he's married? I mean, it's not fair to dump all the guilt on Kelly!"

I don't want to tell Paige that we overheard her and Kendra at the castello; that would lead to an explanation of why Kelly and I were hiding behind a sofa, which I certainly don't want to give. I'm hoping I can point out to Paige that she should have looked after Kendra a bit better, deflect some of the aggression she's directing at Kelly. But though Paige's eyes flash at this, it just causes her to go more on the attack.

"But she *told* on Kendra!" Paige's voice rises, and she puts her hands on her hips. "She *told* Catia where they were so Catia could go down and catch them! Can you *imagine*!"

"*Buon giorno, ragazze!*" Elisa says, strolling into the dining room, her legs looking like toothpicks in her impossibly tight white jeans, a smirk as wide as the Cheshire Cat's on her face. "*Tutto bene?*"

"Everything okay?" she's asking. Ugh, what a cow Elisa is. She was out last night during the huge Luigi-is-married-plus-his-wife-is-pregnant melodrama, but clearly Leonardo or her mum has filled her in. And she's enjoying, tremendously, the knowledge of Kendra's humiliation, and the sight of us all at loggerheads.

Kelly rips the napkin from her face and does her best to look as calm as possible. We all keep blank faces, determined not to give Elisa any more ammunition to fire at us.

"*Povera Kendra!*" Elisa says, and then switches into English. "Poor Kendra! She must be very sad today. It is very much a shame. She feels stupid, yes? *Molto sciocca.* Of course, she knows that she is not the first girl. Luigi, he has another stupid foreign girl two years ago. *She* cries a lot too when she finds out that he has a wife—"

Paige stands up, shoving her chair back with a scrape along the floor.

"I'm not staying here to listen to this," she says. "I've got better things to do. Like going to pee."

"Yes," I agree, standing up too. "I think I might go for a wee too. Good idea, Paige."

Elisa isn't as disconcerted by our deliberate vulgarity as we hoped. She's homed in on the weak link in our chain, and now she leans in to focus on Kelly, whose face is still damp.

"And you, Kellee?" she asks sweetly. "What will you do—cry some more?"

"Shut up," I snap, as Kelly does indeed heave a sob at this. But I'm eclipsed by Paige, who loathes Elisa at least as much as I do, and clearly needs a truly satisfactory outlet for her fury at what's happened to Kendra.

"*You,*" she says to Elisa, rounding the table with the whirling-dervish fury of a tornado in wedge heels, "*you* stay away from us, you hear? *All* of us. I've totally had it with you sticking your nose in the air and thinking you're better than us just because you're practically anorexic! You're only dating Luca—if you even *are*—because Violet turned him down! If you say a *word* to any of us that isn't just hello or goodbye or pass the salt at dinner, so help me, I'll haul off and smash your skinny ass through the nearest window, don't think I won't! Right in front of your mama, too!"

I think I'm sort of in love with Paige at that moment. Of course, if you asked me, I would totally say that violence is wrong and people shouldn't menace other people, and that I'd be very sorry to see Elisa go flying through a french window.

But, you know, the first word Elisa said when she saw us lying out by the pool was "pigs." She and her friend Ilaria have been nothing but mean and nasty as far as we're concerned, and now that Kendra's in such a vulnerable state, I am absolutely, one hundred percent behind every word that Paige just said to Elisa.

"You heard her," I say to Elisa, narrowing my eyes. "Piss off and leave us alone."

Elisa is shocked, looking from me to Paige, who's looming over her, but she doesn't turn to leave, and Paige's fists are clenched. I remember her smacking Luigi in the face yesterday, and I panic: what if Elisa says something that makes Paige so angry she goes too far? I reach out and grab the handle of the jug of water on the table. If Paige lunges for Elisa, she'll get the entire contents full in the face. That should hold her long enough for Elisa to get away.

My fingers grip the handle tightly. Paige isn't backing down, Elisa isn't backing off, the tension's so thick I can feel it all around us—

I don't know what would have happened if Catia hadn't come back into the room just then. But it's with huge relief that I loosen my grasp on the water jug. For all Paige's brave words, she isn't actually going to punch Elisa in front of her mum.

"Kendra has gone to her room to pack," Catia announces, and I gasp.

*Kendra's being sent home?* I didn't think that would happen. I really didn't. It would be an admission of failure on Catia's part, that she can't keep control of the girls who are in her charge. Not only would it be a huge deal, Catia would probably have to give back at least some of the money Kendra's parents had paid to send her here; and she definitely—from what Leonardo's said—relies heavily on the fees from summer schools to keep Villa Barbiano going. Plus, Kendra's parents, apart from being very strict, are really high-powered professionals who would go absolutely mental at the knowledge that Kendra had been messing around with a married man hired by Catia to teach us girls. Let alone a married man who'd done the same thing before!

I'd have bet pretty much anything on Catia's hushing this entire thing up and assuming that Kendra, Paige, and Evan would never breathe a word of it, as long as she kept Luigi and Kendra well separated for the rest of the summer. So I'm gobsmacked at this news.

Judging from their gasps in unison with mine, Paige and Kelly are equally shocked; we clearly all thought it over and reached identical conclusions. Which, from Catia's words, we got completely wrong.

But we weren't idiots; Catia's own daughter also looks completely taken aback.

"*Veramente, Mamma?*" Elisa asks, her eyes wide.

"And Paige, Kelly, Violet, you will go to pack as well," Catia continues.

Now we all really do exclaim.

"What? No *way*!" Paige says.

"*No!*" I hear myself say forcefully, rather to my own surprise. "I don't *want* to go home yet!"

And Kelly bursts into tears once more.

"*Andiamo a Venezia!*" Catia raises her voice to be heard over the din. "Okay? Oh, you girls and your constant drama!" she exclaims with exasperation, flapping her hands in a very Italian gesture. "You are not going home, none of you! We are *going to Venice*!"

Four girls gasp as one. It's the only sound we have ever made simultaneously. But I'm sure that my reaction, though it sounds identical, is very different from the others'. Because the first thought that popped into my head on hearing this utterly unexpected announcement was:

*Mum! What about Mum? She said to hold on, but she must be almost nearly on her way over here, she must! She wouldn't leave me for much longer, without her, waiting and waiting and getting closer and closer to totally freaking out. She loves me too much for that! I have to let her know, in case she turns up here and finds us all gone.*

*I have to let her know to come to Venice.*

# He Kissed Me

"It's like San Francisco," Paige breathes at our incredible first view of Venice.

Which breaks the spell for a moment. We wrench our eyes away from the Grand Canal and turn to gawk at her instead.

*"San Francisco?"* I ask. *"Really?"*

I mean, I haven't been to San Francisco, but I've seen it in lots of films. Amazingly steep streets, cable cars, Alcatraz Island out in the bay, a huge red bridge they call Golden for some reason. Does she mean Venice is like San Francisco because of the *bridge?*

"Never a dull moment with Paige," I mutter to Kelly as an aside.

"*Well,*" Paige starts enthusiastically, "when I went to San Francisco, it was, like, *amazing*. You wander around the whole time going, Oh my God, this is *awesome*. And I saw it in the movies tons of times, but it was way beyond anything I imagined from the movies. Do you see what I mean? Like, Florence, and London when we came through, were really cool, but they were just like I knew they were going to be from movies. But this is like San Francisco—*way* more stunning than you expect. You know there's going to be rivers—"

"*Canals!*" Kendra interrupts, rolling her eyes so hard it looks painful.

"Okay, whatever, canals. You know there's going to be canals. And gondolas. But *seeing* them in real life is *way* more amazing than any movie ever!"

I'm grinning now because I actually know what Paige means. In the train from Florence, coming up the spine of Italy, Catia had told us that arriving by train is by far the best way to see Venice for the first time, and now I get why. You don't see any of Venice from the train at all; you have a last stop on the mainland, and then the train takes off on a track over the lagoon, dazzling blue water spreading out on either side, dotted with tiny, uninhabitable islands. On the right-hand side is a road parallel to the train tracks, cars buzzing along it, and bright-orange city buses, which seem really incongruous in the middle of the sea. But that's all you can see: the lagoon, the road, and the terminus, which is a totally normal, boring train station.

So you get off the train, handing your suitcases down to one another in a chain, looking around you with high excitement, and you walk through the station, a bit confused that this looks exactly like Florence station—surely Venice should look different? And then outside the huge arched entrance doors, you see bright glittering sunshine and a burst of color, like a carnival, and the next thing you know you're through the doors and at the top of a flight of marble steps leading down and right in front of you is the Grand Canal, and you all gasp and bump into one another as you stop dead to stare your eyes out at the most amazing sight you ever saw in your life.

In her eccentric way, Paige has nailed it. No matter how many pictures of Venice you see, how many films set here, it just doesn't prepare you for the extraordinary, beautiful, magical reality.

Boats jostling past one another on the water, sliding under the low bridges. Gondolas, water taxis, small private ones barely bigger than dinghies, bigger ones crammed with people that we come to learn are the equivalent of buses here, called vaporetti. Palazzi, behind them, elaborately carved and hung with red and burgundy draperies. Rows of wooden mooring poles, painted bright candy-cane red and white, like the stripy T-shirts of the gondoliers. Golden buildings, shimmering in the sunlight. Heat bouncing off the stones and wrapping itself around us, a shock after the air-conditioning of the train and the cool station.

And people, people everywhere. Florence was crowded, but Venice is absolutely packed. The arching white stone bridge over the canal is crammed with tourists; the promenade in front of the station is equally busy. People are pushing past us to get into the station, muttering crossly in Italian. I try to budge up and see that lots of other tourists have done exactly the same as us: stopped dead to stare in wonder at the sight before them.

*"Venite, ragazze!"* Catia calls, and we snap to attention, bumping our cases down the steps. All along the promenade are boats, moored up, and I realize that the bigger docks are actually—

*"Bus stops!"* Kelly's realizing it too. "Look!" She points up at the colored bands that run along the floating white glass-fronted structures. "Those are the bus numbers! Wow, this is *mental.* Imagine living here and taking a boat to work every day along the canal!"

"So romantic!" Paige agrees, before she forgets that she isn't talking to Kelly.

You can't walk a straight line in Venice. There are just too many people. We weave our way through the crowds to the water's edge, past several bus stops, a little way down from the front of the station, to a little pier with TAXI written above it on a wooden sign.

*"Sbrigatevi!"* Catia's calling. "Hurry up." But how can we possibly? There's so much to gawk at! The stalls selling Venetian carnival masks, from small ceramic ones that would fit in the palm of your hand to big silk ones with ribbons to tie at the back of your head, beautifully painted and decorated with glitter, plumes, sparkly stones. Lace fans, unfurled and pinned open to show how pretty and delicate they are; and glass—colored glass necklaces and bracelets hanging from long poles, trays of rings set out enticingly, glass figurines, one stall with what looks like an entire orchestra of miniature black-glass musicians each playing their own perfectly executed tiny instruments—

*"Violet!"*

I jump, Kelly tugging my elbow; I'm the last girl onto the pier. The taxi driver smiles at me as he takes my suitcase and throws it blithely into the well of the motor taxi. It's beyond luxurious: shiny polished pale wood, chrome rails running all around the open back, a white padded cushion on the seat. The four of us girls sink onto the backseat, exchanging awestruck glances as the driver unties the boat from a stanchion, tosses the rope into the boat, jumps in fluidly, and takes his place at the wheel. Catia has taken her place in the cabin, too cool to sit outside—or not wanting to be deafened by our shrieks of excitement as the boat backs out into the water, turns, and starts to buzz down the Grand Canal.

Salty sprays of water splash up on either side of the boat. We bump over the wake of the water-buses; we watch the gondolas slipping elegantly in and out of the smaller canals that feed into the wider one, the gondoliers, in their straw hats, ducking smoothly under the low bridges; we point at the seagulls perching on the mooring poles. On either side Venice rises up, one building more beautiful than the next, castellations, balconies, private gardens with stone walls around them. Grand hotels, art galleries . . .

"Ooh! The Prada Foundation!" Paige gushes as we pass an exquisite white building with rows of white balconies and elegant dark-green shutters: a discreet gray banner declares its name. "Can we go? I *love* Prada handbags!"

"I think it's an art gallery, not a shop," Kendra says dryly.

"Oh," Paige says, disappointed.

"They'll still sell stuff, even if it's an art gallery," Kelly points out. "All the galleries we've been to have shops."

This is absolutely true, and Kendra and Paige nod in unison before they remember that not only are they not talking to Kelly, they're not listening to her either. I really hope this wears off soon; I'm already over it. They've made their point, they've punished Kelly, can't they just let it go?

I turn my head away from them and pretend they're not there. I fill my eyes with Venice. I see two water-buses on the same line—the N, it looks like—going in opposite directions down the canal, but needing to use the same stop: one's pulled in, people flooding off and on, and the other one is hovering midstream. The first one chugs away from the stop, weaving its way around the other one, which waits for it to pass and then turns toward the stop. The buses have huge black rubber bumpers around them, and so do the stops, so they can thwack against the sides without worrying; as the bus pulls in, someone—a sailor? Bus conductor?—on board slides a gate open, jumps onto the pier, swiftly winds a rope around a stanchion, and signals that passengers can start walking off down the little gangway.

Old ladies pulling shopping trolleys. Businessmen and -women in smart suits. Kids with backpacks tucked under their arms. Normal people, going about their everyday lives, tuning out the hordes of tourists with cameras and baseball caps. It makes me wonder what it would be like to actually live here, to catch this bus back and forth to school or university, to live a life on the water. . . .

We stop, swivel, pause in the middle of the Grand Canal. We're waiting for another water taxi to emerge from under a bridge, and once it's gone we pass through, the buses slipping past us, a gondola too, the gondolier angling his pole skillfully under the bridge; everyone seems to know how to get past everyone else with no obvious rules, no traffic lanes.

"Imagine a pileup," Paige comments. "Everyone would drown."

The sky above is dazzling blue: when the boat pauses, you realize how hot it is. And then we chug beneath the bridge, a moment of damp coolness surrounded by stone, and barely thirty seconds later we stop in front of a little dock outside a palazzo.

"Is this the only way in?" Kelly asks, tilting her head back to take in the lines of the building. "Can you imagine if it was? If you didn't have a boat, you'd be completely stuck!"

"There must be another way to get in," I say as the taxi driver ties up the boat and hands us all out onto the pier, passing up our cases. But the big Gothic-shaped doors, which are open to receive us, do look very like a new entrance, and the tiled hallway inside, high, arched, painted with frescos, definitely looks like the kind of posh entranceway in which Venetian aristocrats would receive their guests.

"*Eccoci!*" Catia says, after paying the taxi driver and shutting the doors. We all sigh in disappointment at the amazing view of the canal being blocked off. "We are in Venice! We are here as the guests of the di Vesperi family, or rather, of the principessa's family, the Giustinians. They have been kind enough to let us stay here."

"How long are we here for?" Kelly asks bravely.

We haven't dared yet to ask Catia a single question about our sudden trip: we were too relieved that no one was being sent home in disgrace. She said to bring lots of clothes, so we all crammed our suitcases, but she didn't give us any more information, and we kept our mouths shut and our heads down. She did tell Evan, whom she's really taken to, that he could stay on at the villa with Leonardo and Elisa, but Evan said he wouldn't dream of it without his sister there, and he ought to be heading off to rejoin his friends anyway.

I miss Evan. We're friends on Facebook now, of course, and before he left he asked me to swap mobile numbers, at a time when no one else was around. We gave him a lift to the station, and he sat next to me and I felt his arm hovering over my back, sinking slowly, cautiously, faux-casually, to avoid startling me or having any of the other girls notice. But it settled eventually, and for the last twenty minutes Evan's arm lay along my shoulders, warm and heavy, a secret that we were sharing in plain sight.

I liked it. I liked it a lot. It made me feel . . . secure. Steadied. As we drove through Florence, with all its distractions to look at, he closed his fingers around my shoulder in a gentle clasp that turned the arm around me into something definite and made me shiver a little with pleasure. And when we all said goodbye, hugging him one after the other, I felt his hands tighten around my waist and he kissed me, swiftly but unmistakably, on the side of my head that the other girls couldn't see.

I was the last: he'd already shaken Catia's hand and said his polite thank-yous to his hostess. So after the kiss, he bent down, picked up his big rucksack with the guitar slung on the back, and strolled off to find the bus terminal and buy a ticket to Arezzo, where he was meeting his friends at a jazz festival. And as I watched him make his way through the crowds, girls' heads turning to look at the big, tall, handsome blond boy, I felt a spike of jealousy, the last confirmation, if any were needed, that my feelings for Evan had passed from friendship into maybe, just maybe, the possibility of something stronger.

"We'll see" is the only answer Catia gives Kelly to her question about how long we're staying in Venice. And just then a smartly dressed lady bustles into the hallway, exclaiming:

*"Ma siete già arrivate! Avete fatto veramente veloce!"*

She's the housekeeper, Bianca, and she wastes no time in sweeping us upstairs to our bedrooms, past a series of huge and rather empty reception rooms whose walls are covered in delicate frescos and smell a bit damp. When we realize we have bedrooms overlooking the canal, with balconies just about big enough for two of us to stand on, we're too excited to think about anything else. Kelly and I are together, of course, Paige and Kendra next door, and we wave to each other from our respective balconies, whooping with delight.

"Girls! Please behave with decorum!" Catia calls from the corridor. "We are guests in the home of the principessa's family. We do not want the neighbors complaining to her that you are all shrieking like hooligans!"

Grimacing, we pull horrible faces at one another.

"Now please unpack, and bring a swimsuit each and some sun lotion and be downstairs in half an hour," she continues. "We have been sitting still all morning, so I have decided to take you to the Lido beach to swim this afternoon to let off some energy. The taxi will come back in thirty minutes, so be in the front hall by then."

We all shoot back into our rooms, galvanized by this,

and dash around, calling dibs on beds, unzipping suitcases, and fighting over who gets more hangers.

"Catia sounds really happy," Kelly comments to me as we divvy up the drawers. "I know she's trying to sound stern, but actually I think she's really happy."

"Because of being in Venice, do you think?" I ask. "It *is* amazing. Even if you've been here before it must still be massively exciting to come back."

"Well, I've been thinking," says Kelly, and now I'm all ears, because whenever she starts that way something interesting's coming. Something I haven't been clever enough to think of myself.

I make an encouraging noise.

"Coming to Venice, taking taxis—" she continues. "I looked at the map of Venice last night, and the Lido's like a beach quite a way across the lagoon, it'll take quite a while to get there—I bet there are buses we could take—"

"It's expensive!" I say, having caught on faster than usual.

"Right," Kelly says, folding her T-shirts neatly. Sharing a small council house with a big family has made her very tidy and efficient at fitting into a small space; I'm an only child, so I sprawl out everywhere and have to work at making sure we split the available room evenly so I don't take advantage of her. "And coming to Venice wasn't in the budget, was it? She can't ask our families to chip in any more dosh—it's pricey enough as it is. I'm sure we could have taken a bus from the station to near here. There were stops everywhere. Same for the Lido. But instead she's throwing money around, when we know from Leonardo that she doesn't actually have that much. And she seems really cheerful, considering the whole Kendra mess. And here we are, suddenly staying in the principessa's family house, which is a big deal. . . ."

I stare at her, sinking down to sit on my bed as I take this in. The springs squeak horribly and the mattress feels like horsehair.

"Someone's given her some money," I say slowly. "To get us out of Chianti."

"We all go to the Castello di Vesperi," Kelly says, putting her shoes in the huge painted cupboard. "And the principe gets a good look at you. And then maybe Catia rings up the principessa to have a fit about the Kendra thing, let off some steam, or the principessa rings her, but either way they hatch a plan that sends all of us well away from the castello, across the country, and Catia's spending money like water, and we know the principe has a ton of money—"

"They sent *me* away," I say. "This isn't really about getting Kendra away from Luigi—that was just a convenient excuse. It's about getting me away from the whole di Vesperi family." I take a deep breath. "Which means—which really does mean—"

"It's just a theory," Kelly says quickly.

*Which means that Luca really is my brother and the principe is my father. A father who doesn't want me around–who positively wants to get rid of me, so much so that he'll pay Catia to bundle me away.*

I texted and emailed Mum, of course, to say where we were going. I was dying to ring her, and it would have been the perfect excuse. But I couldn't bear the idea that my call might go to voice mail—that she might freak out, seeing my picture pop up on her screen, and not pick up, because she isn't ready to talk to me yet. It's the first time ever that I've imagined Mum not wanting to hear my voice, and it's such a painful image that I pushed it away at once.

Or tried to. Because it keeps on coming back. Especially because all I got in response was a text saying:

> Lovely, so glad you're going to Venice! Have a wonderful time. Will see you very very soon darling, hold on. Love you SO much, please just hold on a tiny bit longer!

Which wasn't exactly the satisfaction I needed.

"Hey!" Paige bursts into our room, a huge smile on her face. "Are you two ready?" She's so revved up that she's forgotten she's pretending Kelly doesn't exist, and as soon as she continues I realize why.

"We're going to the beach!" she carols. "And you know what that means? Tons of boys! Plus, *lifeguards! Hot Italian lifeguards!*"

# A Really Worthy Adversary

Wow. Lounging by a private pool in Chianti with a couple of boys hasn't prepared us in any way for an Italian beach in the full height of summer. It's packed as full of tanned and oiled Italians, their skins as dark as cherrywood from this long hot summer, as the narrow Venetian streets are with tourists. Catia's picked a *stabilimento,* which has a bar, an open-air restaurant, and its own stretch of beach; you have to pay for lounger and umbrella hire to get in, and the guy who's leading us to our group of chairs weaves through a throng of happy, swimsuit-wearing, chattering Italians who are standing around in groups everywhere, waving their hands as they talk, pushing back their hair, and all looking so cool that by the time we get to the loungers, we're relieved just to sit down in the shade and get our bearings.

This is glamour central. Or maybe it would be more accurate to say confidence central. It's like walking into a party where everyone knows everyone else. You look around and slowly realize that people are in small groups, that there are couples together and maybe even some lone singles, but the overall impression is utterly intimidating.

"They're all so—" Kelly starts.

"I *know,*" I say.

It's totally unlike any English beaches I've ever been on, or any Scandinavian ones; when we visit Mormor and go to the lake in Norway, the locals are much more reserved. And *covered.* With a lot of the guys here, I just don't know where to look. There are a *lot* of Speedos. I didn't expect that. Leonardo and Andrea, by the pool, always wore looser swimsuits, sort of like boxers, and Evan has those typical baggy American shorts—American boys seem much shyer than Italian ones about showing off their bodies, as far as I can see.

"See! Told you!" Paige sings out, pointing up at a wooden tower, on top of which a lifeguard is lounging, smoking a cigarette, talking on his mobile phone, his skin tanned so dark he might be Indian, wearing nothing but a tiny, shiny pair of red Speedos.

"But *Paige,* his *swimsuit!*" I object.

Paige tosses her head.

"*Actually,* Violet," she says, "I think you're being really sexist. Why should girls be able to wear bikinis if boys can't wear Speedos? Boys like to tan too!"

"My dad calls them budgie smugglers," Kelly volunteers, and I snigger at this.

So does Paige, when she figures it out. Then, however, she shuts it down, because it came from Kelly. Turning away from us pointedly, Paige pulls off her T-shirt and skirt and lies back on the lounger in her pink crocheted bikini. I sigh. This whole snubbing of Kelly is already exhausting me, and if I feel like that, how must Kelly be reacting? Before, with the four of us, there was always a good flow of conversation. Kelly and Kendra might have the occasional flash of competitiveness, but it would be only a momentary hitch, easily caught up and smoothed over by myself or Paige.

"Paige," I say, standing up, pulling off my dress and draping it over one of the struts of the umbrella, "let's go and see how warm the water is, okay?"

Paige glances to her side, at Kendra, but Kendra's just lying there, sunglasses on, not doing a thing or saying a word.

"Okay," Paige says, standing up and stretching to draw attention to herself, which has the desired effect. Thank goodness, at least I tan fast, so I don't feel like a small white garden gnome toddling along beside her. I'm not as dark as the Italians, but I blend in well enough. I'm bravely wearing my polka-dot bikini, and as long as I remember to keep sucking in my tummy, I feel relatively fine.

"Paige!" I hiss, momentarily distracted. "Look—those girls are topless!"

"Wow," Paige says, looking over in the direction I'm indicating discreetly. Three girls are strolling along the edge of the water, in the damp sand, wearing nothing but small bikini bottoms. "You wouldn't see *that* back home!"

"Not in England either," I assure her.

"Though," she adds, "those girls can get away with it because they don't have much up top. If you or me tried to walk around topless, we'd be going *boing-boing-boing* like yo-yos."

I snigger at this vivid image. The sun is deliciously warm, the sky's blue as an Easter egg, the sea is aquamarine, the sand is golden and bouncing back heat, and the Adriatic Sea, when we dip in our toes, is pleasantly cool, just enough to be a lovely contrast to the heat all around us. It's a perfect day, and we're in Venice. Even if we're all—apart from Paige, as usual—struggling with our own issues, we should all be blissful in this moment, and when I open my mouth, that's exactly the point I plan to make.

"Paige, look," I say. "This is gorgeous, right? We're the luckiest girls in the world."

Paige, who's eyeing a group of boys complacently, nods in agreement. We walk into the sea, oohing and aahing with the initial chill as the water rises higher up our legs.

"So can we just drop this sending-Kelly-to-Coventry thing that you two're doing? You've made your point, okay? She gets it. She knows she was wrong and she's said she was sorry."

"Sending to Coventry?" Paige asks.

"Not talking to her."

"Oh, a freeze-out! Why is it called—"

"*Paige!* This is important! I don't know why it's called that, okay? Just start talking to her again!"

Paige drops down suddenly to her bum.

"Ooh!" she exclaims, water lapping around her chest. "I

love to sit in the sand and splash around! I'm not a big swimmer," she adds cheerfully.

She's so infuriating. It's like talking to a slippery eel. But if you can't beat 'em, join 'em. I plop down next to her, gasping in my turn; I'm considerably shorter than she is and the water's up to my chin. I tilt my head back and submerge my skull completely, bubbling air out through my nostrils. It feels wonderful to be underwater after all the hot sweaty traveling of today. When I come up, I spit out a stream of salty water, pretending I'm a dolphin.

"You're so brave to get your hair wet," Paige says, primly patting her own pinned-up locks.

Sometimes I think Paige is actually a lot cleverer than she seems; she's doing a brilliant job of distracting me from the serious talk I'm trying to have with her.

"*Paige!*" I yell loudly, casting around me for a way to make her listen. I glance back to see if Kelly and Kendra have heard me shouting, and I see Kendra still lying there, slumped on her lounger, unmoving.

"You don't need to shout," she says. "I'm right here. Oh, look at those cute kids!"

"Look at *Kendra,*" I say strongly. "Just look at her, okay? Does she look like she's all right?"

Paige glances back for a second.

"Well, of course she's not all right," she says, sounding a bit more sensible. "She's all messed up. You should hear what that creep told her. He was in love, she was the only one he'd ever felt like this about, she was the most beautiful girl in the world—*you* know."

I don't, actually. No boy has ever said those words to me. But I nod as if one has.

"I mean, she had *no* idea," Paige continues. "None at all. And it was bad enough finding out, but like *that*?"

She doesn't need to lower her voice; the wash of the waves, the happy chattering of the Italians all around us, the seagulls squawking overhead, means we can talk normally, which is a real relief.

"Did they—um—how far did they—um, you know, did they actually—" I'm asking this completely out of curiosity, it's none of my business, but Paige doesn't snub me for it.

"No," she says, rolling her eyes. "Could you *imagine*? But they would've. He kept pushing for it. And she sort of wanted to."

"*Yuck*," I say reflexively, thinking of hairy old Luigi.

"Right," she agrees.

I go in for the kill now that we're on the same page.

"She must be in pieces," I say. "Which is exactly why I'm asking you to start talking to Kelly. Don't you see, it's just drawing things out for Kendra? If she's holding on to a grudge like this, and you're egging her on, she won't get over this whole Luigi thing. She needs to recover, not dwell on it."

Paige shoots me an unexpectedly sharp look.

"You sound like someone on daytime TV," she says. "Next you'll be telling me she needs closure."

*Paige,* I decide in that moment, *is clever. Not academic-clever, but she's smart. I should be careful not to underestimate her. I think this whole bouncy-blonde thing is an act she puts on to get what she wants.*

"Well, *doesn't* she need closure?" I ask. "I'm not saying it won't take time. Probably loads of time. But rubbing in what Kelly did over and over again isn't going to help Kendra in the long run."

"It's sort of helping in the short run, though," Paige observes, pinning up a lock of hair that's fallen down.

Paige is turning out to be a really worthy adversary. I'd be impressed if it weren't so frustrating. She turns to look at me face-on. Suddenly I feel that we're rival generals, armies massed behind us, negotiating a peace treaty.

"Kelly doesn't have all your advantages," I say, my last card to play. "She's poor, she's not posh, and she doesn't have your confidence. I'm not defending what she did, but you can understand, a bit, how she'd feel jealous of Kendra with all the boys after her."

"Andrea never would have looked at her, whether Kendra was around or not," Paige says with devastating frankness.

"So have a bit of compassion, okay? It was really hard for Kelly, crushing on someone she couldn't have, watching him pretty much throw himself at Kendra's feet. And Kendra's so gorgeous," I say. "Think about it."

I hope I've wrestled Paige to a draw, at least. But I sense that I shouldn't push this any more.

"He hasn't been in touch with her," Paige says, changing the subject a little, signaling that the Kelly subject is no longer up for discussion. "Not at all."

I know she means Luigi and Kendra.

"Isn't that a good thing?" I ask, a little confused. "Wouldn't it be worse if he was still in touch with her?"

"Well, *nothing*'s pretty harsh," Paige says, sighing. "She got really beaten up by this. Not even a 'goodbye, I'm so sorry, I had real feelings for you,' you know? *Nothing*'s basically 'I was just using you to have a good time.' Which makes her feel extra stupid."

I nod. I feel really sorry for Kendra, but what can I say? Like Luigi, I have no words.

I need to move; I'm feeling restless. Standing up, I promptly scream as what feels like a pound of wet sand falls out of my bikini bottoms. It must have worked itself in there while we were sitting in the sea.

"Hahahaha!" Paige cracks up laughing. "It looks like you pooed yourself!"

"Yes, thanks, Paige—"

"It really does! It totally looks like you—"

"*Thanks,* I think we all get the point!"

I dash into the sea as fast as I can, more gobs of wet sand tumbling down my legs, looking and feeling almost exactly like—well, like poo. When I'm waist-deep, I pull the bottoms down and shake and scrape out a big handful of sand. Without any hesitation, I throw it directly at Paige. To my great satisfaction, it lands bang in her cleavage.

"Hey! You have poo on your boobs!" I say happily.

"Aah!"

Taking this in the spirit in which it's meant, Paige scoops it out and hurls it back at me. I jump back, giggling, as she crab walks deeper into the sea, stands up, and starts fishing handfuls of sand out of her own bottoms to throw at me. We're both laughing now, not aiming to hurt or hit the other one in the face, just letting off steam, and it feels wonderful. The stress, the tension, the perpetual worrying about who I am fade away; I realize that negotiating with Paige on Kelly's behalf has helped too.

*Remember this,* I tell myself. *Looking after other people. Visiting somewhere new. Splashing around in the sea, throwing wet sand at another girl's boobs as you both scream with laughter. These are all really good ways to distract yourself from freaking out about things you can't do anything about.*

Up above, on his tower, the lifeguard's standing up and looking down at us, hands on his hips. Laughing too.

"*Vai bionda!*" he's calling. "Go blondie!"

Paige hears it too, and understands—she's called "*bionda*" here so much it might as well be her name. Turning around, she waves at him flirtatiously, which distracts her enough that I can bend down into the waves, grab a fresh handful of wet sand, and chuck it so it splatters all over her back. She screams, the lifeguard laughs harder, and people look in our direction, Paige hamming it up hugely, loving the attention. Boys start drifting over; she's a magnet, and she adores it.

But on their loungers, Kendra and Kelly haven't moved. They're still lying down, showing no signs of coming to join us. Our once-happy group has splintered in all sorts of ways. But at least Paige and I are enjoying ourselves while Kendra and Kelly slump depressively in their own separate misery bubbles.

*Please don't let this last,* I pray. *Please let everyone cheer up. I don't have the energy to make Kelly feel better–it's all I can do to put a smile on my own face.*

"*Ciao, ragazzi!*" Paige is saying to a couple of smooth-skinned, darkly tanned boys who've got up the courage to approach her.

"*Ciao, bella!*" one says back eagerly.

*Oh,* I think wistfully, *if we could all be as light and easygoing as Paige, the world would be a much happier place!* Paige wouldn't have thought twice about it if she'd spotted a portrait that looked just like her in a museum! She'd have said "Cool," taken a photo, made it her Facebook profile for a few weeks, and then forgotten about it completely. She's not only the queen of this beach, she's the queen of living in the moment, not worrying about things she can't control.

*That's what you should be doing, Violet,* I tell myself. *Live in the moment, okay? Stop looking over at your phone on the lounger, wondering if Mum's about to ring or text. You're in Venice on the beach in the summer sunshine! Enjoy it!*

Paige and her new friends are throwing around a big stripy ball, the boys' lean bodies jumping and twisting in the air like slim brown dolphins, Paige's boobs jiggling in a way the boys doubtless intended when they produced the ball. The lifeguard's attention is so focused on the contents of her bikini top that a whole family could be eaten by sharks, screaming for help, without his having the faintest idea.

*Live in the moment.*

"Hey," I yell. "Chuck it to me!"

And I run up the wet sand toward them.

# Not Exactly Birds Eye Fish Fingers

Catia specified two things we absolutely had to bring to Venice—a swimsuit and sensible shoes, because we'd be doing a lot of walking. But you don't realize how much that's truly going to entail in a city where, most of the time, walking is literally your only option. The water-buses actually only go down the Grand Canal; all the other canals are too narrow, have bridges too low, for them to pass. The taxis are expensive, and not practical for nipping around town. You can't bicycle—there are way too many bridges. You absolutely, positively have to walk, and often you have to walk extra far because of the difficulties of getting over the canals at the right place. The buses zigzag back and forth, so you can use those, and they also have these cool crossings with gondolas called *traghetti;* if you need to cross the Grand Canal between bridges, there are little piers at which you wait until a group of you has built up. Then a scruffy gondolier—not in the full stripy T-shirt, black trousers, and straw hat—will hand you into the gondola, in which you stand up, balancing, as he poles you over to the other side. The trip itself barely takes a minute, but we love it; we'd do it again and again if it didn't cost a euro per person each time.

We also like it, to be honest, because it involves standing still. Yesterday by the beach was blissful relaxation; today has been nonstop rushing. Catia's hired a local guide to whisk us around, and, I suspect, instructed him to tire us out so thoroughly that we wouldn't have much energy for sneaking off with lifeguards, boys from the Lido, or art teachers. Certainly, though the guide's a man, Catia has picked one who won't be any temptation to a group of single teenage girls. He's a skinny, hollow-chested academic type who wears a sweater and tweed jacket even in this hot weather.

It's just really unfortunate that he's also called Luigi. Every time Catia says his name, Kendra flinches.

"You'd think she could've found someone with a different name," Kelly mutters to me as Luigi Two bundles us briskly over the wooden bridge in front of the Accademia museum.

I nod emphatically. "This is *not* helping," I agree.

The trouble is that as long as Kendra's in a miserable, depressive slump, Paige will keep punishing Kelly by freezing her out. I don't actually think Kendra's consciously sending Kelly to Coventry anymore; I think she's so down now that she barely has a word to say to anyone. Kendra's initial anger has all ebbed away, leaving almost nothing. She's completely withdrawn, and so is Kelly: Kendra in grief, Kelly in guilt. Paige and I are effectively dragging around two millstones, and it's totally knackering.

We do the Accademia and Ca' Rezzonico, two stunning museums close to each other on the same side of the Grand Canal, so rich and lavish and breathtaking that we're already done for the day after seeing their glories. But it's only lunchtime, and Luigi Two makes us walk for ages down a series of narrow, crowded, hot streets, buildings rising high on either side so you'd have to tilt your head right back to see the sky, past an endless series of restaurants and pizza places where we'd be more than happy to get some food; but no, Luigi Two has a destination in mind, which turns out to be the fish market.

It's open-air, stone colonnades and pillars holding up a high vaulted ceiling, on a bend in the canal; beyond it, boats ply up and down, people surge on and off buses at a stop, the sun beats down, making the wide ribbon of canal water glisten dazzlingly. What's particularly amazing is that the market is surrounded by wine bars, their wooden frontages looking hundreds of years old, their big windows wide open as people gather inside and out, gossiping and drinking as the stallholders pack up the last bits of fish, seagulls clustering as thickly as the wine-bar patrons, cawing for scraps of fish gut.

Maybe the most amazing thing is how nice the fish smells. Not pongy at all: it's like seawater, salty and clean and fresh.

"It's not exactly Birds Eye fish fingers, is it?" Kelly says, jolted out of her silence by the sight of a whole crate of squid, white and violet with purple tentacles, arranged in overlapping rows.

"This is gross! But kind of interesting," Paige comments, which is actually quite positive for Paige looking at a lot of raw fish.

As we walk by one stall, a guy behind it slices off a piece of bright-orange salmon, squeezes a lemon over it, and eats it just like that. Kelly gasps.

"Sushi!" Paige says, giving him a thumbs-up. "Ooh! Can we have sushi for lunch? I *looove*–"

"Sushi is not typical Italian," Catia says, shaking her head. "Luigi is taking us to a typical Venetian lunch."

It's lucky we're tired and hungry, as typical Venetian food is pretty challenging. Shrimp fried in batter for a starter sounds nice, until you hear that it's been chilled and served in a vinegar and sugar sauce with raisins and onions. I quite like it, but it takes some getting used to. And when the pasta course comes out—a huge, heaping plate of spaghetti with mussels—Kelly goes pale.

"This is the specialty of the trattoria," Luigi Two announces. "*Spaghetti con cozze e parmigiano.* There is parmesan cheese also on the pasta. It is very unusual and interesting."

*"Unusual and interesting" might be okay in a modern art museum,* I think, *but not for food! We're teenage girls–doesn't he realize we'd much rather have pizza?*

Thank goodness, because I have a Scandinavian mum, I'm used to all kinds of seafood.

*Okay, your mum's from Norway,* comes the thought, *but what about your dad? Where's he from?*

I push the question away instantly and dig my fork into the plateful of pasta so energetically that its tines scratch on the china.

"It's actually really good," I reassure Kelly after a bite. "Just have the pasta if you can't deal with the mussels."

"I can't!" she says miserably. "I don't even like fish fingers."

Swiftly, I scoop all the mussels off her plate and onto mine.

"Just eat the spaghetti, as much as you can—"

"I *can't*!" she says, the tears now visible. "I feel sick!"

"Oh—" I bite back a curse. "Okay, just eat the *bread*," I hiss at Kelly. "I'll have your pasta too. And stop crying!"

The tears are falling down her cheeks now. I pick her napkin off her lap and shove it at her to dry them. Catia's still absorbed in discussion with Luigi Two; they don't notice as I twiddle Kelly's pasta onto my fork in a series of swift, gigantic twirls, and dump it onto my plate with her mussels. I'm going to be absolutely stuffed. Even Paige is managing to clear her plate, her head ducked. Thank goodness, dessert is lemon sorbet—not even Kelly can complain about that. But by the time we emerge from the restaurant, I feel sick from overeating, Kelly's in a haze of unhappiness, Kendra's even further slumped over in silence, and Paige is eyeing every pizza shop even more longingly.

"You're still hungry?" I mutter to her. "You ate everything!"

"Are you kidding?" she hisses back. "I dumped it all in my napkin!"

"Oh, I wish I'd thought of that! I had to have Kelly's as well as my own!"

"This had better not keep up," she says grimly. "I'm going to need some pizza *soon*."

We're passing distractingly pretty shops and market stalls selling more masks and glass and fans; in Florence the specialty is leather, in Siena it's paper, but here it's clearly carnival masks and Venetian glass. In front of us rise a series of wide steps over the canal, leading to a bridge lined with little shops: the Rialto.

Luigi Two leads us up to the top, gathers our group around him, and launches into a long description of the history of the Rialto Bridge, raising his voice to be heard over the competing Japanese and French tour groups, the backpackers lounging all around the heavily graffitied backs of the jewelry and glass shops, and the Venetians themselves, walking as fast as the tourists are moving slowly.

"Designed by Antonio da Ponte, which is amusing, as 'is surname means 'bridge,' in 1591—'e won a competition for 'is design, beating even the famous Michelangelo. . . ."

Gondolas, motorboats, water-buses, and taxis pass along the canal and disappear under the bridge; a wide-bottomed barge carrying a cement mixer and a digger wallows slowly toward us, and I realize that this is the only way anything can be transported through Venice at all. We saw an ambulance boat earlier today, speeding down a canal with a light flashing above it; somehow it seems so much nicer going to hospital in a boat, though I suppose the Venetians are so used to boats they don't seem exciting.

"Many Venetians said it would never last, and that they needed a bridge with many arches," Luigi Two is saying. "But the foundations 'eld the weight, and as you can see, it 'as been 'ere for nearly five 'undred years! And now, we go to Piazza San Marco."

Catia always let us have a siesta back in Tuscany. Right now, it's the hottest time of the day, Venice is unbelievably crowded, and we're all either queasy from overeating or hungry. I glance at her and see her mouth set in a firm line. No siesta for us; it's Piazza San Marco in the blazing afternoon sun. Yesterday, sunshine and swimming exhausted us thoroughly: we got back to the palazzo, wolfed down dinner, slapped on aftersun, and fell into bed. Today being dragged around Venice will do the same. Catia's marching us all over town until we're too knackered to even contemplate sneaking out to meet boys.

And after what happened in Tuscany, I honestly can't say I blame her.

# We Have an Emergency on Our Hands

Darling, hang on. I think of you all the time. I'm moving heaven and earth to get to you. It's more complicated than you know, but I'm on my way and I will be there, I promise, and I'll explain everything and all will be okay, I hope and I pray. Love you so very much! Hold on! I'll be there really, really soon! Love you up to the sky and back again! Mum x x x x

As I've observed before, Mum's never quite got the hang of texting. She tends to write letters instead. I scroll down the screen, taking in the whole epistle. It's the same as before, really. She's coming, but there are complications. No mention of Dad—and that's what's surprising me. Because I'd been thinking that what's been taking so long is that Mum wanted to see Dad first, maybe, to talk over what I wrote to her, and Dad is thousands and thousands of miles away in Hong Kong. Maybe she flew there, or he flew to London, and it was hard for him to take time off work.

But then why not tell me that? What I wrote to her about obviously includes Dad too. And he must know about it. I absolutely, one hundred percent refuse to believe that Mum had an affair and didn't tell Dad. Before she descended into miserable-zombie status, Kelly dared to hint at this possibility, and it was all I could do not to bite her head off.

"You don't know my mum," I snapped. "You just don't. She's never lied to me, ever. She's like a pane of glass; you can see right through her all the time—everything's written on her face. She would never have done that to Dad. She loved him so much. And she could never have kept a secret like that from him, never in a million years. Not for two seconds," I added, getting my time metaphors all mixed up in my fervor to explain what Mum's like. "Honestly, it's literally impossible."

I don't know if Kelly believed me; without knowing Mum, you might not. But I'm sure of it. If there's any secret about my parentage, Dad knows it too. She isn't breaking any awful news to him. They were in this together.

*So why not write "I have to see your dad first and so I'm flying over to Hong Kong"?*

There's something else here. Another part of the puzzle. And, rack my brains as much as I can, I can't picture what it is. I can't even get a rough sense of its shape.

To compound things, I no longer have a confidante. Kelly's checked out of everything. Or out of everything here. As soon as we eventually limped back to the Palazzo Giustinian, exhausted, boiling, completely overloaded with culture, and having learned that Converses, though cool, aren't actually that comfortable for spending the day tramping over stone, Kelly retreated into her previous life. She's plugged into her phone, on her bed, in knickers and T-shirt, crying and texting, texting and crying, obviously letting people back home in England know what a totally miserable time she's having.

*I mean–in Venice! Which is a free extra to an already amazing trip to Italy!*

I'm so over her. I've tried everything I can, right from the very first day, to help her feel more happy and secure and confident. It's her own fault she's in this mess, her own fault that she let jealousy overwhelm her and went tattling to Catia—her own fault that she can't just bolt down some spaghetti, or be like Paige and cunningly hide it in her napkin.

Unlike our quarters at Villa Barbiano, the palazzo has no communal rooms we can sit in. No rec room with TV, no sitting room with sofas. The only way to get away from my grumpy, sobbing roommate is to go out onto the balcony and sit down, the stone warm under my bum, my legs dangling through the iron balcony struts, hanging over the canal below, my feet feeling swollen and hot from the day's walking. I wrap my arms around the iron, equally warm from the hot sunny day, and rest my forehead against an elaborate piece of metal, looking down at the boats passing below.

"Hey," says Paige, and I look right to see her sitting on the adjacent balcony. Being very keen on comfort, she's brought out some cushions from the chair in their room and strewn them over the stone, and is lying on them in her bikini, doing what she calls catching some rays.

"Hey," I say back.

"How's yours?" she asks.

"Crying. How's yours?"

"Oh boy." She pulls a face. "She got this email from him. Saying he loves her and that she's the only one."

I scowl. "The only one? After his wife and that girl from two years ago?"

"I know, right? The only one right now. Or when he was writing the email. *Pig.*" Paige is scowling too. "So she's all psyched up again. I swear, it's pathetic."

"His wife's *pregnant*," I say hopelessly, because it seems to me such a huge deal—another baby coming!—that it should stop dead any debate Kendra's having with herself about whether she should believe Luigi.

"I *know*! But she's reading the email over and over again and playing Adele and Amy Winehouse," Paige reveals.

"Adele *and* Amy Winehouse? Oh *no.* We'd better keep an eye on her," I say grimly.

"What *happened* to us?" Paige laments. "We were having such a good time!"

She averts her gaze from me—usually an indication that someone's about to make a personal comment and doesn't know how it's going to be received.

"I don't know what went on with you and Luca," she observes, "but you seem okay about it. . . ."

I can't help huffing a dry, unamused laugh. *If she only knew.*

"It's complicated," I say.

"Well, but you're getting on with things," Paige says. "You're not letting it define you," she adds, in the American therapy-speak that occasionally pops out of both her and Kendra.

"I *can't*," I say. It comes out more passionately than I meant it to, and I bite my tongue.

"Sometimes you just have to shove stuff away until you can deal," Paige observes. "I get that. You pull it out when you're ready."

I nod, temporarily unable to speak.

"I just want us all to have a great time in Venice!" she says, moving on from the Luca subject with a swiftness for which I'm grateful.

"Me too," I say, in heartfelt tones. "I think that if we throw ourselves into being here, we won't, you know, dwell on the bad stuff."

"I know! I mean, *look* down there!" Paige sits up and points through the balcony at the canal below. A little boat is chugging by, entirely filled with flowers. "Geraniums! It's a flower boat!"

I can't help giggling at the enthusiasm with which she yodels "Geraniums!" Craning my neck, I look down through the bars; the boat is a riot of pink and red and white blossoms.

"Oh wow," I say, and run for my phone to take a photo. Luckily, the boat stops in midcanal so that its driver can have a chat with what I think is a postal boat coming in the other direction, and I manage to get some good snaps.

"Look, Kelly," I say, going back into the bedroom; she can't hear me, but I hold the phone in front of her face. "A flower boat! Cool, eh?"

She takes out her headphones, raises her swollen eyes to me, and says:

"I'm not coming down to dinner."

"Oh, *Kelly,*" I sigh. "Don't *do* this."

"Paige and Kendra aren't talking to me, you're sounding all cross, and I think I'll throw up if Catia makes me eat fish stew," Kelly says, her lower lip wobbling. It doesn't help when Catia announces in advance what we're having for dinner: it just makes the dread of anticipation worse for Kelly. "I *can't*. I just need to be by myself."

I don't have any energy left to pump into the uphill task of convincing her.

"Okay," I say resignedly. "I'll try to smuggle back some bread."

"Ta," she mutters, and puts her headphones back on.

I mean, *whatever*.

Kendra's in a weird mood over dinner. Elated, but almost speechless. As if someone hit her over the head but she liked it. She toys with her food, and Catia makes some snippy comments about hoping she's not becoming anorexic, which, considering that her own daughter seems to live entirely on espresso and cigarettes, is a bit rich. Kendra excuses herself as soon as dinner's over, saying that she's tired and wants to go to bed early, and Catia reveals to me and Paige the existence of a room with a billiard table, in which she suggests we amuse ourselves after dinner.

To my surprise, this cheers Paige up immensely. I

wouldn't have thought she'd know how to play snooker. But then, thinking about it, I realize that people are always doing it in American films and TV series.

"In Britain, it's kind of an old-guy thing to do," I explain as she gleefully chalks up a cue stick.

"You're kidding! We have them in all the bars where I live." She pantomimes a big theatrical wink. "Not that I've been in any, of course. Here, I'll teach you to play pool. Though 'snooker' is a really cool word. Snooker!" she says, and it sounds hilarious in her accent.

Who'd have thought it—me and Paige. If not BFFs, we're certainly BTFs. Best Temporary Friends. I certainly didn't see that coming. But we're united, at least, in refusing to withdraw into the kind of slump that both Kendra and Kelly are indulging in. It may be unfair of me, but I think it's selfish of them. We're all in this together, away from home, and though the group could cope with one of the four throwing a wobbly, two is unquestionably a downer.

Thank goodness, Paige teaching me pool is a lot of fun, especially as she keeps showing me how guys put their arms around girls from behind to do what I call copping a feel and she calls doing a booty rub. We laugh, a lot. We laugh so much that Paige's mobile rings four times before we hear it, and she only just answers it before it goes to voice mail.

"Hey, Ev! No, I wasn't ignoring you—Violet and I were playing pool. She calls it snooker! Isn't that such a great word? I— You're *what?*"

Evan's actually managed to make her shut up for a moment. Go, Evan! I practice hitting the cue ball, though I'm a bit nervous because of seeing an old Peter Sellers comedy film years ago where he rips a big hole through the green baize. The mere idea of tearing up the principessa's family's billiard table is terrifying, and probably why I'm not managing to hit the ball hard enough. I click my tongue in frustration, try again, and only just manage to send the white ball into the red one I'm aiming at with the limpest of clicks.

"Yay!" Paige is caroling in my ear, and I jump.

"Evan's here!" she sings. I keep saying that Paige sings, carols, yodels, and she really does. She can't actually carry a tune, but the enthusiasm with which she communicates makes her voice go up and down so much that it's weirdly melodic.

"Here at the palazzo?" I ask, dropping the cue on the table and turning to look at her.

"Here in Venice! Cool, huh? He met his friends and they all decided to come see us! I mean, who doesn't want to come to Venice?"

"Kelly and Kendra," I say sarcastically.

"Ha!" She rolls her big brown eyes. "Okay, apart from those losers! *Sooo* they just got off the train and want to meet up."

"I don't think Catia'll be okay with letting them stay here," I say cautiously. "I mean, it's not her house. And Evan's got people with him."

"No, they booked a hostel online, and they dumped their stuff there already. They just want to go hang in—you know, the main square, where we were today."

"Piazza San Marco?"

"Yeah! The one with the pigeons! It's only nine. Ooh, I hope Catia lets us go out and see him!"

"It's nine-thirty," I say, following her as she eagerly scampers off to find Catia.

"So what? Everyone in Italy stays up past midnight!" she says unanswerably.

It's true; in the summer, Italians tend to crash, aka have a siesta, in the hottest hours of the day and then stay out late in the cool evenings. I've noticed that in all the cities we've visited—Florence, Siena, Venice—tourists hugely outnumber the locals by day, but rarely by night.

Catia, found in one of the smaller sitting rooms reading a very intellectual-looking book, is surprisingly okay with the idea of us going out with Evan.

"He must come here, though, to collect you," she specifies firmly. "And he must bring you back no later than eleven-thirty. Are you taking the other girls with you?"

It hadn't even crossed our minds.

"I don't think they'll want to come," I say frankly.

Catia huffs a small laugh.

"If they do," she says, "you must keep a very strict eye on Kendra."

She's wearing glasses, and she lowers them to look at me and Paige in turn. It makes what she's saying extra-serious.

"I know you both understand *exactly* what I mean," she says. "I cannot keep her under lock and key, but you are friends of hers, and the last thing you will want is for her to do anything catastrophic with her life. Evan will understand too. He's a sensible young man. I would not let her go out in the evening without Evan being there, and knowing *precisely* what her situation is."

We nod so hard our heads nearly come off.

"*Thank* you!" we breathe, overwhelmed with anticipation at being out in the warm Venetian night.

"And don't order *anything* from the bars on Piazza San Marco," she advises. "I don't want to get a phone call from you saying you're being brought back by the *carabinieri* because you can't pay your bill. They charge eight euros at Florian's for a coffee and another eight for the orchestra fee. Per person."

"*Oww,*" Paige says with feeling.

"If Kelly wants to come out with us," I say firmly as we dash upstairs to get ready, "you have to talk to her. Deal?"

"Oh, okay," she sighs. "Deal. I was kinda over the not-talking thing anyway. And Kendra won't care—ever since she got that email, she hasn't noticed whether anyone else is dead or alive, let alone who's talking to who."

Evan and his friends are getting a water-bus to the closest stop to the palazzo, so we probably have fifteen minutes to doll ourselves up. And yes, there's a curfew of eleven-thirty, but Catia's always been lax on curfews before. I bet if we're back around midnight, she won't make any sort of fuss.

"Kelly!" I say, bursting into our bedroom before I realize the lights are all off. *Honestly, she's gone to bed by nine-thirty? This is ridiculous.* I turn on the overhead light and say:

"Evan's in Venice, with his mates! And Catia says we can go to Piazza San Marco with them! Come on, get up! You don't want to miss this!"

She's turned away from me and doesn't stir. There's a pillow pulled over her head to shut out noise. I heave a deep sigh and contemplate just letting her lie there sulking. Then my conscience pricks me, reminding me that I forgot to bring her up the bread I promised from dinner, and I stride over to the bed to sit down and coax her up and out. I'm thinking the fact that she'll be able to get pizza by the slice, or pastries and ice cream from the infinite number of bars in Venice, will be all she needs to convince her to join us. Kelly really likes her food; she didn't eat much at lunch, and she skipped dinner. She must be starving.

"Kell, don't be silly," I say, and reach out to touch her shoulder.

And then I scream. Because my hand goes right through the sheet and into something horribly floppy, as if a serial killer's somehow got into the Palazzo Giustinian while we were having dinner, slaughtered Kelly, taken out all her bones in the bathtub, and then put her deboned body back into her bed again.

I really have to stop reading those awful crime novels where girls get killed in all sorts of horrible ways.

Jumping up again, I drag back the sheet. Kelly has very cleverly managed to squish her bed pillows, plus the chair cushions, into the shape of a body. And under the pillow I thought was covering her head is a small decorative globe that was on the chest of drawers, giving just the right shape to mold the pillow into looking as if there's a human skull beneath it.

*Very clever, Kelly.*

If I'd come to bed later, I wouldn't have turned on the main light. I would have sneaked in quietly, switched on my small bedside lamp, got undressed in its soft glow, and gone to bed. I would have whispered a goodnight, but it wouldn't have occurred to me to be suspicious because she didn't reply.

I spin around the room looking for clues as to where she's gone, something, *anything*. I can't believe she left without saying a word to me. She won't have texted or emailed because I might have checked my phone or laptop tonight; she'll have wanted time to get away. I swing all the way around again, having completed three hundred and sixty degrees, till I'm looking at the bed again.

Kelly's very clever.

An idea strikes me. I rip at the pillows, pulling them off the bed one after another. Sure enough, under the last pillow of all, the one farthest down, is a folded piece of paper with my name on it.

> Violet, I'm so sorry but I just couldn't bear it any longer. I'm really homesick and Kelly and Paige are being so mean to me. And it's my own fault so I feel even worse. And then YOU got cross with me, and I felt so alone!!! I'm going to try to get a cheap flight home. Hopefully see you in London. I'm so sorry. K x x x x

*The silly cow! The silly, silly cow!*

Absolutely livid with her, I crumple up the paper, throw it at the wall, and dash next door to tell Paige and Kendra that we have an emergency on our hands.

# Girls Can Pull and Tear and Rip at Each Other

It feels like only a minute later that the door knocker sounds: Evan and his friends are here. Paige dashes downstairs to stop them coming in. We need to shoot out as quickly as we can, not waste time as Evan makes polite conversation with Catia while we're desperate to get out and start searching for Kelly. Kendra follows: I take an extra, crucial few moments on the laptop before slamming it shut and tumbling down the stairs myself. Catia will just think our hurry is because we're keen to explore Venice by night.

Besides, her attention's entirely focused on the possibility of Kendra running away; she isn't remotely worried about Kelly. Hearing that Kelly's sleeping off her headache, Catia nods briefly, tells us to stick together—with significant glances at me, Paige, and Evan—and shepherds us out into the soft, warm Venetian evening.

The atmosphere is completely different after sunset. This is the *passeggiata,* where locals come out after dinner to stroll through the streets, stop at coffee bars, chat, meet up, flirt, fall in love; you hear all these songs about love being in the air, but this is the first time I've actually felt it. From the moment we step outside the palazzo—and yes, there is a door to the little street behind it, though a much smaller one than the grand entrance onto the canal—I feel the romance wrapping around us all. The narrow streets, the pretty bridges, the water lapping gently at the stone borders of the canals—in Venice by night, you should be walking hand in hand with someone you love, not sprinting along in a sweaty group to try to rescue a friend from making a really big mistake.

We're racing to Piazza San Marco: my frenzied researches on the laptop have told me this is the main stop for the airport water-buses. Kelly has a head start of almost two hours, and she might well have managed to get on a water-bus by now, but we have to go there anyway. Someone at the ticket office might remember a lone redheaded English girl buying a one-way ticket for the airport, a girl who looked as if she'd spent the entire day crying.

Of course, I've tried to ring her, but her phone's turned off; it goes straight to voice mail. I've left messages, texted her, begging her to ring. But so far, no reply.

"The cool thing," Evan says to me, striding along, not remotely out of breath, "is that there are signs everywhere to Piazza San Marco—look."

He points to a corner, where a little plaque with directional arrows tells us which way to go for Piazza San Marco and which for the Rialto.

"As long as you keep to the main drag," he says, "you can navigate really well. We worked that out already coming from the station."

"Phew!" I pant, half jogging to keep up with him. "We went everywhere today but we had a guide—I thought we'd get lost a hundred times trying to get to the piazza."

"If we're lucky, *she'll* have got turned around a few times," he says. "Maybe she isn't that far ahead of us."

"I hope so!" I say, grateful to Evan for being so positive.

"Why did she run off like this?" he asks. "She seemed like she was having a good time! Did you girls have a fight?"

Evan's not an idiot. He hasn't grown up with Paige without knowing how girls can pull and tear and rip at each other till they can make their victim feel like they're going insane.

And suddenly, there's nothing more important to me than Evan knowing I'm not like that. I'm not one of those girls.

"She didn't fight with me!" I say as fast as my pattering feet. "I even ate all her mussel pasta at lunch so she wouldn't have to!"

Evan laughs. "That was nice of you."

He grabs my arm. "Here, this way. Look . . ."

He's pointing at another plaque, indicating that San Marco is to our right. We turn and start down the street—well, they're really lanes, they're all so narrow—which is lined with illuminated shopwindows filled with glittering glass. Multicolored chandeliers; clear bowls ribboned with orange and green, filled with fruit, apples, oranges, lemons, all made of beautifully blown glass; more tiny orchestras; miniature animals. Luigi Two explained today a bit about glassblowing, one of Venice's main art forms (the other one is lace-making). It's breathtaking to think that each of these pieces was made by a man blowing air into hot glass down a tube. I can't get my head around it.

"The glass is crazy, isn't it?" Evan says, reading my mind. "I really want to take something back to the States."

"What are you going to get?"

"I thought a little guitarist," he says a bit bashfully. "You know, one of the musicians."

"Oh, cool!"

He's still holding my arm, and it's nice. Not pulling or pushing, not like one of those bossy boyfriends who likes to move their girlfriends around with a hand in the small of their back. Just a light clasp guiding me along because he's taller and can see the plaques better.

We pass under an arch and emerge into a loggia, a covered walkway with columns: we're in Piazza San Marco. It opens out in front of us, sparkling gold and bright with lights from the bars flooding out into the square. The orchestra of the Caffè Florian, the marble-tiled, gold-walled bar that Luigi Two told us today has been here for almost three hundred years, is playing under the loggia farther down. If I thought Venice was romantic before, this is enough to make me want to cry. There are some couples waltzing slowly in the piazza, wrapped in each other's arms, and as we dash past I can't help staring at them longingly.

Pigeons fly up as we shoot across the piazza; today we saw

kids feeding them from bags of corn, putting the kernels in their palms, even on their heads, so the birds could perch and nibble. It explains why the pigeons don't move till you practically land on them; they're tame enough to be fed by hand. But a stampede of large Americans—plus one smaller English girl—tearing across the square sends them all up in a cloud, flying toward the domes of St. Mark's Basilica on the far side. It's lit up by night, glowing pale gold, and we all catch our breath at its beauty.

Now it's me who knows where we're going, having lugged around here today. I steer us past the big brick bell tower, which, thank heavens, Luigi Two didn't make us climb. The Grand Canal's in front of us, the basin that opens up to Giudecca Island and the Lido beyond. A big boat chugs across the lagoon, a brightly lit beacon moving across the dark water: the Lido car ferry, which we saw going back and forth from the beach yesterday.

"Wow," says Stu, one of Evan's friends. "This is *unbelievable*."

"I *know*," says his girlfriend, Andi. "It's *magic*."

Those few precious minutes I spent scrabbling on the laptop told me that the airport bus line is called Alilaguna. And the main stop is along to the right, on those new, posh-looking piers I spot as we race along the waterfront, past the stalls and the outdoor bars and the people turning to stare at us, because who runs like this in Venice, when you should be strolling arm in arm, eating ice cream and falling in love. . . .

"There!" I'm almost out of breath, but I point to the sign I recognize from the Internet, the Alilaguna logo, two wibbly-wobbly blue lines like drunken seagulls on a white background. We run onto the wooden pier and look around frantically for (a) Kelly and (b) the ticket office.

"Kendra, you ask the ticket office about her," Paige instructs. "You speak Italian best. Stu and Andi, you go with her. The rest of us'll search around here for Kelly, in case she's waiting for a boat."

Evan agrees. "All split up and meet back at the ticket office in ten minutes. That way we'll stop her if she's just about to board."

I nod, catching my breath, and head off to the far side; it's really confusing to work out which of the stops are for people arriving or people departing. There are three colored lines here, blue, orange, and green, and I didn't have time to check which one Kelly would want. But because the stop is new and modern, every wall is a single sheet of glass, which means it's pretty easy to see who's waiting in the separate areas. I dash around, weaving my way through various groups of people gathered around their suitcases. I want to make sure I've covered every single place she could be. I know Kelly didn't take her suitcase, that poor, beaten-up cheap thing she got from the market in London; it was still under her bed. She walked out with just her handbag, which means she really was in a bad state, because she wouldn't want to leave her clothes behind.

My heart's sinking. I don't see her anywhere. I even nip out onto the stone waterfront again, to see if she went to get something from a bar while waiting, but I doubt she'd have gone far—she wouldn't have wanted to miss her boat. After a few minutes searching, I give up, trudging disconsolately back to the ticket office again.

Paige and Evan are returning from unsuccessful searches too. And Kendra, turning away from the window of the ticket office, says:

"She was here maybe a couple of hours ago, buying a ticket. One of the women remembers her, because her eyes were all red—like her hair, she said."

"A couple of hours!" I feel my heart drop even further. Now it's roughly on a level with my stomach. "She'll have had plenty of time to get on a boat then, right?"

Kendra nods.

"I think the blues go every half hour," she says, "and the oranges every hour—though I might not have got that bit right. They talk really fast. But anyway, there's no way she isn't on her way to the airport. She could easily be there by now."

"Oh *no*," I sigh, though it was only to be expected. Kelly might have been in an awful emotional state, but she's practical, efficient, and smart; she found her way here, she bought a ticket, she would definitely have boarded a boat.

"Are there flights out tonight?" asks Andi. "She's going to London, right? Stu, check to see if there are flights from Venice to London."

Stu thumbs at his phone, and announces:

"There's a British Airways that leaves at eleven-twenty-five. Hate to say it, but if she doesn't have luggage to check in, she could make it."

"Kelly doesn't have enough money for British Airways," I say quickly. "How much is it?"

"Uh—three hundred euros, give or take," he says.

"Oh, no way could she afford that!" I say.

Paige says with brutal frankness, "That's a point, Violet—how could she buy a plane ticket at all?"

"She's got a prepaid card for emergencies," I say, "but I don't know how much is on it. Not *that* much, I'm sure."

"The question is," Evan says, "should someone get on a boat for the airport? By the time we got there she could be checked into a flight."

"A water taxi would be a lot faster," Paige says. "But that'd cost a fortune."

There's no question among any of us that we want to get Kelly back if we possibly can. For which I am hugely grateful.

I haven't had to muster any arguments about not letting her quit, because her school and community did a ton of fund-raising to pay for this opportunity so that it would give her a more level playing field in her competition with much more privileged students for a place at Cambridge, where she wants to go to university and make her community proud.

I haven't had to say that I'm scared that if she leaves, all her dreams will be lost forever. That precisely because she doesn't have the advantages of money and class that we other three girls possess, this failure to stick it out will haunt her for the rest of her life. She probably won't even apply to Cambridge, and if she does, she won't have the confidence to impress her interviewers enough for them to accept her. She won't have the career of an art historian, which has been a dream that's blossomed during this visit to Italy. And if she loses her dreams, she'll be lost herself.

I don't know how much of this anyone else but me understands. But we're all teenagers—or just-stopped-being-teenagers, in Evan, Stu, and Andi's cases—bonding together to protect one of our own. Stopping her running away after a silly fight. Making sure, at the very least, that she has time to think about what she's doing, not just throwing this opportunity away in a hysterical impulse.

"Can you pay for a water taxi with a credit card?" Kendra asks.

"You must be able to," I say. "It's got to cost at least a hundred euros—maybe even double that. Not everyone has that much cash on them. But I don't have a credit card."

"*I* do," Kendra says, fishing in her bag. "Come on. Let's go find a taxi rank."

I'm so shocked that all I can do is shake my head back and forth slowly.

*"Kendra,"* I breathe. "I don't *believe* it."

"What?" she says, not meeting my eyes. "My mom gave me a card for emergencies too. This is one."

"But she snitched on you!" Paige, very annoyingly, exclaims.

"I don't like to think where I'd be right now if she hadn't," Kendra says soberly. "She kind of did me a favor, in a backhanded way."

*"Really?"* Paige gasps. The wind is rising on the lagoon, and a gust blows through our hair, the wind scented with kelp, fresh and salty.

"I just checked Luigi out on Facebook," Kendra tells her sadly. "I looked at photos of him with his wife and little girl. She's really cute. And you can tell his wife's pregnant.

There's a photo of them all together at a friend's wedding, just last week. Hugging and kissing. When he was telling me he loved me and I was the only one." She swallows hard, tears coming to her eyes. "I would have—I *know* I would have—" She catches herself. "*Anyway*, let's go get Kelly! She did the right thing for the wrong reason: I'll do the right thing for the right reason. Where's the damn rank?"

I can't help grinning at Kendra's pompous words, her need to be superior to Kelly, even in a crisis: but I wouldn't dream of pointing that out to her.

"There's a taxi pulling in," Andi says quickly, turning away from Kendra, giving her time to stifle her tears. Andi's pointing to a sleek pale wooden boat visible through the glass walls. It's turning, backing up to a pier just before a low stone bridge. "Can we grab that? Do you just, like, hail them like a cab?"

"Worth a try!" I say. "Come on!"

Grabbing Kendra's hand, I dash out of the water-bus stop and along the waterfront. The taxi is gliding smoothly in reverse, docking at the pier.

"Let's just hope it isn't picking people up," I say. "But there's no one waiting, is there?"

"No, it's dropping off—there're people in the cabin," Kendra says as dark shapes emerge onto the steps of the boat, one of them pulling money out of his pocket for the driver.

"Great! Kendra, thank you *so* much—"

We're on the taxi pier now, and I pull up, waiting for the previous passengers to disembark, but my heart's racing, frantic to jump on board and get going.

They're stepping onto the pier now, a man helping a

woman off, putting his arm around her as they walk toward us. The light's behind them, so I can't see anything but their shapes; I have a brief rush of envy, another happy couple in Venice, just come off a romantic water taxi ride. . . .

And then I shriek, loudly. Kendra echoes me a second later.

Because the people walking toward us, the girl leaning heavily on the boy's arm, are the last two people in the world I expected to see.

It's Kelly. And even more shockingly, Luca.

# Wings of the Lagoon

It's awful to admit, but the first emotion I feel on seeing the two of them is rabid, uncontrolled jealousy. Luca, so close to Kelly, his arm around her, taking some of her weight; Kelly, leaning on him like the heroine of a nineteenth-century novel too fragile to walk on her own, looking up at him worshippingly as he speaks softly to her. So absorbed in each other that they haven't even noticed us yet.

*It should be me beside him!* I think with raging envy. *If he's going to put an arm around a girl, ride with her in a water taxi, walk through Venice with her, it should be me!*

They're practically on top of us now. Luca looks up, sees us, and stops dead. For a brief moment he stares at me, and, taken completely by surprise, without a chance to compose his usual cynical, careless expression, I can see his true emotions. He's looking at me with so much longing in his blue eyes that if this were the end of a romantic film I would be tearing across the few feet of pier that separate us, throwing myself into his arms, knowing that they would lock tightly around me and his mouth would come down on mine.

I know then that my attraction to Evan, nice, down-to-earth Evan, is nothing compared to what I feel for Luca. Evan's come up behind us, towering over me, solid and secure. I must be the biggest idiot in the world to prefer Luca, sarcastic, shrugging, dismissive, moody Luca, to sweet, even-tempered Evan. But I can't help it. I learn in that moment that you can be attracted to more than one boy at a time, but it doesn't necessarily mean anything. Not if, when you look into the eyes of the boy who means the world to you, you know with absolute certainty that he's the one.

Luca is the one. And from the way he's gazing at me, I know with equal certainty that he feels the same. That I'm the one for him, as much as he is for me.

But life isn't a romantic film, as I've learned this summer with horrible force. Kendra, standing beside me, has had to absorb the same lesson. Both of our Italian romances have crashed us hard into brick walls; we're bruised, shaken, battered, having found out the hard way that we're characters in something a lot more gritty and realistic than a simple love story.

I can't run to Luca, throw myself into his arms. And still, the jealousy that's surging up in me makes me want to grab hold of Kelly and physically pull her away from Luca. Falling for someone turns out to be not romantic at all. It's raw and primitive and completely illogical.

Luca and I can't say a word: we're staring at each other, tongue-tied. It's Kendra who exclaims:

"Kelly! I'm so glad you came back!" so sincerely that Kelly promptly bursts into tears.

"*Madonna*," Luca drawls, recovering his usual worldly-wise pose. "I spend such a long time making her calm, and now you make her cry all over again. *Grazie tante*."

"Kelly!" Paige, thundering up behind us, crashes past me and Kendra, throwing herself on Kelly. "Yay! You came back! OMG, we were *soo* worried! Kendra was going to pay for a taxi to the airport to try to find you!"

"Really?" Kelly sobs. "Really, she was?"

"Yes!" Paige hugs her. "It's all okay. Bygones are gone. That's not right, is it? Anyway, you're back! Hooray!"

I still can't speak. Seeing Luca like this is like something slammed into my chest. I didn't know if I would ever see him again; if bringing us to Venice was to keep me away from the di Vesperi family. For all I knew, Catia would make sure we didn't ever go back to Villa Barbiano. I had done my best to convince myself that we would never meet again, to tell myself I was okay with it.

And now I'm faced with the fact that I've been lying to myself. I wasn't okay with it at all.

It's Kendra who asks him bluntly:

"What *happened*? Why are you here?"

"I was at the airport," he says. "I check in, and I go to

get a coffee, and I see Kellee by the wall, crying, and I ask what's wrong. And she says she wants to go home but she doesn't have the money, it costs more than she thought. So I buy her a coffee and we sit down and talk, and I say maybe it is better to go back and finish what she has begun, here in Italy. That she should stay in Venice, one of the most beautiful places in the world. And that girls often fight—*che vuoi, è normale*."

Kelly raises her blotchy face from Paige's shoulder.

"He said at least Elisa isn't here to be mean to us," she says, sniffing hard. "And that should cheer me up a bit."

"Hah!" Kendra, beside me, starts to laugh. So does Paige. I can't, but the knot in my chest loosens until I can breathe properly again. I didn't realize it, but I must have been taking really short, shallow breaths.

*Luca knows what Elisa's like. That means he can't be dating her.*

It doesn't leave us any better off, though. I'm a dog in the manger. I can't have him myself but I don't want anyone else to have him either.

*Wow. The more I learn about myself, the more selfish I turn out to be.*

The wind is stronger now, the breeze ruffling all our hair. The taxi boat is pulling away, and the rumble of its engine, the slap of the water against the wooden poles of the pier, briefly drown out whatever any of us might say. I close my eyes for a moment, inhaling the salty air; I wish suddenly that when I opened them again, I'd be alone, the pier stretching out in front of me, and that I could walk to the end of it, sit down, dangle my legs over the lagoon, and just be still and quiet, listening to the waves. Black water and black night.

So much for wishes. I'm surrounded by people. We're all turning now, walking back to land, with Paige still cuddling Kelly; I'm glad, because no better proof could be provided that Kelly has been forgiven.

"What were you doing at the airport?" Paige is asking Luca. "I mean, why are you in Venice?"

Thank goodness for Paige's directness. I was curious too; what on earth is Luca doing here? And where was he going? Not back home; it would be crazy to get a plane from Venice to Florence, when the train is so fast.

"Oh, family business," Luca says. "Nothing important."

I notice he hasn't really answered either question, but it's not my place to say so. I notice, too, that he doesn't have any bags. He wouldn't have left them at the airport—he would have got them back from the airline on deciding not to take his flight after all. Which means he was traveling really light. All he has is a leather bag, like a small, elegant satchel, slung across his narrow chest.

But it's not my place to ask about that, either. In fact, I'm determined not to speak a word to him.

"And you missed your flight!" Paige exclaims. "You missed your flight so you could bring Kelly back!"

"I couldn't let her come back on her own," he says lightly. "We thought I would bring her back here, walk back to the palazzo, and ring one of you on a mobile to let her in, quietly, so that Catia does not suspect."

"That's really nice of you," Kendra says, glancing at me to see how I'm reacting to all this.

I nod, clamping my lips together.

"What a coincidence we bumped into you!" Paige comments. "That was crazy lucky."

"Oh, Venice is tiny," Luca says, shrugging. "*Un piccolo paese*–a small town. Even smaller than Florence. I see people I know five times a day here."

"Wow," Andi comments sotto voce to Stu. "Isn't it cool to hear how real Italians live?"

"How did you know I was gone?" Kelly's asking us.

"Violet found your note and came to get us," Paige blurts out. "We figured you must have gone to the airport."

"And Kendra, you were really going to pay for a taxi?" Kelly asks.

The two girls look at each other, face to face, the breeze lifting their hair. Kelly shivers a little—not, I'm pretty sure, because it's cold, but because of this moment of confrontation.

Kendra takes a step forward, and Kelly flinches. I see Luca's hand come up to pat her reassuringly on the arm, and my stupid jealousy flares up again, hot and bright.

"I was going to," Kendra says. She swallows. "Kind of as a thank-you."

"A *thank-you?*" Kelly repeats, baffled.

"If you hadn't told on me," Kendra continues, "I honestly don't know what would have happened. But nothing good." She shakes her head slowly. "Nothing good."

Kelly seems about to speak, and then she meets my eyes: I know what she's about to say, that she made exactly this point to Paige when the latter was having a go at her the morning after the big scene on the lawn. I shake my head swiftly at Kelly. It would be like rubbing it in, a "told you so."

She gets the hint, thank goodness. Instead she says simply:

"I still shouldn't have told on you."

"Well, you shouldn't," Kendra agrees. "But it ended up being the right thing to do. The wrong way to do it, but the right thing to do."

"*Thank* you," Kelly says, and the words truly sound as if they come from the bottom of her heart. She takes a tentative step forward, and Kendra does too: they reach out to each other, awkwardly, making it really obvious that they've never hugged before.

As they do, Kelly's red head leaning into Kendra's dark one, Paige, beside me, nudges me in satisfaction. I turn to grin at her, feeling suddenly like we're two mums in the playground watching our daughters finally get on. They pull apart and Kendra links her arm through Kelly's; I see with great happiness that Kelly's pale skin is flushed with excitement and pleasure at this definitive burying of the hatchet.

"We'll let bygones be bygones, as Paige nearly said," Kendra comments, and she smiles, the first genuine smile I've seen on her face since the whole Luigi mess, as they start to walk down the pier toward land. "I'm really glad you didn't get on a plane."

"I thought there was a cheapo flight," Kelly says, "but it didn't go from the main Venice airport, but another one, miles away. I didn't realize there were two. So I was stuck—

there was a British Airways one—but it was *so* expensive! I just got hysterical—I couldn't face going back on my own—and then Luca found me."

"You were really lucky," I say quietly.

"I'm sorry I was such a cow this afternoon, Violet," Kelly says to me. "It was really nice of you to eat my pasta."

"Paige put hers in her napkin," I say.

"Oh really?" Kelly manages a giggle. "I should do that next time."

"Hey," Andi says as we pass the Alilaguna stop on our way back to Piazza San Marco. "I just figured out what 'Alilaguna' means: 'Wings of the Lagoon.' I love that! Doesn't it sound like a romance novel?"

"Totally!" Paige agrees enthusiastically.

*"Wings of the Lagoon!"* Andi continues. "A beautiful American girl comes to Venice in the nineteenth century and gets swept away by a handsome gondolier . . ."

"Only her rich and powerful parents are way too snobby to allow them to date . . . ," Kendra chimes in.

"So they run away together in the gondola," Andi says, "but get caught up in a terrible storm . . ."

"And her parents think they're dead . . . ," Kendra adds.

"So they send out a search party and find them floating in the gondola, arms wrapped around each other," Kelly suggests. "Still alive, but barely . . ."

"And the parents forgive her and say they can be together . . . ," Andi says.

"And then it turns out he's the son of a Venetian duke who was going to have an arranged marriage, but he ran away to be a gondolier 'cause he wanted to find a girl who loved him for himself . . ." Kelly's voice is getting stronger and more confident.

"And they both live happily ever after!" Paige carols happily. "I *love* this story!"

She, Kelly, Andi, and Kendra exchange high fives.

"It's nice when a story has a happy ending," Luca says softly in my ear. I hadn't realized he was so close to me. "In real life, it's not so easy. . . ."

I swallow hard at the sound of his voice, at his words. All I can do is shake my head vehemently. *No. It's not so easy. You come to Italy and meet the son of a Florentine prince and you don't live happily ever after. Not at all.*

"Shall we go get gelato to celebrate?" Stu asks.

"Yeah! Gelato!" Andi says enthusiastically. "We've been eating gelato all over Italy, haven't we, Stu? What's the best place to get some in Venice?"

"Near here, it is Gelato Fantasy," Luca says. "I can take you."

"Don't you need to get back to the airport?" Evan says, the first time he's spoken since Luca and Kelly got out of the water taxi. "I mean, if you've got somewhere you need to be . . ."

Luca turns to flash him the most dazzling of smiles, pushing back his black hair with his long pale fingers.

"*Ma no!*" he says, so charmingly that I know he's being totally fake. "*Per niente!* Now it is too late, my flight has gone. And I am very happy to show you all where to find some good gelato. *Andiamo!*"

"Wow," Andi sighs as Luca leads us into the piazza. "Luca's *hot.* I mean, I love you, Stu, but that's just how I pictured Italian men. *So* handsome and sophisticated."

"He's a prince, too!" Paige says enthusiastically.

"Oh my God, you're *kidding*!" Andi exclaims. "Kelly, you got rescued by a prince! That's crazy!"

"I was so lucky he was at the airport," Kelly says in heartfelt tones. "I don't know *what* I'd've done without him."

"We'd have turned up!" I say, for some reason finding it almost intolerable to hear Luca praised to the skies. "Kendra would've got a taxi, and we'd have come and found you. You would've been okay."

"I'm just saying he was really nice," Kelly says quietly to me.

I nod as we cross the square. The orchestra's still playing a waltz, and Evan says to me:

"Violet, do you want to dance?"

I know he's pitched it so Luca can hear; I see Luca's shoulders stiffen. Because of course, I'm looking at him, not at Evan.

"I'm a bit knackered from all that running around," I lie. "Another time."

And I smile up at Evan, because he's really nice, and because he likes me, and because I have to stop obsessing about Luca, about how much I would like it to be Luca asking me to dance. . . .

"Stu?" Andi says to him wistfully. "Just this once?"

"Oh, *Ev*!" Stu says to his friend reproachfully. "You *had* to go ask a girl to dance! Now you've dropped me in it!"

"Sorry, dude," Evan says, not sounding remotely remorseful.

"*Stu,*" Andi wails to her boyfriend. "It's *so* romantic. . . ."

"Jeez, Andi," Stu says, wrapping his arm around her. "You know guys only dance with chicks to get—uh, to get to know them. Once you've, uh, got to know them, you don't need to dance anymore. Right, Ev?"

Evan falls back, and Stu emits an "*Oof*" that sounds as if Evan's smacked him on the head.

"Dropped you in it right back, buddy!" Stu says cheerfully.

"Oh *wow,*" Paige breathes; we've gone down another narrow street and have stopped in front of the aptly named Gelato Fantasy. "This is *amazing*. Look! Meringue mousse! It sounds like a face cream, doesn't it! Mmm! Strawberry cake!"

"Yellow peach and crème caramel," Kendra says dreamily.

"Ooh, I might get a Nutella crepe," Kelly says. "Or *three*. I'm starving."

"I bet," I say. "You barely had any lunch and you skipped dinner."

"Luca got me a sandwich at the airport," she says. "But I was all wound up and I couldn't eat it." She looks at me, her face illuminated by the bright light pouring from the window of Gelato Fantasy, making the brightly colored ice creams and sorbets gleam orange, blue, green, deep red. "He was really nice, Violet. He got me a cappuccino and just sat and listened to me whine and cry all over him, and then he took my hand and said that I was really lucky to be here, and I shouldn't just throw it all away. And he said that it was my fault Paige and Kendra were cross with me, so if I didn't come back it would be like insult to injury, cause their time here would get all messed up worrying about me."

*Wow,* I think. *Well played, Luca.*

Kelly hesitates, and then plows on.

"And he said I should come back because you would need me. 'Cause you were my friend here and that, the way things were going, you were probably going to need a friend."

*It's true. Luca knows he's my half brother. There's no doubt anymore.*

Blindly, I put out a hand to steady myself, leaning into the slightly damp stone wall of the ice cream shop.

"I'm going to have milky cream and fondant chocolate!" Andi's saying. "That sounds *amazing*!"

"What does '*Puffo*' mean?" Stu's asking. "That blue one?"

"It means 'Smurf,'" Kendra informs him. "We saw that in Florence. Isn't that great? It's Smurf ice cream!"

My stomach has closed up. I can't even think about ice cream, let alone eating Smurfs. By this time, I was more or less sure that my guess about my parentage was true, because of my mother's stalling, her refusal to offer a clear denial; but the gap between guessing and knowing was wide enough to let me fill it up with a big bucketful of hope.

Now that gap has slammed closed. I look over at Luca. He's gazing at me, and I can see all too clearly that I'm right. His father must have said something to him, confirmed what we suspected. His deep-blue eyes often seem to change color: they can light up, or glint bright with cynical amusement, a clear sapphire. But now they're so dark they're nearly black. Like mourning.

I'm mourning too. Just when I've seen such a nice side of him, one I hardly knew was there. Just when he's taken care of Kelly, found just the right things to say to her, shown a level of empathy and understanding I had no idea he possessed . . . just as I'm more impressed with him than I've ever been—that's when I've realized, for sure and certain, that I can never have him.

"I'm so sorry, Violet," Kelly says. "I'm so sorry."

And I don't reply. Because there's nothing at all for me to say.

# All I Care About

The next day is as gorgeous, glowing, and sunny as all the other days we've had in Venice. I wish it were pouring rain. I wish there were thunder, lightning, a massive electrical storm crackling over the water. Sleet. Hail. Biblical plagues of frogs and blood and locusts. I totally mean that. Almost.

I've woken up in the worst temper I've ever experienced in my life. I slept very, very badly, tossing and turning, waking up in a cold sweat from a nightmare that involved getting stuck in a plunging lift with two faceless girls who were trying to strangle me. I have no idea what it meant, but it wasn't good. Now I'm pacing up and down the room as Kelly's in the bathroom taking a shower: I've been up for ages, showered, dressed, ready for today's excursion, and I have not pent-up energy, but pent-up anger to discharge.

Because I really am angry. Furious. The other girls have sorted out their problems and made peace and wafted hearts and flowers all over one another—last night was a total lovefest as we got ready for bed, all "No, *you're* cleverer and nicer," "No, *you* are!" and it completely made me want to puke. I went to bed in a foul mood and woke up even nastier. I want to punch through a wall, stamp a hole in the parquet floor, jump off the balcony into the canal.

It's Mum and Dad I'm so livid with, of course. How dare they leave me for days and days without anything but some feeble texts telling me they love me and to hang on? Don't they know, can't they *imagine,* how utterly awful I'm feeling? How much longer am I supposed to wait in limbo like this? It's *beyond* unfair of them, and I honestly don't think I could be more wound up, more on edge, than I am right now.

No more waiting. No more being Miss Nice Daughter. I ring Dad in Hong Kong: I don't even work out the time difference. If I wake him up in the middle of the night, that's his own bloody fault. I get the answering machine, horrible Sif's stupid voice on it, of course, to make the point that she and Dad live together: well, she certainly gets an earful, because I scream down the line that Dad has to ring me *now,* this *second,* the *moment* he gets this message. I ring his mobile, get voice mail, and scream louder. Then I ring Mum: same thing, both home and mobiles, her recorded voice but not her. I'm hoarse by the time I finish, every message angrier than the last. Kelly comes back from her shower in her dressing gown, takes one look at me, and zips her lips shut, seeing that I'm in a foul mood but locked into myself; she's smart enough to know to leave me alone till I reach out to talk to her.

I don't. I'm over talking to anyone but Mum and Dad, the two people who can actually, finally, get off their bums, come to Venice, and tell me the truth about myself. I barely say a word all day, and it's particularly annoying that I'm in such a strop, because normally there's nothing I would have enjoyed more than another fast, bumpy, exhilarating ride in a water taxi to two of the prettiest islands you could ever imagine. Murano is the glassblowing one, and according to Luigi Two, until a few centuries ago, all the glassblowers had to live here so that they could make sure their secret techniques were preserved. Burano is the lace-making one, though the lace-makers seem to have been free to travel around and live where they wanted, so they were luckier. Both the islands are, as Paige comments, like something out of a Disney film: ridiculously pretty, with canals running through the center of them, lined with brightly painted little houses, their colors as vivid as the ice creams from last night at Gelato Fantasy. Luigi Two says the fishermen painted their houses such vivid colors so that they could see them from far out on the water; there are quite a few that the girls gleefully call "*Puffo* Blue."

We go to the glass museum and the lace museum and the little leaning tower of the Church of San Martino on Burano. The peace pact last night has had the effect of us all bonding together to say we don't want to have to eat weird fish dishes, like spaghetti with parmesan and mussels, anymore: presented with this united front, Luigi Two and

Catia sigh, roll their eyes, and agree to take us to a restaurant that serves risotto, which makes everyone whoop with happiness.

Apart from me. I couldn't care less if they were serving us spaghetti with sawdust and rotten eggs: I can't eat anything anyway. I push my risotto around my plate to make it look as if I've eaten some, and tell Catia I'm feeling too hot to manage more than a few bites. *I must be at my absolute lowest point,* I reflect grimly. The risotto, with peas and parmesan ("Cheesy peas!" Kelly's yodeling in amusement), looks delicious, and I never, ever lose my appetite. I'm not one of those girls who drops seven pounds whenever she has a breakup or a heartache: I'm too greedy.

But what heartache can't do, existential angst about my parentage, plus a heaping side order of complete and utter fury with my mum and dad, clearly can. Catia would have to force-feed me to get any more risotto down my throat, and I'm almost surprised she doesn't try: she's usually quite strict about us eating what we're served—more strict than she is with her own skinny daughter. But she shoots me the oddest look when I mutter my excuses, nods, and lets it go without another word, which is very unlike her.

*Maybe,* I think, *she's decided not to fuss over little things like someone losing her appetite now that the whole atmosphere among us four girls is so massively improved.*

Everyone's talking to everyone else, laughing, giggling, exclaiming at how lovely Burano and Murano are, what lace they want to buy to take back to their mums, what glass they want for themselves. It's as if there were a cork stuffed in a bottle of bubbles ever since Kelly betrayed Kendra, and now the bubbles have all burst forth, effervescent and sparkling. Paige, Kelly, and Kendra are blissfully happy not to have the stress and tension of fighting.

And the icing on the cake is that it turns out Kelly has been secretly making an online scrapbook of our stay here, which she planned as a combination diary for her and gift for us all at the end of the stay. Given the big reconciliation last night back at the palazzo, where the three of them fell into one another's arms, hugged, cried, and told one another how fabulous they were, Kelly decided to show it to us early, and we were incredibly moved and impressed. It's truly beautiful. Not only is it full of funny little observant details about all of us, it also has tons of photos: Kelly's been snapping away on her mobile phone, it turns out, since the moment we arrived. Paige and Kendra clutching their pillows and dragging their suitcases, me laughing at the funny bronze sculptures at Pisa airport that looked like crocodiles climbing out of the grass—she's been documenting this trip all the way along, tagging each photo with a clever caption.

Not only do I stare at it in awe as we click through the pages, it occurs to me immediately that this diary is the perfect proof that Kelly was born to be an art historian. She's found images on the Web of every museum, every historic place, every artwork we've seen, and annotated them all with really thoughtful, interesting comments: I tell her that if she makes a separate folder with all the art stuff, that will be an ideal addition to her university application. I honestly can't imagine anyone who sees this not giving her a place—

maybe even a scholarship—on the spot. She goes red with excitement and asks me if I really think so about twenty times. I've never seen her so happy.

So everyone's blissful. Well, Paige and Kelly are blissful: in Kendra's case, it's more that she's at peace with knowing she's done the right thing, closed the book firmly on Luigi forever. The three of them are so content, in fact, that my own utterly gloomy state of mind is more or less hidden under their release of high spirits.

But not quite. Catia has noticed something, I'm sure. She's different with me today, very careful, as if I need special consideration. She's quizzing everyone else on their Italian, on what they've learned so far about Venice and its history, but she barely asks me anything, and when she does, it's so easy that it's what Paige calls a "softball": the rest of the girls groan that they weren't asked that question.

I have no idea why she's treating me with kid gloves, and I'm so grumpy that I don't much care. The answer only becomes clear when the water taxi, on our return from Murano, doesn't take us directly back to the palazzo, as we all expected from the itinerary Catia outlined for us that morning. Instead, it slows down as we pass the Piazza San Marco, then the Alilaguna stop, and turns in a semicircle so that it can back into the same pier where Luca and Kelly's water taxi moored last night.

Catia's been inside the cabin, on her mobile phone, for part of the trip back; now she emerges, clicking the phone shut, and says to me:

"Violet, you will get off here. There is someone ready to meet you."

I've been curled up, slumped, really, in the corner of the seat, watching the water splash up against the side of the boat as we slice through the waves; my brain is so dulled with unhappiness I don't even realize, the first time she says it, that she's speaking to me. Catia has to repeat herself, and even then Kelly, beside me, has to elbow me to get me to focus.

"What's going on?" I say, looking around me blankly.

"You're getting off here!" Kelly says, as all the girls crane around to see who's waiting on the pier. "Violet! Is that—is it—"

For some reason, I think it must be Luca; but that's just because he's on my mind so constantly. I'm caught in a vicious circle of telling myself not to think about him ever again, which of course makes me think about him all the time. But it can't possibly be Luca. I swivel around, kneel up on the white cushion, and prop my hands on the chrome bar that runs along the back of the boat so I can twist to see down to the end of the pier.

Then I shriek my head off, jump down, run up the steps, and literally throw myself onto the pier even before the boat is properly moored. The driver yells at me but I don't care; behind me, I hear the girls loudly speculating about who it is. The taxi starts up again, pulling away, but that's all a million miles behind me already.

Because all I care about is tearing down the pier and throwing myself into my mother's arms. She smells just like she always does, the most wonderful, comforting smell in the world, a mix of Elizabeth Arden Beauty perfume, Chantecaille powder, apple shampoo, and herself, not necessarily in that order. I'm crying, but it's out of pure happiness and relief, as if I've had my own cork in my own bottle, and it's finally popped.

"Darling," she says again and again into my hair, bending over a bit, because of course she's quite a lot taller than me, being model-height. "Darling, darling Violet, I'm so sorry I couldn't come sooner. I'm so, so sorry. . . ."

We cry and cry and cry in each other's arms. Mum's tears make my hair wet; mine are soggy against her silk blouse. It feels wonderful. We're sagging against each other, propped up, I think, just by leaning our bodies together, like two pieces of wood stacked at an angle that means one would crash down if you removed the other. Goodness knows how long we stand there. Ages, it feels like. Until we've sobbed everything out that we possibly can, until we're hiccupping as you do at the end of a crying jag, pulling back to blow our noses—mums always have tissues in their bags for this kind of thing—and smile blearily at each other as we mop our faces.

"I missed you so *much*!" I say. "I was *freaking out* about not hearing from you. Did you get my messages today? I couldn't have waited any longer! I need to know, Mum—I need to know what's been going on, I need to know *everything, now. . . .*"

Mum grimaces, twisting her wide mouth into a comical shape. Because she never wears much makeup, she hasn't smeared anything, but she pulls another tissue out of the packet, licks the edge, and starts dabbing around my eyes, as obviously my liner must have got smudged.

"You'll understand very soon," she assures me. "I promise, darling."

"*Very soon?*" It comes out as a high-pitched squeak. "Why not *now*? Mum, I feel like I'm going mad!"

Mum finishes cleaning my face, takes it in her hands, and kisses my forehead.

"Come with me," she says, linking her arm through mine, walking me along the pier. "I can't talk about it without—" She draws a breath. "There are some other people that—there are some other people waiting for us."

"Is Dad here?" I ask eagerly.

"Yes." She squeezes my arm. "Yes, he is."

"And Sif the loo cleaner?"

Mum laughs: usually she ticks me off for being rude about Dad's girlfriend, and the fact that she's letting me get away with it speaks volumes for her state of mind.

"No! She's not here! Isn't it *lovely*!" she says confidingly.

I heave a big sigh of relief. The thing about Sif is that she seems incredibly resentful of the fact that Dad was married and had a daughter when she met him. Once she got him to leave Mum for her, it's like she tried to erase his past, to pretend that he didn't have a life before meeting her. That makes seeing him when she's around really hard for me, as she acts as if I don't exist even when I'm in the room. Once I visited Dad and her for a week, and she said loudly over breakfast on the third morning that in her country they have a saying that guests are like fish—they start to stink after three days. Charming, eh?

"It's absolutely nothing to do with her," Mum says firmly

as we walk along the waterfront. "And to give your father credit, he completely understands that too. He didn't even suggest bringing her."

"She must be *fuming*," I say with great satisfaction.

I assume we're going to the hotel, where Mum and Dad are staying; so I'm surprised when, after barely a minute, Mum guides me onto another little dock. Or rather, stops in front of a very smart gate, beyond which blue, red, and gold pillars run down the length of the pier. Mum presses an intercom button and says:

"It's Mrs. Routledge. Could you please send the boat back for me?"

"Eet is already on eets way, *signora*," buzzes a voice through the intercom, and the gate clicks open; we step through.

"We're staying at a hotel over there," Mum explains, pointing across the lagoon.

"On Giudecca," I say, showing off the local knowledge I've learned.

"Yes, it's called the Cipriani. It's very lovely, Violet. You can stay there with us if you'd like. There's a swimming pool! You'd like that. Really, you can have anything you want, darling . . . anything at all. . . . We're *so* sorry. . . ."

Her voice wobbles dangerously: I squeeze her arm and say swiftly:

"Mum, don't cry! Don't! It's all right. I love you."

She pinches the bridge of her nose hard and takes a deep breath. A water taxi is coming straight toward us, like an arrow fired from Giudecca Island directly to the dock; as it gets closer, I see HOTEL CIPRIANI painted in white letters down its side. It slides into the pier, a very smart couple dripping in Gucci and Missoni step off, and Mum and I are handed in by the smiling, liveried driver. We sit in the back, our arms around each other, her long blond hair blowing across my face, and don't say a word for the entire short trip.

I'm in suspension, waiting for the big revelation. I'm terrified, of course, how could I not be? But having my beloved mum with me makes me feel stronger and more secure than I have in absolutely ages. I know I wanted to stand on my own two feet, and I think I've done pretty well while I've been in Italy. But sometimes, even if you're growing up and trying to be adult, you really need to run back to your mum and hug her and smell the special mix of scents that are so familiar they mean home and love and security to you. . . .

The boat pulls up in front of another little dock with the same blue, red, and gold pillars: very smart. And as the driver hands us up, and we walk down the dock, beautiful gardens open up in front of us. On the right, through high planted bushes, I can just about glimpse the bright artificial blue of swimming pool tiles. The hotel is directly in front of us, a beautiful white building with a plush, red-carpeted reception; white walls with every molding detail picked out with gilding; smiling staff behind the big reception desk; and Mum guiding me over to a bank of lifts. There's even a lift operator in a cap and more livery, who slides the cage doors open for us and takes us up to the floor Mum tells him; this hotel is beyond five-star.

*Dad is definitely paying for this,* I think. *No way does Mum have this kind of money.*

We go down a thickly carpeted corridor lined with the gilded tables and elaborate flower arrangements that posh hotels always seem to feature, and halfway down Mum stops in front of a door and presses the small gold bell set into it. It swings open almost immediately, and standing there is my father, his face lighting up with happiness to see me.

"Violet! My darling!" he exclaims as his arms open wide.

I thud against his chest, wide and solid, and hug him; after Mum's very slim frame, Dad seems huge. I can't get my arms to close around him; he's put on a bit of weight. He hugs me back so tightly that I can barely breathe. I pound his back with my fist, and he loosens his grip. I'm giggling—Dad always does this after I haven't seen him for a while.

"I don't know my own strength!" he says, looking down at me, as I say simultaneously:

"You don't know your own strength!"

It's a long-running joke of ours, and we both laugh at it.

"Darling daughter," he says with enormous tenderness. "My darling daughter."

And then, as these words sink in, they emphasize exactly the reason that we're all here, and we both fall silent.

All I've seen so far is Dad, his big bulk looming in front of me. But now he puts his arm around my shoulders protectively and leads me out of the lobby and into the sitting room of a suite, all brocaded and padded out and tasseled and hung with curtains over other curtains, the way posh ones always seem to be.

Then I stop dead. The suite is so crammed with furniture and occasional tables and big gilt-framed pictures that it's taken me a moment to realize that there are other people in it. They're sitting on one of the sofas, staring at me. Not together; at opposite ends of the sofa, as if they want to make it clear that they don't want to be close to each other. And after everything that's happened, that isn't really a surprise. I wouldn't exactly have expected Luca's mum and dad to be sitting next to each other holding hands.

Beyond them, I see movement on the balcony, a trail of cigarette smoke rising into the air, and I freeze.

Is it Luca? Did he come back here last night after we left him in the Piazza San Marco? I honestly don't think I could bear to see Luca with all our parents here. To be told that he's my half brother. To be expected to hug him and say how happy I am to have a half sibling . . .

*And besides,* I think idiotically, *Luca promised me he'd stop smoking!*

And then the person on the balcony drops their cigarette to the marble floor, stubs it out with a diamante sandal that is definitely not Luca's, takes a deep breath, and rounds the brocade sweep of curtain to step inside.

I'm holding Dad's hand, and my fingers clench on it as tightly as if I'm trying to break his bones.

Because the person smoking outside was my aunt Lissie, and she's looking at me with such an awful, guilty, hangdog expression that suddenly the last piece of the puzzle falls into place.

And I understand absolutely everything.

# Some Sugar Would Be Good

"We were in Milan, for the shows," Aunt Lissie is saying.

She's sitting next to me on the sofa, holding my hand; Mum's on the other side, holding my other hand. Aunt Lissie smells of cigarette smoke, her Lola perfume, and hair spray; the combination is stronger than Mum's, drowning her scent out. I realize that I'm fighting an impulse to crawl onto Mum's lap, wrap my arms around her neck, and bury my face in her hair, as I used to do when I was little—even though I probably weigh more than she does by now.

"That's me and Daisy," she adds quickly, looking over me at Mum. "Daisy was modeling, and I'd just started as a junior editor on *Vogue Italia*. We were very young," she says rather sadly, and, across from us on the other sofa, I see the principessa flinch. "Daisy was modeling for—"

"Versace," I say. "We saw some photographs in the castello." I manage to look over and meet the principe's eyes briefly. "You were at the Versace show. Mum was in the picture too."

"*I* was in the picture?" Mum asks. "Oh, Violet! You must have thought—oh, *darling* . . ."

"It's okay, Mum," I say, managing a smile for her. The relief in her eyes as I call her Mum is incredibly sweet.

Aunt Lissie heaves another sigh.

"So, we were in Milan," she continues, "and I met Salvatore." She looks over at the principe, then back at me. "Oh, Violet!" she adds in a sidebar. "I'm so sorry you've been having to wait so long after emailing Daisy, but it was my fault. Your dad came straight over from Hong Kong, but your mum had a really hard time getting hold of me because I was on a meditative yoga retreat in Thailand and had my phone and iPad switched off. . . ."

I can't meet her eyes. I'm looking down at my lap, concentrating on keeping my knees together, my skirt pulled down decorously, as it's a cargo mini I wore to go to Murano and Burano and it feels too short for such a serious occasion. It gives me something else to think about, some other small distraction from what I'm hearing Lissie tell me. What I know is coming.

I notice my mum jerk her head at Lissie a bit impatiently, as if to say *Get on with it*, and Lissie says quickly:

"So, yes, we were in Milan. I met Salvatore at a party,

and we—well, we had an affair. Like I said, Violet, we've all discussed this already, all five of us here. So you don't need to worry that anyone's being surprised, or will get cross about anything I'm telling you. Well"—she says ruefully—"anyone but you."

Lissie takes a deep breath.

"We had an affair," she says. "Not a long one. We agreed that we weren't going to hide anything from you, and that you can ask any questions you want. So, I'll tell you honestly that he was married then, and I knew he was married. And it was wrong, and we shouldn't have done it."

I writhe, because there's nothing more embarrassing than adults apologizing to you, confessing their faults, asking for your forgiveness. It makes me want to dig my nails into my palms till it really hurts. Like when Mum and Dad were getting a divorce, and sat me down to tell me about it, and explained about people falling out of love with other people but still caring about them, and that nothing would change between them and me, and a whole lot of other rubbish, frankly, that made me really angry and sad and frustrated all at the same time.

*Yes. Well. No point thinking about that right now.* Aunt Lissie has misread my flinch, and has paused, staring at me nervously; I give her a quick nod with my head to say *Go on,* because words are pretty much beyond me right now.

"And I got pregnant," she says bravely. "With you, Violet."

It's as if there were a huge invisible pressure in the room that has suddenly released, as if everyone were holding their breath and has let it out all at once. Because it's been said.

We've all heard the words and we've all survived hearing them.

I feel like a deflated balloon. I've been wound up as tight as a coiled spring with so much stress and doubt and uncertainty: and now that the doubt and uncertainty have vanished, the stress has released along with them. I sag back against the sofa cushions, floppy and exhausted all of a sudden.

Aunt Lissie pushes on.

"I didn't know what to do," she says. "I wasn't in touch with Salvatore any longer, and I didn't want to tell him. I mean, he was married, and he had a little boy."

I manage not to flinch again at this.

"So of course, I went running to Daisy," she says, and the warmth in her voice when she talks about Mum, her sister, is lovely. "I always went running to Daisy when I had problems. And she said—she offered—Robert too, he was wonderful, you were both wonderful—" She's looking at Mum and Dad now.

"We had been trying to have a baby for a while," Mum says, clearing her throat and forging on as Aunt Lissie loses it for a bit. "And we just couldn't get pregnant. The doctors couldn't tell us why. They called it unexplained infertility. So as soon as Lissie told us she was pregnant with you, I thought instantly that we should take you and bring you up as ours. And Robert agreed."

"It felt like it was meant to be," Dad says simply. "We couldn't believe it, really."

Lissie and Mum nod emphatically.

"You were theirs from that moment," Aunt Lissie says.

"Honestly, I felt as if I were being their surrogate. That's what I told them. This is your baby, and I'm its aunt. I'm just carrying it for you two."

I am *not* going to cry in front of the principe and principessa. So I swallow really hard at how lovely it is of her to say this, and nod again.

"We agreed that I would just be your aunt when you were growing up," Aunt Lissie says. "Well, I *am* your aunt, as far as we're all concerned."

"We were going to tell you when you were eighteen," Mum says quickly, and Dad nods vehemently. "I read up on all the stuff about adoption I could find, and they said that you either tell the child straightaway, so it grows up taking for granted that it's adopted, or you wait till it's old enough to process everything."

"And this probably sounds ludicrous," Dad chips in, "but we honestly barely even *thought* of you as being adopted, Violet my love. You were already ours, a few months after Lissie conceived you. It was as if she were carrying our baby for us, just like she said."

I find myself looking up now, at the principe, who's sitting directly opposite me. At my biological father.

"Were you going to tell me about—" I can't manage to say "biological father" out loud. "About him?"

"We didn't want to. But we knew you would have to know," Mum says with her usual honesty. "We'd decided it would be the three of us to tell you, and then we'd all discuss what to do about contacting the principe, if you wanted to, darling. It was going to be left to you to make the decision."

"Salvatore, please," the principe murmurs.

"We didn't think there would be the issue of you"—Dad glances from the principe to me—"looking so much like your biological father."

It was obviously very hard for him to get those last two words out; he stumbles over them, determined to do it but almost stammering in the process.

"*You're* my dad," I say passionately, the words tumbling out. I jump up and run over to him; he's been sitting in an armchair but he stands up swiftly and catches me in his arms, hugging me. I feel his heart pounding in his chest, thumping against his rib cage as if it's trying to break his bones; I know my own is doing just the same. "Mum's my mum," I say firmly, "and you're my dad."

"We didn't think of the resemblance issue at all," Aunt Lissie says, sounding guilty. "I mean, Daisy and I look so alike we could almost be twins. We just assumed there wouldn't be any problem. We did the paperwork, of course—we legally adopted you. But in all of our eyes, it was just a formality."

"And as soon as you were born, you were just *you*," Mum chimes in. "Our beloved daughter. We never thought about it or noticed it at all."

"But *I* did," I observe, pulling a little away from Dad. "I always noticed that I was different. I'm not blaming you at all!" I add swiftly, as Mum looks horrified. "But I noticed I didn't look like anyone on either side of the family. And I'd hear when people would comment on it."

"We should have said something," Dad says soberly. "But we'd made the decision all together, and we thought we should stick to it."

"And you're so nearly eighteen!" Mum practically wails.

"It was getting so soon, the deadline to tell you! And you kept having exams, so we didn't want to stress you—and you were always so happy, so secure, you didn't seem to be feeling anything odd or negative—"

I don't want to let them know how aware I've always been of how odd-person-out I've felt in my tall, white-skinned, blond family. That the sight of a picture in a gallery in London was enough to send me on a quest for my origins, when another girl, one whose relatives looked much more like her, would have just thought *Oh, how cool!* and dragged all her friends back to show off how much she resembled a random girl from the eighteenth century.

"It was going to the castello that set it off," I lie. "Everyone saying how much I looked like the family portraits."

"It's true," the principe says quietly. "The resemblance is very strong. This is almost always the case with my family. The di Vesperi face comes down through the generations practically without fail."

The principessa hasn't uttered a word yet, though she moves a little on her side of the sofa. Eventually she says: "This has 'appened, and it cannot be changed. We all know life is full of temptation. But we also care about family." Her face is even whiter than usual, but she seems as poised as always. She can't be much older than Mum and Aunt Lissie, but she looks as if she comes from a different generation because her style is so old-fashioned, with her Chanel jacket and jewelry and her Ferragamo shoes, her hair smoothed back tightly to her scalp.

"Yes, family is the most important thing," the principe agrees. "Donatella and I have of course discussed this," he continues, glancing sideways at his wife. "She was sure almost immediately, when she saw Violetta, of the true situation." He spreads his hands wide. "I have not been a very good husband, I must admit this."

*Oh no, please,* I think frantically, *no more adults beating themselves up! I really don't want to hear it!*

"But that is not for Violetta's ears," he goes on, earning my eternal gratitude. "I think the best thing to say here is that Violetta, you must take time and decide for yourself how you feel. Your *mamma* and *papà* are your parents, not me. It is for you to say how you want to go ahead with anything in the future as far as I am concerned."

Aunt Lissie looks at him directly and prompts:

"And can you tell her—can you say what you told me about—"

"Ah yes!" The principe nods. "Yes, Violetta, I also must say that I understand very completely Lissie's reasons for not telling me about you."

Hearing an Italian say "Lissie" is so funny that it actually makes me smile a little, something I never would have thought could happen in this situation. Catia's been teaching us that, to pronounce Italian correctly, you have to pronounce every letter of every word; the principe turns my aunt's name into "Leess-ee," lengthening it out till it sounds as long as an entire sentence.

"She was correct to not tell me," he says, smiling diplomatically at Lissie. "Or rather, it was for her to decide. I accept that completely."

"Thank you," Lissie says gratefully.

I'm still standing up, and I'm fighting the urge to pace

madly back and forth across the room. From being exhausted, I now feel very restless, itchy, overwhelmed with information and emotions to process.

"Should I order some tea?" Mum says, going very English. "Tea and cakes? Some sugar would be good, wouldn't it? We must all be feeling very . . . well, shall I order tea? Violet darling, is there something you'd like?"

I realize that all of them are staring at me, and they're all looking nervous. I must be wearing a very odd expression on my face.

"I think I need to go outside and be by myself for a bit," I say.

There's a hubbub of fuss and people saying that I must do exactly as I feel and to take my time and that it's totally okay for me to want to be alone and they'll be right here and blah blah blah, et cetera et cetera. They're still babbling as I walk across the sitting room into the foyer, concentrating on keeping my steps even, telling my legs to walk straight. Once the door closes behind me, I start to run. I'm heading for the lift, but when I see a fire door I dash through it instead and down the stairs, taking them two at a time, the relief of some physical action huge; I hammer those steps so hard that by the time I'm down however many flights there were to the ground floor, I'm breathing hard and feeling at least a little better, as if some tight knot has loosened itself inside me.

I can see daylight and sunshine flooding through the glass doors of a bar area, so I walk toward them, white-jacketed waiters smiling and nodding at me as I pass. Emerging into the fresh air, seeing the green grass of the garden, with its stone fountain playing into a lily pond surrounded by a deep-red circle of rich geraniums, instantly makes me feel calmer. Set into the stone wall built along the boundary of the island are a series of wrought-iron embrasures with white cushions in them, and I sink down on one, kicking off my sandals, curling up into a ball, wrapping my arms around my knees. I stare out over the blue lagoon, listening to the waves slapping against the stone foundations below, breathing in the salty air, listening to the seagulls.

Trying to make a small quiet place in my head where I can just be. Letting it all sink in.

*Luca is definitely my half brother. We're related by blood.*

Ironically, everything else that I've discovered today is hugely positive. I couldn't possibly have imagined a better solution to the mystery of the way I look. My mum is my mum. My dad is my dad. My aunt is, very firmly, my aunt. Nothing, truly, has changed. I'm testing the ground beneath me and finding it firm and solid. No holes for me to fall through.

Apart from . . . Luca.

Eventually, I realize that my hands are cramping, my legs getting stiff. I straighten up and emit a little yelp at the sight of the principessa standing by the fountain watching me. She starts to walk toward me, slowly, tentatively, as if she thinks that I might bite, or scream, or run away if she startles me.

And though I want to run away, I slip my sandals on and I wait. I have no idea what she wants to say to me. But if there are any more secrets, anything else that needs to be said, I want to hear now, today. To wake up tomorrow morning with the knowledge that nothing else is hanging over my head.

"*Ciao, Violetta,*" she begins cautiously. "I know you must feel . . . *strana. Confusa.*"

"It's okay," I mutter. "What is it?"

I know I'm not exactly being gracious. But she can't really expect perfect manners under the circumstances. A waiter glides elegantly down the gravel path toward us, pauses, takes in the awkward atmosphere, and demonstrates his five-star training by swiveling on his heel and gliding away again rather than disturb us.

"May I?"

She gestures at the seat beside me. I nod abruptly.

"I 'ave something very important to tell you," she says, smoothing down the back of her skirt, lowering herself neatly onto the cushion, and sitting with as straight a back as if she's in a full corset. Her face isn't white anymore, or at least not all over. Her cheeks are bright dots of pink, and on her neck I can see a red flush rising, ugly, nervous blotches.

But she was right. What she proceeds to tell me, in a halting mixture of English and Italian, truly is very important. More than important: crucial.

Because it literally changes everything.

# *L'amore è bello*

I'm going back the way I came, on a high-speed Silver Arrow train tearing down the spine of Italy. From Venice to Florence, the train rocking with speed, the landscape shooting past. And it still isn't fast enough. Nothing would be. I want to be there so urgently that I'm biting my lip, tapping my foot, fidgeting so much that eventually Paige threatens to throw her phone at me if I don't calm down, and I smile reluctantly.

It's just me and Paige, sitting in the dining car, drinking cappuccinos and feeling hugely grown up. After yesterday's dramatic family reunion, both my mum and dad and the di Vesperis pretty much threw themselves at my feet and asked me how I felt, what I wanted to do, what they could give me to make up for all this. I probably could have grabbed a Tiffany catalog and circled everything in it.

But as it happened, I knew *exactly* what I wanted. And I made them go along with it without even asking why.

Only the principessa knows why I'm rushing back to Chianti. No one else. I haven't confided in any of the girls. I'm lucky that it was Paige who volunteered to come with me, because the only stipulation my parents placed on me setting off first thing this morning was that I had to have a travel companion. Kelly, amazingly, has performed a hundred-and-eighty-degree turnaround; she said she'd messed up by moping through her first days in Venice, and wanted a chance to really enjoy it before Catia packs them all up and onto a later train back this evening. Kelly and Kendra are going out together to do the Ca' Rezzonico again, and then a couple of modern art museums they've chosen together.

Whereas Paige was extremely, enthusiastically keen to give up a last day in Venice and get up at the crack of dawn to throw herself on a train to Florence. Not only that: she hasn't even asked why I want to head back so badly. She's too busy texting and fiddling with her phone and smiling to herself, playing with her hair and repeatedly touching up her makeup. It's a relief, but it's also a bit disconcerting not to be asked a single question about why I'm so keen to make this trip. I was braced for an interrogation, and yet Paige, bizarrely, seems entirely uninterested.

Which definitely isn't normal. She's the only one who hasn't asked a single question. Last night, when I got back to the palazzo after having a quiet dinner at the Hotel Cipriani with my mum and dad and aunt Lissie, Kendra and Kelly were dying to know why I'd been whisked away, why my mum had suddenly appeared. And I couldn't, or wouldn't, tell them. Not yet. Not until tonight, when they all get back to Villa Barbiano. When, hopefully, the last piece of the puzzle will have been put into place.

I can't wait. I just can't wait.

"Stop *tapping*!" Paige says, widening her eyes at me. "You're like Road Runner in a cage! You're driving me crazy!"

She grabs my cappuccino and pulls it away from me.

"No more caffeine. That's the *last* thing you need."

"We're nearly there!" I say excitedly, looking at my watch. "We stopped at Bologna ages ago. I think there's only about twenty minutes more, if we're on time. . . ."

"Yeah," Paige says, sipping my cappuccino and looking thoughtful.

"So, look," I say, "Giulio will be waiting on the platform to collect us"—Giulio is the husband of Benedetta, Catia's cook—"and he'll drop you at Villa Barbiano, and then he'll take me on to—"

"Here's the thing," Paige says. "I'm actually not coming with you to Villa Barbiano. Not, like, right now."

"You're *what*?"

"You're going to need to cover for me. Say I decided to spend the day shopping in Florence. I'll meet Catia and the girls off their train and get a ride back with them this evening."

I stare at her blankly. This makes complete sense; Paige would much rather shop in Florence than laze around the villa with nothing to do. But why is she just springing this on me now?

"Paige," I ask, and for the first time since all of yesterday's family drama, I realize that I'm not thinking about myself. "What's up?"

She's looking serious now, but her eyes are sparkling.

"You have to have my back, Violet," she says firmly. "I came with you today, and you couldn't have come without me, because no one else wanted to, they wanted an extra day in Venice—"

"Paige, tell me!" I lean forward, planting my elbows on the smart brown fake-wood table of the restaurant car, my voice rising so much that the waiter looks over at us. "What on earth is going *on*?"

I have absolutely no idea what she's about to say. And even so, her answer absolutely gobsmacks me.

"I'm engaged," she says.

The train jolts. My elbows bounce painfully on the table. And I barely even notice. I'm staring at Paige, who looks positively transformed; she's glowing. Her face is prettier, more gentle, than I've ever seen it.

"My folks are *completely* against it, of course," she says calmly. "They say we're much too young. Which is *way* hypocritical, 'cause Mom was twenty-three when she had Evan. But you know, blah blah blah, I have to go to college and have a life and date a lot before I'm ready to settle down, and you know what? I *want* to go to college and have a life, I just don't want to date a lot! I want to be with Miguel."

I'm so taken aback by all this that I focus on the least important part of her entire speech.

"Miguel?" I echo. "Is he Spanish?"

"Hispanic American," Paige corrects, rolling her eyes.

"He graduated West Point last year, and now he's a second lieutenant in the army."

"He's in the *army*?" My voice is getting weaker and weaker.

"He's been serving in Afghanistan," Paige says proudly. "When he finished his tour he was shipped back to Germany, to a military base. But he's wangled some favor or something, and he flew into Pisa this morning. There's a big US base there called Camp Darby. So he got the train down and he's at Florence station now, waiting for me. We're going to spend the day together."

I shake my head slowly in disbelief.

"I just—" I say feebly. "You totally didn't act like you had a boyfriend, at *all*, this summer. Fiancé!" I correct myself. "You *totally* didn't act like you had a fiancé! You were so flirty with everyone!"

"*Exactly*," Paige says complacently; I'm hugely grateful she didn't take offense. "I was flirty with *everyone*. I let off steam but I didn't do anything with *anyone*. Did I?"

She raises her perfectly groomed and penciled eyebrows. "All I did," she points out, "was have fun."

I think about it; she's quite right. Paige flirted madly, but now I think about it, I never even saw her kiss a boy at a party. I nod slowly.

"Was it all an act?" I ask, a bit confused.

She tilts her head from side to side, blond ringlets bouncing.

"Yes and no," she says. "I really did want to have a good time. And I couldn't see Mig anyway, because he was overseas. And I knew my mom had told Catia that she was sending me off to Italy to distract me from thinking about Miguel." She pulls a face. "Mom thought if I met some sexy Italian boys I might decide I wasn't ready to settle down after all. Mom and Dad really like Mig—he's one of Evan's best friends—but they don't want me to get married so young. And that he's an officer in the army freaks them out. I mean, they're really proud he's serving our country and all, but they're worried about how I'd cope. Which is *stupid*! I'll go to college, I'll be fine. I'm tough. I don't panic. I can totally deal with having a husband serving overseas."

Her jaw is set determinedly: she looks like she'll pick a fight with me if I don't agree. But I'm already nodding. I think Paige will cope brilliantly as a military spouse.

"How do you know that's why they sent you to Italy?" I ask curiously.

"'Cause I heard Mom on the phone to Catia," she says instantly. "I knew something was going on, so I was super sneaky. Believe me, I'm really good at that when I need to be."

"Honestly, Paige," I say, shaking my head again in disbelief, "I really underestimated you. Does Evan even know?"

"Well, he knows about Mig, but not that we're meeting up today. Look, I'm not super clever, not like Kendra and Kelly," she says frankly. "But I'm really good at getting what I want. And I know I'm not going to change my mind about Mig. He and I are meant to be together. *But*, if Catia tells Mom that I had a really good time in Italy, and went out with tons of boys, and partied my head off, Mom's going to relax and think I forgot about Mig while I was away. And then it'll be way easier for us to see each other when we're back in the States. They won't be watching what I do or where I go all the time."

The train is slowing down. We're coming into Florence.

"Paige," I say slowly, "I'm beyond impressed. Oh!" I realize something else. "*That's* why you yelled at Evan when we went swimming in the river—why you got cross and told him not to say you were showing your junk all over town! You didn't want him saying anything to, um, Mig."

"*Exactly!*" she says in a heartfelt tone. "Can you *imagine*? Ev knows how serious I am about Mig, and he was totally messing with me. *Brothers!* I could have slapped him!" She shakes her head crossly as she remembers his teasing. "*Soo*"—she leans across the table—"you're going to cover for me, right? We'll go meet Giulio, and then I'll say I'm staying to shop—meeting Catia and the girls when they get in tonight and coming back with them. You act like it's all totally normal. He won't care."

I nod. Giulio won't give a toss; he's as taciturn and grumpy as his wife is vivacious and chatty. Besides, it *is* totally normal that a teenage girl like Paige would grab the chance to spend the day in Florence hitting the shops.

"Okay, Violet?" she asks, grabbing my hands. "Please? This is so important to me—I haven't seen him in months, and we're dying to have some time together in Florence; it's going to be so romantic. . . ."

What can I say? One thing about Paige, she's incredibly practical. Look at the way she's organized this whole thing, volunteering to come down to Florence with me, arranging with Miguel to meet her here, covering her tracks so smoothly no one suspected a thing.

"Was he always going to come to Florence?" I ask, suddenly curious. "I mean, if I hadn't decided I wanted to come back here, what would you have done?"

"Oh, I had it all planned out," she says instantly. "Mig was always going to come see me, but when we got packed off to Venice he was going to catch a train up there instead and I was going to pretend I was sick and then sneak out while you were all off on one of the day trips. Lucky Italy's so small!" she adds, grinning. "You can, like, get anywhere on a plane or train in a couple of hours! But this worked out even better. I get the most time possible 'cause I don't have to keep worrying about how long you're going to be out for. Catia's train doesn't get in till eight tonight—we have *ages*."

She heaves a big, happy sigh. The train comes to a halt, and we hear the hiss as the pneumatic door locks disengage.

"*Firenze Santa Maria Novella!*" the guard says, walking through the restaurant car. "*Signori, signore, Firenze Santa Maria Novella, siamo arrivati! Prossima fermata, Roma.*"

"We're here!" Paige jumps up. A tall figure appears in the aisle, almost filling it completely.

"Paige!" he says, and she turns, sees her Miguel, screams, and throws herself against him with an audible thud. They're pretty much the same height, especially with Paige in heels; I can't see much of Miguel, just his wide frame, his arms wrapping around his fiancée, and a shaved dark head. They're kissing madly.

"*Ah, l'amore è bello,*" comments a woman sitting across from us.

"Love is beautiful." I have to agree with her.

"Guys?" I tap Paige. "We better move, 'cause the next stop is Rome, and none of us wants to go there. . . ."

Locked together, Paige and Miguel move along. We jump down at the far end of the platform. Squinting, I can see Giulio leaning against the buffers at the other end waiting for us, smoking a cigarette, not even looking down the platform; the lovers are pretty safe from being spotted—by him, at least. Because almost everyone who's getting off or on the train is pausing to look at Paige and Miguel embracing, and commenting audibly with approval and encouragement. That's Italy for you. If you kissed passionately in public in London, people would judge you as attention-seekers and deliberately ignore you: in Italy, they practically applaud.

"Violet, this is Mig," Paige eventually says. "Second Lieutenant Miguel Ramirez," she adds proudly, detaching herself for long enough to manage a few words. Her face is pink and beaming, her eyes twin stars, and Miguel is in exactly the same condition. It's beyond sweet.

"Nice to meet you, Violet," he says, taking my hand and pumping it up and down, dragging his gaze from Paige for long enough to look at me politely. "We're grateful to you for giving us this opportunity to get some time together."

"It's my pleasure," I say, going all formal for some reason—probably because of his military good manners.

What maybe impresses me most of all about Miguel is that he isn't that handsome, though he has a really lovely, kind smile. Paige has gone for character rather than looks. He's wide and square, with a friendly, solid face that looks as if it might have been in a couple of fights. He seems poised.

Mature. As if he can handle Paige with one hand behind his back. Which is good, because Paige, frankly, needs someone who won't let her ride all over him.

"We should get going," I say, glancing at Giulio, who's stubbing his cigarette out with his foot and starting to look down the platform for us.

"Yes, Mig, get lost," Paige says flirtatiously. "Meet you by the McDonald's."

"Hey, I did *not* come to Italy for a day to eat McDonald's!" Miguel says with a grin. "I'm taking you to an Italian restaurant for lunch. Pizza, pasta, the works."

"Silly! You never eat pizza and pasta together in Italy! You have a *lot* to learn," Paige says, pushing him back into an embrasure in the station wall. "Catch me up, okay?"

"Yes, ma'am!"

He salutes and ducks out of sight as we walk quickly down the platform, waving at Giulio.

"I love him *soo* much," Paige says in a soft, dreamy voice that I've never heard from her before.

"He seems really, really nice," I say.

"Oh, he *is*," she assures me as we greet Giulio and explain about Paige staying on.

As expected, Giulio reacts to this information by shrugging and grunting, "*Moh! Cazzi vostri*," which we know by now is a rather coarse way of saying "Who cares? It's your business."

So I hug Paige hard, which would have raised Giulio's suspicions if he had any natural curiosity, because why on earth am I hugging her like this when she's just going shopping? I follow Giulio out of the station, and just as we're about to turn down the walkway that leads to the underground car park, I look back. Sure enough, there are Paige and Miguel by McDonald's, kissing again, Paige's blond curls clearly visible, both of them still oblivious to the fact that every single passerby is slowing down to gaze and comment approvingly on this excellent demonstration of *l'amore* being *bello.*

I'm horribly jealous, to be honest.

"*Allora, prima la villa?*" Giulio says as we get into the Range Rover.

"*No, direttamente al Castello di Vesperi,*" I say. We're going straight to the castello. And as I say the words, I feel my heart leap and bound in my chest.

Not long now. Not long at all.

Forty-five minutes later, we're bumping up the zigzag of cypress-lined driveway, around the castle, in through the portico, barely even slowing down, though there can't be more than a few inches' clearance for the Range Rover on either side; a month and a half ago, I would have been gripping the armrests in fear, but I'm so used to Italian driving right now that I don't break a bead of sweat.

"*Eccoci,*" Giulio says economically, screeching to a halt a bare foot from the castle's internal wall. "We're here."

I heave open the door, clamber down, get out. He's backing through the open gates almost as soon as I slam the door again. My ride's gone; no way back. But that's okay. I've never wanted anything in my life as much as I want to go forward right now.

I run up the walkway into the castle. The doors are open, letting in light and air, and a maid is up on a high stepladder in the hallway, dusting the hanging crystal light fittings.

*"Il signore?"* I ask. *"Luca? Dov'è?"*

"Where's Luca?" I'm asking. *I'm so close.* I'm trembling as she says:

*"Non lo so, signorina. Mi dispiace."*

She doesn't know: oh well. I don't care if I have to comb the entire castle for him.

*"Prova su di sopra,"* she adds, jabbing the ceiling with her duster; he's somewhere upstairs.

*Oh well, that narrows it down. Only about twenty thousand square feet to search, rather than thirty thousand.*

"*Grazie*," I say over my shoulder as I start to run up the big central *Gone with the Wind* staircase. I take the search systematically, starting with the picture gallery, covering the south wing first, where there are a lot of public rooms. I don't want to run around calling his name; but as I find myself pushing open the double doors that obviously lead to the family's private quarters, I decide that, if I won't call out for him, I'll knock on every closed door. The last thing I want is to barge in on Luca doing something private and start this massively important conversation on a completely wrong note.

I pass another maid waxing the wooden floors, and ask her if she's seen Luca. She, too, has no idea where he is. Never mind: I know he's here. The principessa made sure of that. And I'll find him if it takes all day. I enter a suite of rooms with pale-blue-painted paneling and gorgeous molded golden ceilings, and I guess straight away that these are the principessa's. There's something about the formality of this sitting room, the neat piles of books and magazines, the silver tissue box on the coffee table and the perfectly arranged flowers on the side tables, that indicates the principessa immediately.

Luca won't be in his mother's rooms when she's not here. I pivot to go, but then I hear sounds next door and think it might be another maid I could ask about his whereabouts.

The door's ajar. It leads to the dressing room that adjoins the principessa's bedroom, which I can see reflected in the mirrored cupboards behind the dressing table: a big canopied bed, hung with pale-blue draperies, pale-green rugs that echo the color of the fitted carpet in here. It's enviably pretty and serene, everything built-in, the dressing table stacked with a matching set of white leather jewelry boxes, the kind that lift up and slide open and have lots of little separate drawers and ring stands and different velvet-lined compartments, so you can view all the jewelry you possess, almost at once.

And certainly, the person I heard in here is busy seeing all the jewelry the principessa possesses. It looks as if every lid is raised, every drawer pulled open, every padded, hinged door ajar to reveal its contents. Around the arch of the dressing table are a whole array of built-in concealed lights, which are all illuminated, the faceted jewels sparkling temptingly.

Lit up, reflected again and again in the angled mirrors, is Elisa. She's sitting on the pale-green velvet low-backed chair, bracelets on the wrist of the hand she's holding up, arrested in the process of clipping on a huge emerald earring, pearls and diamonds around her neck, rings on her fingers—and, on her face, the most horrified, busted expression I have ever seen another girl wear.

# I've Gone Mad

Elisa is dumbstruck. I, most definitely, am not.

"What are you *doing*?" I exclaim, staring at her in shock.

Her mouth is open. She flaps her lips like a fish in a tank when it swims up to you looking for food. And, just like a fish behind glass, no sound comes out.

"That's the principessa's jewelry!" I continue. "No *way* do you have permission to try that on!"

"*Sì, invece,*" she manages finally. "I do. She tells me I can come in here to wear them."

I can absolutely one hundred percent tell she's lying. Her eyes, set in their heavily black-penciled sockets, are flickering from side to side, avoiding mine; her hands, which have dropped to the marble shelf in front of her, are twisting together in a fit of nerves.

"*Right,*" I say witheringly. "You're making that up."

She jumps up and turns to face me.

"I am not," she says utterly unconvincingly, her eyes still flickering; I can tell she's trying to think of a way to get out of this huge hole she's in.

"Why are *you* here?" she adds, going for the attack-is-the-best-defense strategy. "You are not welcome in this house! You come in to spy through the principessa's jewels! If you go now, I will not say that you come in here, and you will be safe—"

"Oh *please,*" I say contemptuously.

"You should go now," she says feebly, her hands on her hips. "Luca *tells* me to wear this," she adds defiantly, gathering courage as she works out the best way to get out of it. "He says I may wear his mother's jewelry when I choose. Because he likes *me,* not you. If you go now, I don't tell him that you come in here to spy her jewels."

I know she's lying about Luca; that doesn't even ping my radar.

"Nice try," I say, almost absently, because my attention's distracted by something about her. The light is catching the jewelry she's wearing, blazing off the diamonds and emeralds in her ears, more diamonds at her neck where she's layered a lot of necklaces, pearls glowing against the bare, darkly tanned skin, and . . .

*Wait.*

I stare at her throat. That's the exact same pearl

necklace the girl in the portrait is wearing, the portrait in Sir John Soane's Museum I saw in London this spring; the girl who looks so like me she could be my double. And who, thanks to the book in the Greve library, I know was called Fiammetta. It's extraordinary to think that the very same necklace Fiammetta wore centuries ago, to have her picture painted, has been passed down through the generations to the current principessa as part of the family jewel collection; that it hasn't been lost, or altered in any way. I recognize it because of the small cameo that hangs from it, a carving of a woman's head, her hair piled high in curls at the back. The stone is set in a delicate, diamond-studded gold frame, and there are diamonds placed at intervals through the string of pearls. It's unmistakable.

What strikes me most profoundly is how accurately the necklace was depicted in the portrait. It looks exactly the same. I imagine the painter studying it with great care to make sure it was reproduced perfectly. The precision is breathtaking.

I take a couple of steps forward to look more closely at the necklace, marveling at it; Elisa sees me staring at her neck and raises a hand to her throat protectively. As if the necklace is hers, and she's defending it from me.

Which makes me *really* angry.

Before I can think about what I'm going to say, the words burst out of my mouth.

"Take that off, *now*!" I practically command her, pointing at the necklace in a way that, looking back, I can see was over-the-top dramatic. But by now I identify with Fiammetta, with the necklace; I'm part of this family, which means the necklace is part of my heritage. And seeing it around Elisa's neck is the last straw for me.

There's a moment when it could all have been averted. I see her deciding what to do. And, unfortunately for her, she makes the wrong decision. She pulls herself up to her full height, raises her hand, and hits mine away, hissing:

"*Stai lontana, stronza.*"

"Stay away from me, bitch."

That is *it.* This girl's been the bitch, not me, not any of us four foreigners. She insulted us the first day we arrived, and she hasn't stopped since. I've busted her sneakily trying on the principessa's jewelry, which I'm absolutely sure she doesn't have permission to do, and she's giving herself airs instead of just copping to it and taking it off, like I told her to.

Which I have a total right to do.

*And* she just whacked my hand.

Before I know it, my hands are on her shoulders and I'm shaking her as if I'm trying to actually detach her head. It wobbles madly; one huge, heavy emerald earring flies off and lands on the carpet. Elisa's hands grip mine, trying to pull them off, her nails digging in. I push against her and she staggers back with me following her, my hands closing around her neck.

I've gone mad, I admit it. Completely mad. I'm trying to get the necklace off her, find the clasp, undo it; crazy, because you don't do that from the front, of course, but from the back. And naturally Elisa misunderstands. She thinks I'm trying to strangle her. She starts screaming really loudly, a hysterical, help-me-she's-trying-to-kill-me screech, and her hands flap and slap and pound against me in a desperate attempt to get me off. We rock backward and forward, me scrabbling for the fastening of the strand of pearls, Elisa trying to wriggle free, shrieking like a banshee, howling and wailing at a deafening pitch, but all I can think of is ripping that necklace off her.

She scrambles away, tumbles over on a heel, and tips over onto the carpet. My hands are still tangled in the necklaces and I can't get them free in time. So I fall too, crashing down on top of her body. I will freely admit that I weigh quite a lot more than bony skinny Elisa, and my extra thirty pounds or so land on her like a ton of bricks. The breath is squashed out of her for a moment; I hear her exhale in a violent *whoosh.* My hands are trapped under the back of her neck and I'm struggling to pull them free; Elisa gets her second wind, manages to inhale, and starts the screeching again, thrashing under me, writhing around like a possessed bag of bones in a horror film.

Suddenly I feel hands close around my waist and pull me off her bodily. My fingers snag on a necklace as I'm dragged back and a strand bursts, a chain breaking with the force; it's that or my finger. I'm being lifted up; I manage to get my feet under me on the carpet, standing up again, and for a moment I lean back against the person behind me to get my balance.

I know instantly it's Luca. There's a reaction that happens whenever he touches me, an electric current, fizzing and unmistakable. I catch my breath as my back presses against his chest, feeling his long fingers wrapped around my waist, my head nestling into his shoulder for a brief wonderful moment. I hear him draw in his breath too. And then his hands drag away from me. He steps back and barks:

*"Ma che cosa succede qui? Siete impazzite, voi due?"* "What's happening here? Have you both gone mad?"

*"È lei!"* Elisa screams from the carpet. *"Lei è impazzita!"*

*"Right,"* I say contemptuously, taking a step back so I can see them both. "*I'm* the crazy one."

The sight of Luca takes my breath away. It always does when I haven't seen him in a while. His hair's so black, his eyes so blue, his skin so white, his mouth so red. He's like a boy from a fairy tale, a prince from a winter country. It's his beauty that shocks me: the fact that he's glaring at me doesn't faze me at all. I point down at Elisa.

"Look, Luca," I say. "She's wearing your mum's jewelry. I came in here and found her trying it on."

Elisa is quickly wrenching off the bracelets as she starts to sit up, but it's too little too late. The strand that broke was part of another necklace, pearl and lapis lazuli, and there are pearls and dark-blue beads scattered all over her and on the carpet around her body. I'll pick up every one, crawl over the carpet to make sure I've found them all.

*"Luca,"* she begins, desperately looking for an excuse, *"io . . . guardo, la tua mamma . . ."*

*"Elisa, non ci posso credere,"* Luca says flatly, staring at her. "I can't believe it."

*"Ma giuro–"*

"I swear," she's saying, but he raises one hand and she falls silent, staring up at him as he switches to English, glancing at me to show that the language change is for my benefit.

"I do not believe this, Elisa," he says, shaking his head.

"*Incredibile.* You come here to see me, I tell you I do not want to talk to you and to please go away. But you come to my mother's room and put on her jewels! You must be mad! And no," he cuts in as she tries to repeat what she was saying about his mother. "I know that Mamma does not tell you that you may put them on. *Mai.* Never. That is a lie. These are di Vesperi jewels, for the family women only. They wear them. Nobody else."

He's very pointedly avoiding looking at me now.

"Take them all off," he says angrily. "You must be truly mad."

Elisa's crying as she reaches back and starts to unfasten the clasps of the various necklaces she's wearing. I ought to feel triumphant, I suppose. This girl has tried to destabilize thc four of us since we first got to Italy, make us feel fat and stupid and badly dressed compared to her skinny Italian chic-ness: here's the ultimate victory, her complete humiliation in front of me and the boy she's madly keen to get with.

But all I see, looking at her fumble to pull off the backing to the single earring she's still wearing, to pick up all her borrowed treasure and put it back on the shelf, is a sad girl who is full of anger at her mum and a desire for a boy who doesn't want her.

"She didn't steal anything. She was just dressing up," I say, somehow defending her now.

His shoulders rise and fall slowly under his white shirt. It makes no difference to him what Elisa's intentions were. She's violated his beloved mother's dressing room, and he can't see any extenuating circumstances at all.

Elisa's face is absolutely wet with tears as she turns to

leave the room. She can't look at either of us; her head's hanging, her messed-up hair tangled into her eyes.

"We won't tell anyone," I say to her, and she whispers: *"Grazie, Violetta,"* in such a pathetic way that I feel even more sorry for her than I did before.

Luca and I are left alone as Elisa's slow dragging footsteps echo away down the corridor. I look up at him, bursting with what I have to tell him. But he's striding to the dressing table, picking up something that Elisa put there, holding it out to show me.

I gasp. It's the pearl necklace from the portrait.

"Luca—" I begin, but he's already crossed back to me and is placing it around my neck. The pearls are cool against my skin; his fingers, doing up the clasp, are even colder. I stare at myself in the mirror, my hand coming up to touch the cameo hanging just at the tip of my collarbone.

*"Sei bellissima,"* he says so quietly that I can barely hear him. I think this is the first compliment he's ever paid me. "Come, Violetta. I have something to show you."

"But, Luca—"

He's at the door, walking away, expecting me to follow him. I scurry after him, dying to tell him what I've come here to say; but I can't do it on the run, trotting like this. He's striding so fast I can barely keep up, let alone get anything out that he'll be able to hear. Along a corridor, around a corner, along another corridor, up a flight of stairs, then another, through a door that he holds till I've caught up with him.

There are a lot of planks stacked against the corridor wall, which I have to navigate past, and in a window embrasure, a pile of long nails and a claw hammer. I follow him up an unexpectedly narrow, low-ceilinged, twisting wooden staircase with creaky old treads, Luca ducking his head as he takes them two at a time.

Through another door, and into a round room with unvarnished, wide old floorboards and brick walls. A room with windows running around half its circumference, narrow turret windows with bright stunning views of the glorious sunny day outside, of vineyards rich with green leaves and cypress trees planted in lines to frame the road that twists and turns down the hillside . . .

My jaw drops. The words that were on my lips fade as I turn around slowly, absorbing the sight of this place where Luca has brought me. It's the turret room in which Fiammetta di Vesperi, my look-alike, was painted centuries ago. The turret room from the portrait in London, which I didn't know that Luca had ever seen . . .

I come to a halt where I began, staring at Luca, still speechless that he's led me here, to the place where, in a way, everything began.

"You are a di Vesperi, Violetta," he says to me gravely. "I want to show this to you, to welcome you to the family. I see you recognize where we are."

Formally, he holds out his hand for me to shake.

*"Benvenuta, sorella mia,"* he says.

"Welcome, sister."

# This Is Our Future

As I stare at Luca, I feel like Elisa just now, her mouth flapping like a fish as she frantically thought of what to say. I hate hearing him call me "sister" so seriously, with such acceptance of the situation, and I want to protest. But simultaneously, I'm so taken aback that the first thing that comes out of my mouth is:

"How did you know about—this?" I gesture around the room. "How did you know about the portrait?"

"Portrait?" He frowns, not understanding.

"Picture," I say. "The picture of the girl in this room."

"Her name is Fiammetta di Vesperi," he says, walking over to the windowsill—the one on which, in the portrait, Fiammetta's ginger cat was lying. A wide ray of golden sunshine is streaming onto the slab of stone, warming it, just as it did centuries ago, for the cat to bask in. Luca picks up a piece of paper from the sill and hands it to me.

It's a color photocopy of the portrait. I stare at it, taking in all the details. Before, when I've looked at this image, I've obsessed about her face, Fiammetta's face: because it's mine. Now that the mystery has been solved, I'm released to absorb all the other parts of the picture; the room, the view outside. . . .

"It's identical," I say, looking at the window in front of me and then back down to the photocopy. "The view. It hasn't changed in hundreds of years."

He shrugs.

"Why would it? We have changed nothing. We make wine now, we grow the grapes, just like always."

"Those aren't the same vines," I say incredulously.

He laughs. "No, that would not be possible. But the trees are the same. The *cipressi*."

I stare at the stone frame of the window and, through it, the cypresses marching down the hill in two lines. To think that they're the same trees that stood there over three hundred years ago is mind-boggling. The sheer history overwhelms me for a moment, the knowledge that I'm a descendant of this family, which has owned this castle, these lands for many more than three hundred years. . . .

Luca lets it sink in, leaning back against the wall, propping his shoulders on the brick, crossing his legs at the ankles. The way he was standing when I first saw him, just a month and a half ago, at the Casa del Popolo. I think I fell in love with him that very moment.

"How did you know?" I eventually ask again. "That I'd seen this picture, I mean?"

"I see you come out of the library with Kelly," he says, looking a little embarrassed. "And I am curious. What do two English girls do at an Italian library? So later I go in and I ask Sandra, who works there, what you want, and she says, 'Oh, they do *ricerche*–' "

"Research," I prompt.

"Yes. On your family, she says. And she shows me the book they have with the di Vesperi in it." He shrugs again. "We have a copy of course, but I never look in it. But I open it and there it is. A picture of Fiammetta. Of you."

He looks straight at me for a moment, his eyes a clear blue, filled with acceptance of what he thinks is the truth.

"And I do my own *ricerche* in my family documents, and I see that there is another picture of Fiammetta in a *museo* in London. So I understand a lot of things." He swallows; I see his Adam's apple bobbing. "I do not maybe understand why you did not tell me. Before we kissed. Before we start to feel . . ."

He breaks off, staring down at his shoes. Luca never wears sneakers; they're navy suede loafers, very Italian dandy.

"You kissed *me*," I remind him softly.

He wriggles like a snake pinned to a wall.

"There is no point in talking about this!" he says angrily, kicking back against the brick with the heel of one loafer and probably hurting his foot in the process.

I don't remind him that he started it. I say instead: "So you found this room?"

"Yes," he says sullenly. "I see from the window, the view,

where it is in the *castello*. But many rooms were closed, you know, for many years, while my *mamma* was here with just Maria and me. This one, it was—there was wood on the door—"

"It was boarded up," I prompt, remembering the wood, the nails, the claw hammer downstairs.

"Yes, with nails. I take them off and I come upstairs, carefully, because maybe it is not safe. But it is all good here, the floor, the stairs, no problem. Who knows why it was closed? But now you can see it. My gift to you, as part of our family. To see where Fiammetta painted her pictures."

"She *painted*?" I goggle at him.

"*Ma sì*! She was a *pittrice*. A painter. You did not know?" Luca asks. "That is a picture of herself. What do you call it?"

"A self-portrait," I whisper, staring at the paper in my hand.

*Of course*. Behind her, there's an easel with a landscape painting on it; a wooden palette is propped on the shelf below. She's telling the viewer that this is what she does: she's an artist. That's how these portraits worked back then. Kelly's been studying it. They were like stories, telling you things about the subject, conveying their lives as well as their images.

I was so busy trying to work out who Fiammetta was, what the connection was between her family and mine, that it never even occurred to me to read the clues in the painting, to realize it was a self-portrait. That I might have inherited my desire to become an artist from her, a long-dead distant relative who also loved to paint.

"It was not usual then for a woman," Luca tells me, still

propped against the wall. "I think this is why she works up here, so far away from people. To hide a little, to be secret. Private. Her father probably tells her he doesn't like that she is a painter. That she has to marry and make babies instead."

"She didn't marry, though," I say, still looking at her face. My face. "She died young."

"Yes, the *tifoide,*" Luca says. "I see that in the book. So she died, she did not have children, and her picture was sold to an English lord. With other pictures that the family did not value so much." He grimaces apologetically. "Italy was much more poor then. We needed the money. It is all in the family papers, I found it. I can show you if you like."

I walk slowly across the room, my legs wobbly, and half sit, half collapse, on the windowsill. The idea that I'm so intimately linked to the di Vesperi family that I've maybe, actually, inherited some sort of talent from Fiammetta is overpowering. I'm not saying that I'm as good as her, of course not. This picture is amazing, way beyond anything I can do.

*But I only just started to learn,* I tell myself. *I'll keep going and keep going. I'll go to art school and study really hard and maybe, one day, I'll be able to do a portrait half as good as this one.*

"Violetta?" Luca's looking at me, his mouth twisted with concern. "You are okay? I want to do something to welcome you. To show you the room in the picture." He pauses for a moment, and then says bravely: "To say, I know you are my sister."

I see his hands have tightened into fists as he says the last sentence. And I can't wait any longer. I pat the windowsill next to me.

"Come and sit down," I say.

"No!" he says with great vehemence, shaking his head. He pushes off from the wall, pacing across to the other side of the round turret room.

And now the moment's almost here, I have to admit that I'm relishing this, his resistance at being close to me. Because the violence of his refusal speaks volumes about his feelings for me. His attraction to me.

"Luca, *please*," I say strongly. "You need to sit down to hear what I'm going to tell you. I won't touch you," I add, and I can't help smiling a bit when I say that. "I promise I won't touch you. But I came here to tell you something really important, and you have to listen."

He glares at me, clearly thinking I'm not taking seriously enough the fact that we're related. Gingerly, as if he thinks I'll bite, he walks slowly across the room and lowers himself into the very far corner of the windowsill, legs straight out in front of him, his haughty handsome profile turned to me.

"*Allora?*" he snaps.

"So, I was in Venice," I begin, picking my way through this carefully. "With my mum and dad, and *your* parents. And you know what they told me, that my aunt and your dad are actually my biological parents. But that's not the whole story."

He nods stiffly, a quick, unhappy jerk of his head.

"For me," I say, "my mum and dad will always be my mum and dad. They brought me up, they're my parents, and I love them to death. My aunt gave birth to me, but they're my parents."

"*Certamente,*" he says more gently. "*È normale.*"

He glances at me briefly.

"*Mi dispiace,*" he says. "I'm sorry for my father. He is a playboy, like I tell you before. I'm sorry he makes such a *casino.* A mess. He does only what he wants and he is always hurting people."

I bite my lip.

"It's not just that," I say. "Listen carefully, okay? There's more."

"*More?*" The anger in Luca's voice is chilling. "*Dio mio,* there are more children? He has made more children?"

To my horror, he turns, his hand clenched again into a fist, and goes to punch the brickwork. I lunge over and grab his wrist a split second before it lands.

"No!" I say, struggling with him. "Luca, no, you could break your hand—stop it—"

"*Lasciami!*" he says. "Let me go!"

But I can't let him hurt himself. I wrestle with him for another moment, before his arm goes limp and he slumps back against the window frame. I look at his face, and see there are tears in his eyes.

"Look what he has done," he mumbles. "My father. *Our* father!" he says with terrible bitterness. "Look at how he has made us so unhappy."

I still have his hand in both of mine, and now I keep hold of it, grateful that I'm touching him after all. I think he's going to need comfort for what I have to tell him.

"That's the thing, Luca," I say quickly. "Did you not wonder what I'm doing here? Why I came back from Venice by myself? Why your mum rang and told you to wait for me here?"

"To tell me that we are brother and sister." Tears start to run down his pale cheeks.

"No! It's because of something your mother told me. About you."

Slowly, he turns to look at me.

"My *mother?*"

"Yes!"

His handsome face blurs and becomes his mother's. They're so very like each other, with their pale skin, their high cheekbones, their fine bones. I see the principessa in front of me, her pale face, one hand raised to shade her eyes from the bright sunlight, the other smoothing down the front of her skirt as she perches awkwardly on the seat beside me in the balustrade of the Hotel Cipriani yesterday afternoon. I hear her voice as she tells me, slowly, hesitantly, what she followed me outside to say, and I feel my eyes widening, my jaw dropping, as she recounts her story.

"You have to tell Luca!" I exclaim, almost before she's finished. Impetuously I lean forward, grasping the hand on her lap, enfolding it between both of mine. It's a gesture that would normally be far too forward of me, considering how very formal and reserved the principessa is, but after hearing what she's just confided in me, I did it without thinking. She responds, to my great surprise, by clasping my hands tightly in both of hers.

"I am so frightened to tell Luca!" she says quickly, her fingers wound around mine. "I am not brave. I 'ave tried before, to tell 'im, but I never can."

"But now you *have* to," I say, trying not to panic. This is vital to me, to my whole life. Luca has to be made aware, immediately, *now,* in a phone call, of this crucial information. "Don't you see? Now that we've found out about me—"

"*Sì, sì, lo so!*" she says. "I know." Tears are forming in her eyes. "*Lo so bene! Ma . . .*"

She draws in a long breath, swallowing back the tears. Sits up straight on the seat, her hands still wrapped around mine.

"I will go and tell 'im, but what will 'e think of me? I am so afraid!"

I gape at her, unable to say a word. "He has to be told," I say. "Please, as soon as possible. It's only fair to him." *To us.*

"Luca comes 'ere to see us yesterday," she continues softly. "I ask 'im to come. We are waiting for your parents to arrive. I think I am brave enough to tell 'im, but I do not find the courage. So I tell 'im instead about you, that you are the daughter of my 'usband, and 'e is very angry and 'e will not stay, 'e goes away. 'E says he will go to the *aeroporto* and fly to somewhere far away for a very long time. 'E shouts, 'e cries, my 'usband cries too. *Terribile, orrendo.* They are always like this, Luca and Salvatore. The shouts, the cries. Very bad. But I see one thing, very important. I see that Luca is not smoking no more. I say to 'im, 'I am very 'appy that you do not smoke.' And 'e says, 'It is Violetta. She tell me not to smoke, she say it is *schifoso.* So I stop.' "

I think about this. Luca not only gave up smoking because I didn't like it; he told his mother that I was the reason he did it. That I was important enough to him for him to listen to me. It gives me the bravery the principessa lacks.

"Let me tell Luca," I offer.

The principessa leans toward me, her blue eyes—blue as Luca's—fixed on my face.

"Oh, wonderful! You are good for 'im," she says earnestly. "You 'elp 'im. 'E listens to you. I know that if you tell 'im this, 'e will listen. And then I will come to see 'im when 'e knows. Please. I am not brave like you. And Luca—*ti vuole bene. Ti vuole veramente bene.*"

"He cares about you. He truly cares about you."

My heart fills up. I remember looking into her eyes yesterday, seeing how much she was counting on me. And I look at her son now sitting beside me, frowning, unable to imagine what message his mother might have to deliver. She rang him and told him to go to the castello and wait for me, that I was arriving with something very important to say: but he obviously hasn't guessed—how would he?—that what I need to tell him isn't on my own account, but on hers.

I've practiced this over and over in my head, run through every conceivable way to say it. But of course, I couldn't predict how he would react. I tried to imagine it, but that never really helps. I didn't, for instance, picture us up here in the turret, with Luca having tried to punch the wall and then bursting into tears.

"Did you ever wonder why you look so much like your mum?" I begin, having decided this will be a gentle way to ease into the huge revelation that's approaching. "And not at all like your dad? When, as he says, the di Vesperi face comes down the generations, again and again. I mean, look at me! I could be Fiammetta's twin. And you don't look remotely like a di Vesperi."

His frown deepens.

"I am happy I look like my mother," he says, not getting where I'm going.

I take a deep breath.

"Your mother told me that there's a reason you look so like her, and not at all like the principe," I continue. "It's because . . ."

I still need to pace this. I can't blurt it out all in one go. I do understand the principessa finding that she just couldn't bear to say the words.

"Luca, the thing is—we're not related."

I look at him, waiting for his reaction, but I see that the words haven't sunk in. Maybe I babbled them. Maybe it's just too much of a shock, too impossible to believe, after all we've been through.

"Luca," I say again, "you and I are not brother and sister. We're not related."

Luca's staring at me, his features absolutely motionless, his face white as chalk. I hold my breath. Finally, his lips move, and he says:

"But—*Madonna*—that is only possible if . . ."

His voice trails off. He can't say it. I nod vehemently.

"Your mother had an affair with someone else," I say. "The principe isn't your biological father."

The words spill out of me. The release is unbelievable; no wonder the principessa seems so tense always, so tightly wound. Carrying this secret for Luca's whole life must have been the most intolerable burden. At least my mum and dad could share theirs together: she was alone with hers.

The release for Luca is strong. He grabs me, pulls me toward him, embraces me so tightly that I'm half on his lap. He's crying and laughing, his arms around me. I reach up, twine my hands around his neck, realize that I'm crying too, laughing too. We stare at each other. Luca's palms cup my face, his thumbs stroking my jawline gently as he looks at me, and I can't bear being so close to him and not kissing him. I pull his head down and kiss him, his face, his lips, his eyes, kissing away every single tear, which takes ages, because we're both still crying. His eyelashes are damp on his cheeks, his mouth soft, his hair silky, his hands, sliding down my back, lifting me and settling me fully on his lap, warm now, making me shiver with excitement.

And gradually, through the kissing, I realize that the laughter is stronger than the crying. We keep pausing just to look at each other and smile. Luca tilts his head toward me, rests his forehead on mine, whispers:

"Violetta, Violetta . . . from the first moment I see you . . ."

"Me too," I whisper back. "Me too."

And then we kiss again, and neither of us says a word for a long, long time.

"So!" he says, much later. We're sitting on the floor now. The windowsill is narrow and uncomfortable. We don't care that we may be getting splinters in our bums from the floorboards.

We're curled up, me sitting between Luca's legs, his arms wrapped around my waist, mine around his. His head is leaning on mine, and he's kissing my hair.

"You remember that song by Jovanotti I say to you, in the river?" he asks.

"Yes!" I swivel a little to look at him. "I looked it up, but I couldn't find it."

"'*La Valigia,*'" he says. "The suitcase. The boy is a suitcase, he travels all around, but only one person, the girl, knows how to open the *lucchetto*."

"The lock," I translate, suffused with happiness at this.

"'*Ma chi l'avrebbe detto che la vita/ci travolgeva come hai fatto tu. Tu m'hai aperto come una ferita–sto sanguinando ma non ti lascio più,*'" he quotes.

"'Who would have said that life—'" I start, but that's as far as I get.

"'That life turns us upside down,'" Luca says, "'like you did to me. You open me like a wound. I am bleeding, but I don't leave you anymore.'"

"Luca!" I exclaim in horror, and his body starts to shake with laughter.

"You remember? I say Jovanotti's songs, they are not always pretty," he tells me. "But they are true."

"Still, a *wound* . . ."

"You are half Italian, Violetta," he points out. "You must understand us. We are more . . ." He looks for the right word. "Dramatic," he concludes. "*Esagerati.*"

And then he raises his eyebrows as a thought strikes him.

"You are half Italian," he says, "but me? I don't know. That is very strange, not to know."

"Oh—I can tell you," I say. I wasn't sure whether or not to volunteer this extra piece of information, but since he's brought it up . . .

"Do you want to know?" I ask him: his winged black brows are still up as he stares at me in surprise. "The name of the guy your mother had the affair with? She actually told me that too."

He shakes his head in disbelief.

"She *told* you? My parents are *crazy*," he mutters.

"She's so scared of your reaction, Luca," I say. "She was shaking when she told me. Really shaking. I honestly don't know if she'd ever have said anything if it hadn't been for this crisis with me being—" I break off. "I don't actually like *saying* it," I admit. "My mum and dad are my parents. I don't even like saying 'biological parents.' "

Luca's hands reach up so he can lace his fingers through mine.

"Oh, *carina*," he says consolingly against my hair. I'm *so* glad I washed it this morning.

"She told me to tell you the name if you asked," I say, reluctantly untwisting my right hand from his and reaching into my skirt pocket for my phone. I thumb through the menus and find where I saved it in my notes, holding the screen up for him to see.

He doesn't say anything. Anxiously, I twist around to look at his face; mercifully, he doesn't look upset.

"*Ah, sì,*" he says quite mildly.

"You know him? This Antonio di Meglio?"

"*Sì*, he is in Rome." He shrugs. "He is married, he has

a family too. *Stupendo,* I have some brothers and sisters, I think." He blinks rapidly as he takes this in, his long dark eyelashes fluttering. "I always think he likes my mother, to tell the truth. So now we know."

"Yes," I echo. "Now we know."

I don't ask him what he plans to do, how he intends to let the principe know the real situation, because I doubt whether Luca has any idea at all. He's going to have to let a lot of dust settle before he makes any major decisions. Right now, being together, being able to hold each other, to spend the entire day just sitting on the floor of this turret room, arms and limbs entwined, is all either of us can really think about.

"You realize that truly," Luca says to me very seriously, "truly, this is all yours?"

He waves around him, and I know that he doesn't just mean the room. He means the castello, the land around it, the vineyards, and, extending outward even more, the di Vesperi holdings over Italy; the house in Florence, and probably quite a lot more that I don't know about.

"You are the di Vesperi here," he points out. "Not me. I am just a bastard di Meglio."

"Hey," I say, not wanting him to be too gloomy. "I'm a bastard too."

*"Bastardi insieme,"* he says, hugging me. "We are bastards together."

"Okay, stop with the bastard stuff," I say. "Enough. You do this sometimes, you get all dark and unnecessary."

I frown up at him.

"You have to be more cheerful," I tell him. "Sometimes I think you think it's cool to be, you know, gloomy and brooding. You need to tone that down from now on. Smile more."

Luca's eyes spark bright with amusement.

"You are very good for me, Violetta," he says, taking my hands and kissing them. "You make me happy. You make me smile. You are the only girl that does this for me."

"I hope so!" I blurt out.

"*Eh, sì,*" he says. "*Ti prometto*. The only girl. I stop smoking because you tell me to."

"I *saw* you weren't smoking," I say. "But I didn't want to believe . . ."

"I tell you, I stop," he says. Then he tuts. "I tooold you," he corrects himself. "I need to do the *passato*. The—past?"

"The past tense," I say. Then I shake my head. "That's funny. I mean, ironic funny."

"*Cosa?*" He kisses my fingertips, one by one.

"You're learning the past tense." He's distracting me with his kisses, but I push on. "Of course you have to learn it, but do you see what I mean? It's all been about the past! I'm sick of it! And not even our past, stuff we did—things that happened before we were *born*! I'm *so* over the past!"

I'm panting with the conviction with which I say this, the words pouring out of me. I mean it with every bone in my body. Enough with the past. Enough of Luca and me suffering for other people's mistakes. We need to be free of them now, to start our own lives.

To try to get things right.

"*Basta con il passato,*" I say in Italian for good measure. To make things absolutely clear.

"*Va bene,*" Luca says, wrapping his arms around me, pulling me close. "No more past. I study the future, okay?" He kisses me, so sweetly my heart melts. "Only the future."

I know I'm looking up at him with stars in my eyes, and I don't care. I love that, at last, I can show Luca exactly how I feel, and he can do the same. We're free. Finally, we're free.

"The future is here in this room, Violetta," he says to me. "*Questo è il nostro futuro.*"

"This is our future."

And with those words, I find myself thinking not just of Luca and me, but of the other girls who've been on this Italian adventure too. Vividly, I picture Kelly in a few years' time, having studied art history at Cambridge, coming back to Italy to do more research. Visiting the castello, cataloging its art, becoming a full-fledged art historian. Perhaps even working with Kendra somehow; now they've bonded, it would be wonderful if they realized how strong they could be together, as a team. And Paige—will Paige come back with her Miguel?

I realize I'm imagining myself here: assuming that I'll be in Italy, at the castello. That they'll be coming to visit me as I paint in this room, Fiammetta's turret, mine now. *Maybe I'll get a cat, like her,* I think with a smile. *I've always liked cats.*

Sensing that my thoughts have strayed from him, Luca pulls me even closer, kisses me again possessively.

*I think I will be here,* I decide. *And I think they'll all come to visit me and Luca. That this Italian summer has made friends of the four of us girls for life.*

Who knows exactly what the future will bring? I've had so many surprises over these last few weeks that I've learned it's very hard to predict anything. But one thing I do believe with all my heart: that Luca and I will make our future together.

# About the Author

Lauren Henderson is the author of *Flirting in Italian,* the companion to *Kissing in Italian,* as well as the Scarlett Wakefield mystery series: *Kiss Me Kill Me, Kisses and Lies, Kiss in the Dark,* and *Kiss of Death.* She has also written several acclaimed "tart noir" mystery novels for adults and the witty romance handbook *Jane Austen's Guide to Dating,* which has been optioned for film development. She was born and raised in London, where she lives with her husband. Visit her online at laurenhenderson.net or on Facebook as Lauren Milne Henderson.

"Cute Italian boys, jealous Italian girls . . .
and plenty of tantalizing romance."
—*Publishers Weekly*

"*Flirting* stays true to its title: Henderson delivers lots of crushing and a bit of mystery with a dash of Italian 101."
—*School Library Journal*